T0195580

SHIFTING

SANDS

JANE BYRNES

BALBOA.
PRESS
A DIVISION OF HAY HOUSE

Balboa Press books may be ordered through booksellers or by contacting:

Balboa Press
A Division of Hay House
1663 Liberty Drive
Bloomington, IN 47403
www.balboapress.com
1 (877) 407-4847

Because of the dynamic nature of the Internet, any web addresses or
links contained in this book may have changed since publication and
may no longer be valid. The views expressed in this work are solely those
of the author and do not necessarily reflect the views of the publisher,
and the publisher hereby disclaims any responsibility for them.

The author of this book does not dispense medical advice or prescribe the use
of any technique as a form of treatment for physical, emotional, or medical
problems without the advice of a physician, either directly or indirectly. The
intent of the author is only to offer information of a general nature to help
you in your quest for emotional and spiritual well-being. In the event you use
any of the information in this book for yourself, which is your constitutional
right, the author and the publisher assume no responsibility for your actions.

Any people depicted in stock imagery provided by Thinkstock are
models, and such images are being used for illustrative purposes only.
Certain stock imagery © Thinkstock.

Print information available on the last page.

ISBN: 978-1-5043-0941-7 (sc)
ISBN: 978-1-5043-0942-4 (e)

Balboa Press rev. date: 07/25/2017

CONTENTS

CANADA

He risked a glance at the inert figure beside him. Drunk, drugged or dead, take your pick, all probable, but impossible at the moment to stop and find out which.

The hairpins grew tighter, and the dying sun struck his eyes on every second bend, black ice creating early shadows and the tracks of wheel chains in soft spots showing like scars on the road. It was still at least two hundred metres to the bottom of the gorge and this was surely the only road in safety conscious Canada with no hand rail above the abyss.

Between the strobe flashes of the trees on the lower shoulder of the mountain, he caught a glimpse of the Park gatehouse at the same time as a hand grasped his arm, wrenching the wheel. Desperate, crazed eyes met his as the car speared off the road hurtling them toward the gate three hairpins down.

CHAPTER 1

HELEN

Helen drew the swing back until the tips of her toes took all the weight, and then let it glide, leaning her head and body back to catch the warmth of early spring sun. She closed her eyes and luxuriated in the warmth as the hypnotic rocking of the swing settled her jangled thoughts. A week at a conference in Sydney had left her with a shocking dose of the flu and she felt an urge to kiss the warm tarmac as she walked down the rickety plane steps at Riswell Airport. The two-hour drive home had been interminable and she'd pulled over a couple of times to rest her aching head, not even bothering to lift it as huge semis rumbled past two metres from the open car window. The minute she'd arrived home she'd crawled thankfully into bed and stayed there until her stomach rumbled a starved protest that evening. This morning, the Queensland sunshine was glorious, washing over her in heated waves, with just a drift of jasmine perfume left over from the burst of flower after the last rain. As she lay back she let her hair almost sweep the ground as she stretched cold, cramped muscles.

Today, she was really feeling deathly cold, chilled all over with the remains of the flu, and she'd forgotten to eat, drink, or even move, while she concentrated to finish some work that had built up while she was away in Sydney, living "the high life" as her father would say. Her normally pleasant study with its view over the backyard and down to the creek flats felt as cold as a tomb while the data she was working with kept moving and changing before her eyes. She was sure that the paperwork was performing a square dance, the way each piece she needed kept disappearing.

It had seemed like a sound plan to work at home instead of in the field while she was sick, but it wasn't working at all well for Helen today. This analytical work required intense concentration and attention to detail, and the energy that was required was probably more than a day in the open would take while it didn't feel nearly as productive. Like most active, outdoor people, Helen often felt that she hadn't done anything useful unless there was a physical result, and she sometimes found it hard to come to terms with 'paper shuffling', especially when she wasn't feeling the best. *I'd probably just be better off in bed. I'd recover more quickly and be able to get back to my real work-* she decided.

Idly, she rotated the swing with her weight and listened to the birdcalls in the creek behind the house, just able to hear the occasional car on the highway just over the hill. Jack, his black- and- white dog body laid flat out in the sun, cocked an ear at her and grunted as he dropped back to sleep. His legs twitched eerily, and his lips drew back in a grimace, giving way to funny little yips as whatever he was chasing got away yet again. His eyes half opened with that odd glazed look of being semi- awake, and his mouth drew back in a big, satisfied doggy grin. Helen smiled at him and thought again how peaceful an animal could make you feel. You could never be sad when your dog was so content but she did wish that she could lie down beside him on the warm pavement and soak up the sun too.

His sun-warmed coat shone with health and Helen knew that black fur would be radiating heat like an electric blanket.

Carlisle was a quiet town, and it was this occasional moment of stolen peace, that made working from home a pleasure-at least when Helen was feeling well.

She thought about her current project and frowned. There was no way she could finish the monitoring at the moment since the unseasonal rain last week had brought the creeks up, covering some of their monitoring sites. By the time the creeks went down, it would be hot and every site would be covered in long grass. Although the tall, damp grass and the probability of snakes didn't bother her, the clouds of angry mosquitoes released every time you moved and the sticky seed heads, not to mention the lethal spear grass heads made working in the creek almost impossible later in the year. Ripe spear grass could penetrate the thickest of trousers and Helen had a couple of spears embedded in her calf already simply showing as a black spot under the skin. There were so many stories around about what would happen if a spear grass head burrowed in to a joint that many people were wary, but Helen hadn't met anyone yet who had a problem and plenty of people had them under their skin. She often wondered if the spear grass tale was another Australian tall story.

Three years ago, Cate and Jenny and herself had spent a couple of weeks, setting up the case studies that she wanted to revisit and while it had been a lot of fun, it had also been incredibly hot and humid. The only consolation had been that there was water in the creek and they could cool off occasionally, sometimes even when they hadn't planned it as they crisscrossed on rocky bars and water gates. They'd spent a lot of time with a theodolite and staff, trying to draw creek cross sections and even more time with a measuring tape, counting plants numbers and identifying them to record the state of the vegetation on the creek banks. They'd decided then that future monitoring would be done in spring, just before the storm season started, but this spring had fooled them with out-of-season early rains.

The creeks in the valley were often completely dry, but when there was water Helen was certain there were very few more beautiful places on earth. She loved this area with its flat top plateaus and incised creeks, the tall, stately eucalypts alternating with brigalow flats, rippling with gold and red Rhodes grass and grey-green bluegrasses. After good rain, the cleared brigalow melon-hole country could look like English water meadows full to the brim with clear water edged by lush green grasses. It was the contrast between the wet and the dry seasons, the heat and the frost, that changed the face of the valley every week. She could do the same drive week after week in the area and it never, *ever* looked the same. Here, Helen corrected herself. During the drought, it had looked drearily the same only steadily deteriorating for ten years in a row, with brief episodes of hope when the minimal rains came. The last few years had been wonderful though with solid rains and plenty to look forward to on every drive.

The gentle sound of a purring engine coming up the hill and the crunch of gravel as it pulled in to the driveway next door slid into her thoughts, and then doors opened and men's voices reached her. Rapid footsteps slapped up the drive and she heard the rattle of a key in a lock. Unlike Jack who had leapt to his feet, she opened her eyes lazily, coming back to earth slowly trying to decide if it was worth the effort to see who had come home with David from next door. She could definitely hear at least two men's voices and the slamming of multiple doors. No doubt she would eventually find out anyway.

Deciding she did want to know and that she wanted to know immediately, Helen shot the swing back to the top of its arc in time to see a wheelchair appear from the boot of David's dark green sedan. The young man leaning into the back of the car turned and waved, but continued to assemble the chair, directing laughing comments to his companion in the front seat, although the response seemed less than enthusiastic.

Her moment of solitude broken, Helen moved back inside her own house to prepare some lunch and puzzle over the new arrival. David hadn't mentioned a visitor coming to stay, when she'd spoken with him before she'd left for the conference. They'd spent quite a bit of time together the last time she saw him. David had volunteered to help her with a community awareness day for their latest biodiversity project which had involved manning a display down at the markets. They'd had plenty of time to chat and Helen was certain that there had been no discussion about a potential visitor, especially one with enough luggage to be permanent or at least long term.

With her hands busily cutting haloumi and cucumber for her favourite salad, she watched the driveway from the window as David carted loads of gear into the house, surely far more than a casual guest would need. Helen assessed the man in the wheelchair. He was striking with wavy, dark hair and strongly marked brows. He didn't smile a lot - even when David teased him in his gentle way. He sat in the sun on the driveway in the wheelchair David had reassembled and frowned at the fence that separated the two houses. He turned to David with a question. The reply must have finally tickled his funny bone and as he swivelled to look at the fence again, his face relaxed in to a genuinely amused grin, momentarily banishing the lines of pain and reducing his age by ten years at least.

Helen watched as David bent to talk to his visitor again, this time pointing into the distance at some feature in the direction of town and as David looked up the sun caught his face and outlined his finely cut features. *Wow, I should be so lucky*, thought Helen, *with two heartthrobs living next door*. Both of the men were more than ordinarily good looking, but in very different ways. David had been in town a few months now and had become a friend and perhaps a little more, although just how much more Helen had no clear idea.

At that moment, David moved his hand to touch the other man's arm, an instinctive caring and sympathetic gesture, but it was shaken off with a warning shrug and a sharp turn of the other man's head. Helen winced for David, even more so when the visitor turned his back and wheeled his chair inside leaving David to close the car and follow him inside laden with gear. She knew she shouldn't judge a book by its cover, but it sure seemed a one way friendship from the little she had seen. She would be in no hurry to get to know the new neighbor, in spite of an engaging grin and a well-styled head of hair.

CHAPTER 2

'Owen, we'll need your signature on this before I can take it to the meeting in Riswell today. I know I've left it a bit late but can I call in this morning, on my way through so you can sign it for me?'

Helen pictured Owen on the other end of the phone, with his thick grey hair sticking straight up, and powerful shoulders clad in an old tan work-shirt no doubt.

'Hopefully, I'll have it approved in time for our meeting tomorrow night', she offered as compensation for Owen needing to wait at the farmhouse for her instead of heading straight out on to the farm. It was getting close to wheat harvest and even the most even tempered farmers were usually a little on edge and short of time at this time of year.

Everyone in town, including banks and social hostesses knew not to schedule any events at all for September.

'OK, see you then'. As Helen put down the phone, she sighed, her shoulders drooping just a little. Sometimes, it seemed she spent all her life juggling meetings and people only to have things change at the last minute. Sometimes her job seemed to be miles of driving, always wondering if this meeting was going to be worthwhile or another waste of hours and hundreds of kilometers. Not to mention the time of all the volunteers involved in the projects. She'd given up speeding officially a year ago, deciding that it wasn't worth the heartburn of peering over every hill and around every corner for the radar, as she did 140 kilometres per hour from one meeting to the next. *There was no way,* she decided, *that her work would pay the fine and if she lost all her points, she wouldn't be able to do her job without a licence.* It was much less tiring to just be late to meetings at times, and people would need to understand. Since that day, she had enjoyed the driving a lot more, but it still occasionally seemed to take over her life. *It was better than being locked in a high rise office,* was her one comforting thought.

While the road never changed, at least the country changed every time she drove through, with different crops at different stages and the incredible seasonal changes of the native vegetation. Even the ordinary seeming old grey-leaved brigalow trees could flower most spectacularly, and you never knew which grouping of trees would flower in which year. It was like a long term symphony, with different groups flowering at varying times, one lot here this year, another over there next year, snaking along the creek banks and paddock boundaries. Just when you thought you knew where they all were, another burst of yellow would appear in a totally random spot.

And, while she was working with people like the Kelly's and the projects on properties, everything felt worthwhile. Suddenly, on those two counts Helen felt better.

She truly admired those passionate but sometimes idealistic and pedantic "greenies" as they were known in her industry, but she knew that she could never be that extreme. She had the unfortunate ability to see two sides to every argument and often felt that she was lacking in some sort of vital commitment. She didn't see what everyone else saw- a woman committed to her community and to finding conservation solutions which could work. She didn't count the hours of volunteer work and extra jobs that she took on, just to make it all happen.

Owen Kelly owned a beautiful stretch of land along the lower Carlisle Creek and he was waiting and welcoming as usual when Helen arrived, five minutes early for a change. She stepped out of her Hilux ute, her long legs encased in jeans and her tawny eyes accented by a deep gold work-shirt.

As they walked toward the verandah, Owen removed his hat revealing sweat-plastered, grey hair. Rubbing his hand along his trousers he remarked as usual, 'hot enough for you? Might build to a storm this afternoon.'

Locals were ever hopeful that every hot, sticky day would build to a storm, Helen thought, a little smile turning up the corners of her mouth. 'We must have had enough for the moment, the creeks are only just going down. We need a little bit of dry for the sorghum planting so don't be greedy, but maybe I'll get stuck in Riswell and have to have tomorrow off,' she joked.

'Probably about time, but I bet they'd find something for you to do up there,' he said and went on, 'but at least you'd miss our meeting tonight and that would be a bonus for you. I don't know how you keep going with our meetings the way they are. You'd think that one of these days old Norm 'ud give up and go home. You'd think he could see that he's destroying our credibility'. Owen was simply expressing what many of the local farmers thought and in spite of her flu induced tiredness, Helen warmed at the concern and care in his voice.

She smiled at him and shrugged, 'There'll always be one who's not happy. This one just happens to be nastier than most and anyway, you cop just as much as I do, maybe even more. At least I haven't put up with it since my school days like you have.'

'Owen shook his head. 'Yep, and he has never changed, just as cranky and opinionated as ever and still tries to be the schoolyard bully.'

'Well, it wouldn't still work if there weren't some people who let him get away with it,' sighed Helen, 'they should all just grow up. It's amazing that such a great group of people could let one rotten apple spoil it for all of us. We could do so much more at times.'

'Don't let it get to you, young Helen. We will keep him under control even if we can't keep him totally quiet.'

'Thanks Owen. I know you will and we all appreciate that. It has been much better since you've been the chair, that's for sure. At least other people get the chance to have their say and you have been so sneaky about how you restrict his rants and raves, that I'm not sure he has even realized. I have been watching and taking notes for my own future as a chair some time.'

While Owen signed the papers, Helen's gaze roved over the land she could see from the verandah. Like many farmhouses in the area, the house was built on a slight rise looking down toward Carlisle Creek and its band of blue gums, bauhinia and sally wattle. She smiled with pleasure at the beautifully maintained cultivation and adjoining richly diverse pastures with their brigalow cattle-camps leading up into the foothills.

Even in the dry years, Owen and Jen seemed to be able to maintain reasonable groundcover. They certainly were top class producers and exemplary environmental farmers. Their whole place always seemed maintained with good fencing and a comfortable farmhouse. It was strange how some people just seemed to be able to keep things ship- shape.

Helen visited a lot of properties for her work and she honestly believed that you could tell which property owners would honor the contracts she worked through with them for conservation projects. Some people just seemed to be able to manage everything well and had an innate honesty that made them a pleasure to work with. She loved collaborating with people like Owen and Jen, but she did wonder sometimes how they managed to fit all their work in with the amount of volunteer work they did. They also managed a hectic social life.

'So, have you met the doctor's friend yet'? asked Owen. 'From what I hear he's going to be staying with him for a while. Randall Park was talking to David the other day and seems to think the visitor got pretty knocked around in a skiing accident.'

'No, I haven't met him yet' replied Helen. 'I was away for the weekend and David was gone early this morning. I'm not sure if his visitor went with him or not. I did catch a glimpse the other day when they came home, and I've seen them around the yard once or twice, but I've been coming and going like a yo-yo and just haven't had a chance to meet him.'

'I heard he's pretty good looking. David will have to watch out.'

'Oh, he's certainly that,' she agreed.

Helen wasn't sure if Owen was referring to the

disparaging and homophobic remarks Norm had made about David, and what he would imply about the new houseguest, or if he knew that she and David were slightly more than friends, but she didn't want to follow up either line of thought at the moment. Living in a small town was an amazing way of life as far as a caring community was concerned, but there were times when the community just cared too much and Helen had learnt very early that the less she said, the better, even with a friend like Owen. If there was anything to know, she would certainly tell people but at the moment Helen was not going to start any rumours.

Changing to a safer topic, she said 'Did you know we're getting a new field officer, to help with some of the monitoring and planning work? The interviews are being done this week, and strangely enough, it's all male applicants. That should please Norm. Old chauvinist.'

'Well, I hope the new fellow, whoever he is, stays longer than the last one. You'd think we were in the back of nowhere, it's so hard to keep young people here,' worried Owen.

'Well, from many people's point of view, we are in the back of nowhere,' smiled Helen. 'You know, and I know that we're surprisingly civilized, but I have friends in Brisbane who seem to think they need a four wheel drive and two weeks supply of food to visit me.'

Owen nodded and grinned. 'David was telling me that they had an applicant for a job at the surgery the other day who asked if there was electricity in Carlisle yet. True story! He was astonished when David told him that Carlisle had electricity two years before Brisbane did.'

Owen laughed, 'There are so many stories like that, it

makes you wonder how city folks ever travel overseas. It must be scary for them.'

Owen continued, 'So what do you know about the applicants for our job, then?"

'One of them is a very highly qualified scientist, I've heard, but wants to work in the country. Maybe he'll stay if we get lucky, although I'm not really sure of his reasons. I did hear he'd worked overseas for a while, so maybe he just needs a good dose of country Australia after being away.' She went on, 'He was supposed to be here for interviews this week, but there's been a bit of a hold up and he's still overseas I think. I don't know when it'll be, now. A couple of the others are from around here; you know Josh Larkin and Robert Jackson, don't you? Of course, I only found out who they are through the grapevine but it's usually pretty reliable where local talent is concerned.' Helen paused, 'There are at least two others as well but they're from out of the valley.'

Owen looked down as he moved his hat back and rubbed the back of his neck, 'It's a bit hard that we don't even get to interview them anymore, when we are the ones who have to live with them.' Owen had been on the panel which did Helen's interview and that had been the last one done locally. She was also the only employee who had stayed for more than a year in recent times. The group regularly pointed this out every time the interviews for new employees were done in the regional centre. Not that it made any difference, the interviews were still done regionally.

Helen looked around. Instead of dry grass and dust, which would be more usual at this time of year, the lawn and farmyard was lush and soft, the paddocks full of feed, with every tree reflecting light from clean, shining leaves, washed by recent rain. *At least the country looked beautiful at the moment*, she thought, *and would do for another couple of months*. Usually, in late September the grass would be browned off with frost and no new growth would be visible in spite of the increasing warmth. The wind was often a westerly, straight from the dry plains to the west, bringing dust and smoke from fires and creating the spectacular western red sunsets many people associated with the outback. If it had been a dry autumn, many of the paddocks would have very little groundcover at all but with the rain they'd just had, even the poorest of paddocks at least had a fuzz of new growth, mostly weeds but at least it was green, while the better managed properties were relatively lush. It would be a good beginning for the new man, if pleasant surroundings were important to him.

With Christmas coming up in a couple of months, there'd also be numerous social events and one or two glittering occasions and if it was social life he was after, then maybe, that'd be enough to keep him interested for a while. The constant attrition of trained field officers to livelier surroundings or overseas travel was one of the greatest problems the Landcare groups faced- that, and never having enough money to pay a decent wage.

Country towns this size were a problem, she thought. As towns went Carslisle was extremely liveable, with new-looking, air conditioned shops, a shopping complex and tree-lined streets, a lovely pool complex and entertainment and sporting venues, but it was hard to keep professional people. Doctors, dentists, teachers and engineers all came and went, seeking better job opportunities or educational advantages for growing adolescents. Of the young couples who came as a step in the professional ladder, some loved it and stayed, but many more hated it and moved on. For them and the young singles, it was too far from the beaches, or the shows or the football or something else which was usually unspecified. Often, they didn't seem sure what it was they were missing but they left just the same.

Every small business and group in the country faced the same problems and it was made ten times worse by the wages the mines offered. Why would you work long hours for a pittance when the mines offered twice as much for driving a truck or cleaning the toilets and as a professional could earn in the field for much longer hours? Many professionals also had the responsibility for reporting for Government money in funding grants and this could be become a personal burden for many people as staff turnovers increased and reliance on funding became more prevalent.

It wasn't all negative, though, mused Helen as she got in the car to leave. Every day she could see the changes happening in the landscape, could see that the work she was doing made a difference to the management of properties, to the attitude of Government departments or to the social and economic fabric of the country areas they worked in. She met people from all over the world at conferences, people who were just as passionate and knowledgeable about their regions and who loved to share their successes and who understood what they were all trying to achieve- a sustainable future for as many people on earth as possible.

❦ ❦ ❦

CHAPTER 3

It was some of the heaviest rain Helen had ever seen and it turned the familiar road in to a dark tunnel, constricted to the small patch of light from the headlights, maybe ten foot in front. There was nowhere to pull off and no way of telling how long it had been raining or how deep the flow across the road was. Helen knew she was somewhere near the low spot, where the Carlisle backed up but in the early dark, it was impossible to tell. The road was just a black sheet of water and the headlights coming the other way were high enough to blind her, her nerve endings singing with fear as a curved wall of water blasted against her side window. *One vehicle in 50km and it had to be a truck*, she thought. Trucks didn't ever seem to notice the rain. They just roared on past at a hundred kilometers an hour regardless, spraying gigantic sheets of water both sides. That was one good reason for not trying to stop in the middle of the road, as much as she would love to. The last fifteen kilometers in to Carlisle was never ending and Helen knew she was late. There was nothing she could do but just keep driving doggedly on and hope she made it in time for supper. *At least this way, I don't have to listen to Norm all evening,* she thought to herself mischievously, *maybe I should go even slower.*

Norm was in good form, his bull frog voice booming out to her even as she reached the car park. 'And I won't have that young friend of that girls anywhere near my place, he's not good for much anyway and I know what my neighbours will be thinking. They won't have him either.'

Helen hung back briefly and listened to Owen's defense of David. 'Norm, you don't need to, there are plenty of people who'd love to have such a willing volunteer giving them a hand and believe me, he is very willing and very able'.

Helen silently thanked Owen for his patience and clear sightedness yet again, as she entered what promised to be the meeting from hell, yet again. Too bad she hadn't been a bit later.

Absolutely shattered, Helen pulled the car into the driveway. A drive to Riswell during the day and a nerve-wracking, hair-pulling meeting in the evening had her tied in knots like a boa constrictor. *Why,* she wondered *do I do this? There has to be another way to earn a living and not leave this area.*

Heavy metal roared from next door as she got out of the car and she shrugged her shoulders at all the paperwork waiting to be taken back in to the office. Too bad, it could stay in the car, tomorrow is another day and a coffee was waiting to be made.

'Thought it was you, are you up to a latte? Some nice warm milk to make you sleep and enough coffee to keep you awake long enough to settle down.'

David leant in the car door and gathered up her paperwork, carrying it through to her office. He had to fend off Jack's enthusiastic greeting as he did, his lean legs buffeted by the excited dog's leaps against them. Jack knew better than to jump higher though. Helen would be down on him like a ton of bricks if he did, and he knew it.

Jack had also had a little training with Rhys out at the farm and had illusions of being a working dog. Most of the time he was moderately well behaved, but occasionally he forgot his manners entirely. David took a moment to caress the shiny black head while Jack gave him a blissful goofy grin.

'You are the best. I'll be over in a sec', called Helen.

❤ ❤ ❤

Helen wasn't sure if heavy rock and late night company was what she really wanted at the moment, but she wasn't going to sleep anyway, not with Norm's acid comments and obstructive motions roiling in her brain. How one person could waste so much time at a meeting and justify upsetting everyone else so often was a mystery to her.

She had tried so hard to defuse Norm's influence in the meetings and it was incredible that one person could railroad every meeting so effectively. Owen was a great chairman, very fair and very firm, but Norm still managed to belabor every point and dispute every decision. He had no compunction about making personal attacks either.

After kicking off her shoes and scrabbling her tired bare feet on the carpet to restore their circulation, grabbing a drink of water and a quick visit to the bathroom, she appeared next door with a packet of Tim Tams in her hand.

'Ah, my genie of the Tim Tams, you have three wishes. Your first wish is to meet my houseguest. Helen this is Liam.'

Helen put out her hand to shake, but hesitated. *Did city women usually shake hands?* Then she wondered what had made her think Liam was a city slicker, since there was nothing outward that would tell her. Her hand was taken in a warm grasp and an equally warm voice remarked 'I thought you weren't old enough for coffee, better bring out the milk.' Helen tensed. After tonight's meeting, this was not a good time for remarks on age, experience or gender.

She glared at him; her russet eyes narrowed and chin forward.

David, ever observant, came forward and placed a hand on her arm. 'Helen is twenty seven' he said 'old man.'

Realising that he'd hit a nerve, Liam let go of her hand and raised one dark eyebrow enquiringly, 'Tell you what, I'll get the coffee if you'll forgive me for that,' he murmured and wheeled himself out toward the kitchen.

'I'm sorry, David, I was a bit quick. I hope I haven't upset him.'

'Liam's fine, but what about you?' David's brown eyes assessed her, noting the tiredness and her unusual air of depression. 'That flu hasn't quite let go yet, has it?'

'No, but I'll take it a bit slower tomorrow. Today wasn't one of the easiest days I've had and tonight's meeting was a bit rough.'

'Anything I can help with?' Even as he said it, David knew that anything he did could only make that aspect of Helen's life a whole lot more uncomfortable.

'Oh, just the usual. Norm was on his bike as usual. I tried to ignore him, as usual, Owen tried to manage him, as usual, and several others gave in to his bullying as usual; just another day at the office.'

'Or, in this case, the meeting. Is there nothing you can do?'

'Well we could just forget about it for the moment and I'll give you all the gory details next time I see you. Anyway, it wasn't all bad. John and Owen managed to get some of their points across and we even managed to get some business done. It wasn't a complete waste of time just time consuming and tiring.' Helen paused, and her face lightened. 'In fact, there was some pretty exciting news. One of the groups down south have approached us with some great research they've done that looks like it ties in with one of our projects.'

She looked down thoughtfully, 'But I do feel so sorry for Owen. He works so hard to get things going and Norm blocks everything just for the hell of it, I'm positive. He surely can't disagree with every single thing that anyone else wants to do, can he? Even if he occasionally came up with something of his own, we'd all listen and have respect. There are some people who just get their kicks from knocking the work of others with no justification and that is the joy of an all-inclusive public organization. We can all have a say, some of us at much greater length than others. 'Oh sorry, rant alert'. Helen laughed at herself but David looked concerned.'

'It always comes good in the end, but it makes so much work. If we could just have one meeting where people all pulled together, we could do so much with our time.'

'Wish I could do more for you than listen, old girl but you know I wouldn't improve the atmosphere at all.' They both remembered vividly the one and only time David had gone along to add his support to Helen at one of these meetings. Norm had decided David was a pansy and had attacked him the whole evening, making snide remarks and continually having to be called to order. Since landcare, and local conservation and agricultural issues, were forcibly pointed out to be outside David's sphere of expertise as a doctor, he had wisely decided not to help Helen at meetings anymore, at least until he had a little more local credibility, but he generally turned up when there was work to do- a fact, that all of the regular members, appreciated and acknowledged. Everyone else was completely comfortable with David, seeing in his powerful frame, no nonsense practicality and willingness to work a total godsend for the group. Since Norm never attended working days, there was no fear of them meeting that way.

'Coffee's ready.'

Helen and David filed into the kitchen and for the first time, Helen really looked at Liam.

'I'm sorry I bit at you,' she apologized 'I have no excuse.'

'I'm sure there was,' he corrected 'but apology accepted anyway'. Liam's smile was genuine and Helen felt the warmth of it from the other side of the kitchen. 'So what is it you do?'

'Just at the moment, I don't want to talk work,' Helen replied, 'how about music, sport, politics, anything else, you can think of and I'll tell you some other time what it is I do when I feel a little better about it. Which is most of the time,' she added quietly. 'There's just one evening a month that I don't even want to know about.'

'Rough meeting hey,' nodded Liam sympathetically 'I've survived a few of those myself at times.'

Realising that she'd probably been a bit abrupt, when Liam was obviously trying to take an interest, Helen gave him her full attention and a disarming smile which lifted the corners of her mobile mouth and made her expressive eyes light up, 'One day we'll compare notes then, but how about not tonight?'

David intervened 'Helen went to the UK for a couple of months last year and at the moment she's helping me plan an itinerary for my trip next year. Maybe you can help us with all your travel experience too, Liam. I'll just go get some of the maps Helen has lent me.'

'Was it work or a holiday?'

'Holiday'…Helen's tired face lit up and she launched into an enthusiastic description of her wonderful couple of months.

She'd stayed with a cousin for a while in London, doing all the things that Australian tourists do when they stay for a while. Sandra lived in Sunninghill, near Ascot and Helen had spent a few Sundays walking in the Great Park. During the Ascot races, she'd even managed a conversation with one of the Great Park Farm managers, while waiting for the Queen's procession to leave by the back gate to attend the races. The Farm and the Great Park fascinated her, as did the haymaking equipment that regularly ran down the streets of Sunninghill. A strange part of English life was that rural life never seemed as far away from suburbia as it was in Australia.

'I loved the villages that end suddenly in large farms. In the villages you could live your whole life with very little need for a car and still walk in the country when you want to,' she told Liam enthusiastically.

It was a wonderful country in so many ways and as much as Helen loved Australia, she was planning to go back and work in rural England for a while. Unlike most of the young travelers, she fully intended to come back to Australia and bring her experience back to her own or possibly a similar community. It would also be an opportunity to understand a little more about the early farming practices imposed on Australia and the reasons behind some of them. There were a number of studies at the moment comparing early agricultural practices brought to Australia from England, which were based on what worked in a completely different landscape. Helen felt that by seeing the landscape the farming practices began in, she would understand why they were so wrong for Australia. She had so many reasons for going back.

Liam proved to be a wonderful listener, and entertaining about some of his own travels. Snow skiing was obviously a passion of his, one that David shared and as Helen listened, she realised how much there was to learn about David as well. While she and David had spent quite a bit of time together, it was usually active, outdoor time. They hadn't spent a lot of time talking about his other interests or his life before Carlisle. She knew he played guitar and liked rock music, and they'd talked about travel and work when they'd had a chance to socialize with friends from either of their professions. David had met her parents and lived in her town, but they'd not really talked about his previous life much at all. She knew that he was a caring doctor mainly through the town grapevine, as she was very rarely ill enough to see a doctor herself. Within two months of arriving in Carlisle, he had built a waiting list which included many of the older residents of town, some of whom could be quite critical of new doctors. Doctors and teachers in small towns were under intense scrutiny from the moment they arrived and it didn't take long for word of mouth to damn them or deify them. David was truly deified for the present by most people, excluding Norm and his cronies.

She knew his family lived near Byron Bay and that he had a sister and two brothers. As she listened to the two men talking she realized that he and Liam shared so much and had so many friends in common that she should have known about Liam.

David had never mentioned him, she was fairly certain and she watched the interplay between the two men, until she caught herself, realizing that somehow, Norm had managed to insinuate his opinions into her own psyche. Certainly David had a gentle air to him and he was a sensitive man who was unusually inclined to extend a consoling or protective hand, but Helen knew that proved absolutely nothing. Liam on the other hand presented a much more uncompromising front, only a stray dimple which appeared occasionally in his left cheek, and the odd flash of dry humour or even downright mischief, reduced Helen's initial impression of severity. *Of course, he was in considerable pain and quite obviously suffering from frustration on the job front*, she reminded herself.

Where did Liam fit in to David's life and who was this Jonathon they both mentioned? Before Helen could ask the question, they were all off on another topic, another place, another story.

'Really Liam, you should have seen Katie. She came off the ski lift and somehow the skis just drifted apart.

She ended up sprawled in front of the lift, flat on her face with her legs as far apart as they could get. Just proves embarrassing things can happen to the best of skiers. Katie, at 16 was David's youngest sister and the family had skied together during the winter, down at Fall's Creek. At least Helen knew that much.

'What about the time, Janie and Jonathon connected skis coming down that chute at the Remarkables. I thought we'd all be carted off to the funny farm, we laughed so much. Do you ski, Helen?'

'I have once or twice, but not like you guys. The boarding school I went to in Armidale organized the odd trip, but I spent most of my time riding horses and some of our trips to the Alps were riding trips rather than skiing trips. I've ridden horses over a lot of the country close to the ski fields and even in some of the cross country ski areas. After all, riding was the reason I went to that school, so we had to make the most of it.'

'Boarding school…did you like it?'

'I loved it. It was hard at first, leaving Mum and Dad but they kept in touch and we ran up enormous phone bills. It was also the thought that they loved me enough to let me go to that special place. And it was special. I met so many people and did so many things that I may not have done otherwise. No, I'd never regret it. What about you, did you go to boarding school?'

'Not precisely, David and I went to the same high school in Sydney, and he was a boarder- a little rich boy.'

Obviously this was a standing joke and Helen felt excluded enough not to ask, although she already knew that the school David had gone to was one where many students from the big properties further west went. He had a wide circle of rural acquaintances because of it, without coming from a property himself. A dentist's son from Byron Bay definitely did not qualify in the property owning stakes even if they did have a few acres.

'Well, I think I'll call it a night. See you later…nice meeting you Liam.'

David walked to the door with her and as they wandered outside he said,' Please don't mind Liam being a little bit tetchy. He has just had to put his new job and a lot of other things on hold and he is one of those people who hates to be slowed down and he had to give me some unwelcome news as well.'

'I'm sorry David, I hope I didn't upset him more then.'

'No, you couldn't you know. You are about the least upsetting person I know but Liam was a bit off to start with. He's not normally like that at all.'

Touching her on the shoulder, he opened her front gate and bent to fondle Jack as she slipped through and closed it behind her.

'Well, goodnight. Just give him a little time and I'm sure you and Liam will get on just fine.'

And I never did find out how he had his accident, she thought. *Probably skiing, as Owen had suggested.* It was amazing how accurate the community grapevine could be.

❦ ❦ ❦

CHAPTER 4

DAVID

The car purred, and shimmers rose from the early morning road as they headed over the first rise south of town. David drove easily with one arm on the sill, on the watch for the wedge-tails that were often in the middle of the road at this spot. The great birds were very slow to move off the road, their huge weight and slow reactions, making them hard to miss if you were speeding. It would be horrible to hit one and David held a vivid image in his mind of what could happen if he injured a bird, but not killed it.

He definitely wouldn't be able to capture it, with the huge beak and talons and take it back to the vet and he didn't carry a gun to shoot it. It was the horror of his life that he would injure one of the larger animals and then be unable to help it or kill it. He wasn't exactly sure of the law as far as that went either. As if thinking about it made it happen, a roo shot from nowhere, and somersaulted across the green bonnet with a sickening thud, leaving dirty streaks and broken mirror glass in its wake. It hopped off into the grass on the other side of the road, completely unfazed in spite of the flying lessons. Shaken and annoyed, David pulled over, turning to see Liam resting his head on the dash and breathing deeply, dragging in great sobbing gasps.

Liam shook and sweated as if he'd run a marathon and David could see that the accelerated beat of his heart pressured his head. He could only guess at the nightmare visions that clearly floated behind Liam's dazed and fixed gaze.

'Listen, relax, you're OK, it's OK.' Liam straightened, pulling himself together with a huge effort and gazed out at the sun-dappled paddocks. *Not a snowflake in sight and it hadn't been a deer.*

CHAPTER 5

LIAM

They drove in silence most of the rest of the way to Brisbane, over 400 km of nothing to discuss. *David definitely didn't need this time off from his job*, mused Liam, very aware that he was causing David to lose even more time from his work in caring for himself but it had seemed absolutely essential to let him know what he knew about Jonathon. Liam had ignored his own need for independence in calling David, even while knowing that David would want to look after him once he'd been in contact. As he had expected David had insisted on looking after him because that was who he was.

Liam knew he should have stopped in Brisbane until he was out of the wheelchair and fully functioning again. He'd let himself be talked in to this visit and now he was regretting that he couldn't put off the return to Brisbane, the round of doctors and starting the job that he'd managed to put off. By the time they got tó Gympie, Liam's resilience had kicked back in and he decided to satisfy his curiosity about Helen.

'So, I assume you've only known Helen since you moved to Carlisle?' he asked by way of opening the subject.

'Yes, that's true but it could be forever as far as I'm concerned. She is the most amazing ball of energy and strength, to do the job she does and remain sane.'

'What do you mean' queried Liam.

'Well, I've been along to some of the meetings and field days and there are a lot of strong characters there. There are some who really, really have problem with a female working at anything but baking the scones, if you know what I mean. And there are some, mostly the same, who think that it's OK to say what you think about people without ever checking if it's true."

'So, ignore them."

'I don't think that's an option really. These people went to school together and once a bully, always a bully, and nothing has changed since the schoolyard for some of them. And of course, Landcare has members at the extreme ends of the land management spectrum, just because that is the way Landcare evolved so that there is always going to be conflict. I sometimes think they are all heading in the same direction, but like a badly harnessed team. They zig zag a lot but in the end they get where they are going. Or maybe you could think of it as a broad flowing stream, with lots of individual eddies and some standing waves big bends where you can't see where you are heading and the occasional waterfall.'

'Great imagery, especially for a conservation group,' commented Liam, 'But a bit off the topic of Helen.' He wondered if David was deliberately avoiding the subject and if it was to let him know she was off limits or for some other reason.

He sat for a while and wondered how he could reintroduce her name without being too obvious. If she was David's girlfriend, which was distinctly possible, then he didn't want to interfere, but she interested him, with her honesty and something that he could almost describe as innocence.

'So what have you been doing in your spare time, assuming there has been any?' If he couldn't get an answer about Helen one way, then Liam was going to try for an alternative path to the information.

'You know, just the usual small town stuff. There's a great group of people that Helen works with and occasionally I give a hand with some of the work her group does on the weekends. And there're always plenty of other groups needing volunteers. It's as good a way as any of entering society in a small town.'

'So I've helped with sporting days for the various clubs and maybe I'll think about joining something for myself but I just haven't decided what yet. There's always football but it doesn't really appeal and there is a masters swim team and men's or mixed tennis. One of the smaller towns about ten kilometres away has a really active theatre group and I thought that might be a bit of good fun.'

'What sort of social activities are there?' Liam was fully aware of how small towns differed from one another in their social activities. Some towns seemed to be musical or theatrical with Eisteddfods and Jazz nights happening regularly, while others relied more on sport for social activities.

'Carlisle is a great place. It has a great music and dance scene owing to a couple of very active teachers and the concerts can be really professional. There's also an active group of rock musicians and supporters so there's a festival cum contest every six months which brings in groups from as far away as Brisbane. That's a great night. Or I could get really country and take up pig hunting.'

Liam had difficulty imagining David hunting and killing pigs. It was a ferocious sport and dogs were often killed or maimed, and although the hunters insisted they were serving conservation purposes, David would see it for the inefficient mechanism it was and he would know it really was just an excuse to hoon in the bush and pretend to be super-macho. There was no doubt the pigs were a huge environmental menace, damaging both crops and waterways but Liam just could not see David joining in the posturing. Besides he was far too fond of dogs to risk losing one in that way. Now if there was a helicopter pig shooting crew, Liam could definitely picture David doing that. He was a first class shot and the efficiency of shooting pigs that way would definitely be more appealing than risking his dogs and belting down the bush. Maybe there was a clay target club, that would possibly be more David's style.

He shook his head. He still hadn't learnt much more about Helen.

Brisbane took him by surprise. Once past the suburbs, and on to the freeway in to the city, he realised that the city itself was beautiful, with a feeling of Paris in the wide sweep of the river and gracious old sandstone buildings. It held nowhere near the length of European history of course, but it was just as beautiful and the landscape felt ancient.

Liam's only previous visit to Brisbane had taken him

from the airport in to the city via Kingsford Smith Drive and the Riverside area at night. He'd had the impression of an amazing mix of modern and exciting buildings and elegant history, but nothing had prepared him for the lovely old sandstone buildings on one side of the river and the sprawling but elegant Cultural Centre and museum on the other side, joined by the graceful Victoria Bridge.

'You wait until you see it at night,' said David, 'especially if you get the chance of being there when Victoria Bridge is closed off for celebrations or fireworks.'

'For a Sydney-sider, that's a bit of a turnaround.' Liam gave him a wry look.

'I came here for the River Symposium a couple of years ago, when they closed off the bridge and had a silver service dinner across it,' enthused David. 'It was really something special for what many Australians consider only a grown up country town.'

'I was working in Brisbane then and I came along with a friend who had connections with a group that had been working on a project on the Oxley which feeds in to the Brisbane River further up. There was a lot of industrial pollution, nasty weeds and sediment in the creek and this group looked like being in the running for one of the prizes. We sat with a Canadian Group who were in the running for an International Prize. They were so impressed by the river and the City Cats, and the festival itself, that I believe they went home and tried to get similar things happening over there. My friend still talks to them.'

CHAPTER 6

DAVID

Finding a park on Wickham Terrace, where all the specialists' hide out, was also comparable to finding a park in Paris. In the end David dropped Liam as close as possible to the building for his first appointment, leaving him to make his own way up in the lift, and went to park the car in the large commercial car park just down the hill. He joined Liam for coffee before his next appointment, just to make sure there were no changes to the scheduled order of appointments, then left to visit the Royal Children's Hospital where he had a young patient.

❦　❦　❦

Robbie was eight years old and until two weeks ago had been a normal, happy, energetic eight year old. A badly timed kick at soccer had connected with another child and broken his lower leg. X-rays had revealed some bone abnormalities and Robbie had ended up in hospital in Brisbane with no clear idea of how long he was likely to be there.

He was holding court when David arrived, a group of boys and girls in various stages of treatment and wildly varying dress codes were sitting or lying on his bed, all absorbed in the audio book Robbie's mother had downloaded from the Audible.com website.

This one was the latest in a series that was not available on the shelves in Australia yet, or at least not in affordable paperback. Looking up, he spotted David and immediately hit the pause button. 'Did you bring it?' he asked. Robbie's Mum had promised to send down his guitar hero, to see if it would play on the ward TV, when and if they were allowed. If they couldn't, he'd have it anyway for when they stayed in the apartments in Brisbane between treatments. David flourished the box containing the gear and promptly became the centre of a group of excited youngsters. 'Hello would be polite and maybe even thank you…?' David reminded him. Robbie laughed and a couple of his friends moved over to make a bit of space on the bed for the box.

'Do you think we could try it now?' asked Robbie

'What'll you promise me if I ask the nurses for you?' David asked, looking slyly at Robbie.

Robbie knew what he was after and responded, 'I promise I won't whine about having to have more treatment,' he countered. 'As long as you make sure that Janna is the nurse.'

'Not sure I can do that, but I can ask,' promised David 'You seem to have got more out of that deal than I have.'

He spent an exhausting couple of hours entertaining a ward full of exuberant but easily tired youngsters, with varying methods of improving his skill on the guitar hero. Since David played guitar himself, it was extremely embarrassing to find that almost all the youngsters could double or triple his score by the end of the afternoon.

❧ ❧ ❧

Liam's last visit of the day was to the orthopedic surgeon and she had forcibly recommended that he remain in Brisbane for physiotherapy for a couple of weeks, although not in hospital.

This meant finding an apartment which could accommodate the wheelchair so Liam could look after himself. Tracking one down took most of the next day. Although Liam could move in and out of the chair fairly easily, it was recommended that he stay in it as much as possible. The apartment had to be big enough for the chair to move around in, and close enough to the Wesley hospital for an easy taxi ride.

At last they found one, in Casino Towers in the city, which surprised both of them considerably. It was a two bedroom apartment which meant that David could stay when he came down as well, and was very reasonably priced. Not only was it wheelchair accessible but wheelchair friendly so Liam would be able to cook for himself and use the shower more conveniently, moving easily around the specially designed floor space in his wheelchair. David helped him to bring in enough groceries to keep him going for a while, supplemented by pizza deliveries and the host of other deliveries on offer through Menulog.

David laughingly suggested that Liam become friendly with the Asian students who seemed to populate many of the apartment buildings, since the mouthwatering smell of Asian cooking seemed to be on every floor of every building they had looked at.

Liam could probably manage to eat from a different Asian cuisine every night of the work, just on his own floor, if he were friendly enough, they decided.

CHAPTER 7

LIAM

In spite of having quite a bit of time on his hands at the moment, Liam would have to wait until he was back on his feet to really get on with his new job, and this really did not suit his modus operandi. He was impatient to get on with his life and so far he had nothing but reading he could do before he could start in earnest. His new employers were gratifyingly anxious to have him, so the more he could do from home the better, and home looked like being Brisbane at least until he was out of the wheelchair. There were certainly meetings he could attend more easily in the capital city, which could save others in the regional offices the flight down but he knew that it was only that he was so highly qualified for the job he'd taken that they would even consider letting him work part time like this, especially since he hadn't even made it in to the local office yet. *He wondered how many eyebrows would be raised and feathers ruffled about that bit of privilege.*

When all the logistics were sorted and discussion was no longer centred on practical necessities, the subject both men had been avoiding for weeks had to be brought up.

'Jonathon has no plans to return and said to let you know not to bother to even ask. I'm sorry, there's no other way to say it'.

'Why? That's what I don't understand. There must be some reason not to come back where he can be looked after'.

'Nothing. Not a thing that I know of or that he would tell me…I just couldn't shift him on it'. He won't even let me tell you where he is in case you go over to pick him up and bring him home. He's OK, though it will be a while before he's firing on all cylinders again.' Liam really didn't want to be the messenger, but since he was the only person to have seen Jonathon in the last year, he had the default task of letting everyone know the truth or as much as he knew of it. Jonathon had never been his favourite youngster, even on his good days and they were rare enough in general.

There were times when Liam wondered why they didn't all just let Jonathon go to hell in his own way, since he obviously was trying very hard to and did not want family or friend's interference in his life, especially David's. It would always be hard for everyone to give up on Jonathon. He was the baby they'd all looked after for far too long and David had always had an overdeveloped sense of responsibility where Jonathon was concerned. In some ways Liam could see why Jonathon escaped the family as often as he could but on the other hand, it always hurt them so badly that Liam found it hard to be generous. Jonathon was always forgiven partly because he had a charm which won forgiveness from those whom he had injured in spite of his prickliness, ingratitude and at times just plain rudeness.

CHAPTER 8

HELEN

Helen put down the document she was studying and frowned at it ferociously. 'Really,' she fumed, her frustration making her fierce, 'we need to get these guys up here and introduce them to the real world. The Prime Minister's people really can't seem to see that three months is impossible for a community survey of this size, and that includes the time they plan on taking to analyse it. This gives us two weeks to get it in. Heaven knows what results they'll come up with but I guess we'd better put in our two cents worth so that they know we're here. No use whining about it afterwards when we haven't done our best to comply with their wretched changes.'

Rhys nodded 'Perhaps we'd better organize a committee to get a spread of opinion on it. It's a shame the new bloke's not on board yet. It would have been a good meeting for him to come out from Riswell to find out a bit more about us. That is, if he is going to be based in Riswell. I'm just making an assumption there. Maybe we'll get lucky and he'll decide to live out here in the sticks.'

Helen considered. 'Always possible but not probable based on previous experience, but wouldn't it be wonderful.' For a moment she allowed herself to think of all the amazing things they could do if they had a really well qualified, permanent staff member who was prepared to work from their office instead of the regional office. 'Have you heard any more yet?'

"Just that the one they selected is still overseas, or at least I think that's what has happened. Apparently he did the interview by phone from a hospital bed. It all seems a bit strange to me, but I'm sure he'll be worth it in the end.'

'Well let's just hope it's sorted soon, before our funding runs out and we have to give it back- although, we haven't got the money in our hot little hands yet anyway. It's still sitting with the Regional office or with the State Government until he gets here I gather.'

This was always a worry with funding from the Government, it was always later than they promised, and you couldn't do anything about employing people till you got it, by which time you just about had to be reporting on what the person you hadn't yet employed had done. It was incredibly insulting to then be told that community groups were not professional or not performing since they found it difficult to report on time and this was a constant source of irritation to the Carslisle group, as well as every other community group of all different persuasions in the entire country probably.

Rhys continued 'We need him now, so he'll want to be pretty special when he gets here. You know, it's a long way from the days when we just got a local to do these things and did the advertising and interviewing ourselves. I'm not sure this regional group thing will work out.'

Rhys had been involved with the local Landcare group for a long time, since Helen's parents were still on their property, and he and they were founding members. Helen had been brought up with the Landcare ethic and had always intended to come back and continue what her parents had started. She looked at Rhys and wondered if he minded the changes made by Government in recent years as much as she sometimes did. After all, he'd been there longer and invested even more volunteer time than she had.

In the early days, the group members, who were mostly property owners and local business people employed their own coordinators and applied to the Federal Government to help fund them. Now, all the government funding came through large regional groups and over the years it became obvious that the large regional groups were building in the same restraints as government bodies. They were big and unwieldy, paperbound and fast becoming hidebound, and inhabited by ambitious rather than committed youngsters, who took all the training the groups had to offer and then disappeared to reappear higher up the ladder in other organisations.

It was incredibly hard to obtain information from anyone in the regional organisation, since invariably the people who had made the decision or written the paper had moved on by the time the smaller groups even realized that the research had been done or a decision made. The type of information sharing that had characterized Landcare groups was not as evident, but published work on every little advance or progress took longer to write than the progress itself these days. That and the enormous paperwork required for every small amount of funding was killing small projects and groups.

*Well, it was nearly that ba*d, thought Helen. Possibly she was being just a little unfair since many of the older people in the Regional Groups had started in Landcare and were working incredibly hard to get some great projects running and to work in with the local groups as well. It was just that sometimes, Helen felt like they were forgotten.

Rhys moved toward the phone. 'Oh well, enough with the pipe dreams, let's get on to organizing that committee. I'll start with Owen and Ken…. How about you write down any other suggestions as they occur to you?'

As he put out his hand to the phone, it rang.

'Hello, Rhys Phelan speaking, Carlisle Landcare Office.'

'Yes Brian, what can I do for you'?

'He what….well if you say so but I really can't see the point. We would have liked him at the meeting but I've heard nothing so far. Ok,.see you then.'

Helen looked up. Rhys was unusually angry, 'That was not a good start for the new man. I wish I knew if the request was his or Riswell office doing some anticipating. What's more, Brian wasn't even polite enough to tell me the guy's name or where he is at the moment. Wherever he is apparently, he's doing a bit of work with the regional group first. How are we supposed to work with this?'

'What's the problem……besides Brian?'

'They want a copy of our document before we send it…. So the new guy can assess it before it goes…doesn't make sense to me…what would he know for heaven's sake, he's spent most of his working life in China or somewhere.'

'Well there goes another two days of the two weeks we had left to the survey,' Rhys grumbled.

'Well, at least we know now there is a new guy,' Helen consoled. 'It's more than we knew before.'

'I wonder if he left a vacant spot for me over there when he left?' mused Helen. 'I could do with a change, I think, and maybe the overseas experience would make me more important when I come home. We Australians really have a problem with homegrown experience.'

She brightened. 'You know, on the subject of overseas experience, that meeting in Riswell the other day was really interesting. They had this speaker there from Uzbekestan and although his English was a bit hard to understand, he had a power point presentation on the problems with the Aralskoye and the rivers running into it. It was all about how the five or so Governments involved have deliberately run the lake dry to support an irrigation scheme to grow cotton on the water from the river. The government also takes all the profits from the cotton. The farmers there are just slaves, basically. Imagine trying to negotiate with five governments who don't want to know you, about water rights. It's bad enough dealing two levels of government here, let alone the governments of five different countries. The speaker was a very brave man, if you ask me and from the little I've heard, this new chap may have been working on a similar problem on the Mekong River, I think.'

'Yes, it's certainly getting more complex all the time and the mining boom is not going to make our negotiations any easier in the future either,' responded Rhys, raising an eyebrow at her.

'Yes you're right, the negotiating in our own backyard will soon be just about as interesting as anywhere in the world I would think and it's always that much harder I suspect when you know all the people involved.'

'Why do you imagine Michael Turner has left us to go into law? There's going to be huge openings in environmental law in the next few years.'

'Well, let's get to our own negotiating then. I'll ring if you want to draw up a quick meeting format for us.' Working in silence, Helen reflected how lucky she was to have the support of someone like Rhys, who was a true volunteer. He stood to gain nothing, in fact, possibly to lose from some of the issues their group was hammering out, but he kept at it for the good of the region. His family had irrigated in the area for years but with the water situation at a critical point, he had volunteered to help negotiate water issues for a sustainable supply for the valley. Of course, he was also frantically changing his cropping to alternatives that needed less water, and trying to develop and maintain markets for produce such as herbs and perennial grains. With the cattle part of his enterprise becoming more demanding with quality assurance requirements and more emphasis than ever on workplace safety as well, he was a very busy man, but he still found time to help at the center occasionally.

'So, how's David?' he asked.

'Fine, as far as I know,' replied Helen. 'He did have a friend staying with him for a while, but I only met him once. He's in a wheelchair and David ran him back down to Brisbane last week for more treatment. I haven't seen him around the place since but I think he's had a lot of work to catch up on and has had to put in extra hours for the ones he exchanged with Tom Dwyer so he could run after Liam.'

'Hmm, that sounded a bit disapproving. Didn't you like David's friend?'

'Yes, and no. He was a bit abrupt a couple of times and we got off to a bit of a bad start, but he was good company one night when I had coffee with him and David.'

'So what's happening in the romantic arena?' Rhys was probably the only person, apart from his wife Josie who could ask Helen those sort of questions and expect an answer.

'Rhys, you know there never was a romance. David's fun, and a great neighbor and about the best looking bloke I know, and sympathetic and a good housekeeper, all the things a girl could want, but there's never been anything between us, really.'

'That's not what it looked like to me, you know and if I were you I'd cultivate the idea that there could be a romance. You know old Norman has his theories about David, You'll never shake him and he can make a lot of trouble, the old gossip. For David's sake, I'd make a little romance where none exists, especially if this other good looking bloke is going to hang around for a while.'

'That's easier said than done, Rhys' was Helen's thoughtful reply. 'I've got to catch up with him occasionally to do that.' She frowned. 'What made you think Liam was good looking?'

'Little bird told me.'

'I think you are just fishing. Either that or the grapevine has been working overtime. As far as I know, Liam barely made it out of the house in the time he was here, and yes he is good looking in a stern sort of way, if you like being looked at occasionally as if you'd crawled out from under a rock.'

'So, will he be coming back or didn't you get around to asking that?'

'I didn't think to ask but I think it depends on his appointments in Brisbane and how they go. David said he is a lawyer but as far as I know he's not joining either of the firms here, so I don't know.'

❦ ❦ ❦

CHAPTER 9

HELEN

'Are you going to the Rodeo?'

'Yeah… I'm going to work at the Pony Club canteen for an hour or two. What about you?'

Like a pair of old neighbors, David and Helen hung over the fence in the shade of the palms and gossiped like they hadn't been able since before Helen went down to the conference. So far, they'd covered Mrs Baker's speeding ticket, the sprinkler ban and the local drug raid.

'I'm supposed to work first aid for the first half, since the ambulance are short again because of the football in Munndoo. I wonder if the crowd will be down because of that, or is it different people?'

'Some of the same, I guess, although it's not really my scene. Mind you some of our pony club kids are going to give the junior barrel racing a go, so I'll go and cheer them on.

We've had this wonderful couple from Tangoom coming over and working with the kids on barrel racing and camp-drafting. They're a funny pair really because they run a huge cattle property, but they compete in both camp-drafting and dressage at a pretty high level.

'Do they use the same horses for both?' David enquired.

'I didn't think to ask. Their son is in Vienna as an apprentice rider I guess you'd call it, at the Spanish riding academy there. The story of how he managed to get a place there is absolutely incredible. He was just in the right place at the right time, although there was a lot of work went in to get to that sort of riding level in the first place.'

'Wow, that's pretty impressive for an Aussie country kid, wouldn't you say.'

'I would,' she agreed enthusiastically. 'I wouldn't mind trying camp-drafting or barrel racing one of these days. I mustered at home but I was too wrapped up in dressage and jumping to try either when I was younger. What they've been doing at the pony club looks like so much fun'.

'What do they do? Have they got an imitation bull to chase, or do they use people as cows? I guess that's a bit too risky these days?'

'They've got this in ingenious bull on wires, really very clever and quite lifelike even if it is just bagging. It's amazing how quickly the horses get used to it, and you can even see which ones have a natural ability after the cattle.'

'It's a great thing to watch isn't it- when you see a good horse learning new skills?'

'You sound like you've done a bit of riding David.'

'I thought you'd never ask. Yes, I do, not all that wonderfully but I've been thinking of getting a horse since I've been living in the country and since I plan on staying for a good while. I'd like to go with you when you muster sometimes, if that was OK, once I find a horse of course.

He'd need to be a decent sized animal as well.' David was well over six foot and although he was lean, he had pretty broad shoulders.

'That'd be great, JJ will enjoy the company in the float. He gets a bit nervous traveling by himself, the big sook. And I'm sure that everyone I muster for will be pleased. I can just about hear them saying, 'the more the merrier.'

'Do you want to meet up, say eight o'clock? I should be off duty by then and ready to enjoy the show.'

Was this a date? wondered Helen, but she did put a little extra effort in to looking good. Mind you, wrangler jeans and the obligatory smart, small check shirt always looked good on just about any woman. Helen tied her hair back and used a big blue clamp to hold it against the back of her head in a twisted knot. It would be out of the way around the canteen food but was also chic and emphasised the graceful curve of her neck.

Many women from properties tended to wear smart, well cut jeans and checked shirts a lot of the time. This standard outfit always looked clean and ironed even after a day in town picking up parts for the tractor and bags of dog food and fertilizers. It was almost a uniform, like the business suit was to the woman executive. Denim and ironed cotton stayed clean, through dusty gates, lifting bags, buying the groceries, seeing the accountant and attending the cattle sales- all be in a day's work for a country woman on her one day in town a week if she was lucky.

And there were plenty of them at the rodeo that night.

Here, they wore their best jeans but topped in many cases by beautifully patch-worked or embroidered shirts, some with fancy braids and yokes. Both men and women

51

riders dressed to impress with designer rodeo shirts and superbly cut jeans, huge buckled belts and broad brimmed hats, even though it was evening.

Helen loved the outfits almost as much as she loved the horses, but there were parts of the rodeo that she hated. She refused to watch the calf roping, the cruel jerking of the rope dropping a calf on to his chest, or on to its back, legs waving frantically. The occasional calf would stand still, frozen with fear, shaking and sometimes even lying down preparing to die. She felt so sorry for them, and sometimes for the drafted cattle at the camp-drafts but she loved the barrel racing. The riders sat so unconcernedly on horses leaning close to the barrel, horse and rider forming one straight line at an impossible angle to the ground, eyes focused on the next drum and with their hands relaxed, they never even seemed to guide the horses, much less haul them around the barrels. And the horses seemed to enjoy it.

The bronc and bull riding was OK. At least the men chose to take those risks and strangely, the broncs in particular, were often quiet and happy to be handled when the tickler wasn't on. Some of the better ones had been known to become trick horses in movies and performances later on and were often quite good natured animals.

She met David near the ambulance stand after they had both completed their volunteer rosters and they wandered around the stalls, looking at the competition horses and talking to the competitors who'd finished for the night.

At the burger stand they lined up for the burger and chips and nipped around the corner into the fenced area to buy a rum and coke each, and sit on the grass watching the broncs.

At eight thirty they raced down to the arena to watch the junior barrel racing through the rails near where the ponies were collected before the competition. Helen's little riders looked tiny and nervous as they waited for their turn, as anxious parents hovered out the back. Some of the ponies sidled and stepped around, rolling their eyes and jangling their bits. *On the whole though, they were handling it well,* thought Helen as she adjusted a saddlecloth or patted a nervous pony.

'Toni, hang on, you're doing great.' Helen bounced and yelled. 'David, look at that, 21 seconds, that was amazing!' She grabbed David's hand and dragged him to the competitor's gate.

Her little pony-clubbers mobbed her with excitement, waving their hats, thrilled that one of them had done so well.

She caught David watching her and gave a little smile, her vivid expression making her beautiful in the moment. She could feel her hair coming loose from the bun and framing her face with lacy tendrils, as she leant down and listened to the excited youngsters.

Taking her arm, David steered them back toward the bar, where they met some of the younger people they both knew. Helen was aware all the time of David's hand on her arm, of the gentle way he surrounded her in warmth and approval. To everyone, they appeared as a couple, leaning unconsciously against each other, smiling at others but still together.

There was a band, but at around 11:30, they both decided to call it a night. Since Helen had walked over to the

Pony Club president's house, to help prepare for the canteen and then driven over with her, she was pleased when David offered her a lift home. She really hadn't wanted to ask, although she knew David well enough that she really could have just assumed he would take her home. It was just not in Helen's nature to make the sort of demands on other people that they would make on her without a second thought.

The drive home was quiet and thoughtful, neither of them wishing to put anything into words. Helen wondered if David would want to come in, if she was ready for a relationship with him, if, in fact, that was what she wanted.

When he asked if she wanted a coffee, she accepted but a little guardedly. David made no move toward her. Chatting easily as they always had, he opened the door, ushered her in and moved toward the kitchen to make the coffee. Helen felt a little droop of disappointment, followed by relief.

'Do you know where I could pick up a reasonably quiet horse?' David called from the kitchen. 'I'd like something pretty tall, not too young. I haven't got time for a young one.'

'As a matter of fact, I do,' answered Helen. 'Jenny Muir was in the canteen tonight and told me that she is starting university next year and her big chestnut will be coming up for sale. I didn't get a chance to find out how much they'll want for him, but I'd think it'll be a fair bit, although he'd be worth it. He's an ex-racehorse but he has the most beautiful nature and can do anything you want. Jenny does a bit of everything, including mustering and so far he hasn't missed a trick. Would you like to have a look?'

'What are they likely to be wanting for him?'

'I'd imagine around $4000. He hasn't competed much but he is pretty special.'

'That's fine if he's any good. How about tomorrow? Would there be any chance?'

'What about I try Jenny and I'll let you know in the morning? Shame we didn't think of it earlier, I would have made arrangements there and then. If I can't get her, we can probably call around and talk to her parents anyway. At least get a look at him.'

'I have to work in the morning for a while,' said David. 'Can we go out after lunch? Say I pick you up around 2pm.'

As she left to go home, David leant down and gently kissed her on the cheek across the gate in her fence, and she could feel him watching as she opened the door and went inside.

'Goodnight, see you tomorrow.'

Well, had it been a date? Helen was still not sure.

CHAPTER 10

'That big black fellow…get him….he's ready to go.'

Helen and JJ wheeled, hidden by their own cloud of dust and JJ gave the big black beast the evil eye. One thing about JJ, he didn't let up on the cattle, he kept his eye on the beast even better than Helen did. 'Got him.' They'd pushed him into a corner and he had no choice but to go through the gate.

As he joined the others and bucked his way across the paddock in a great show of bovine arrogance, a huge chestnut rocket shot past on the other side and collected the rest of the mob in one smooth circle. Helen had discovered another of David's hidden talents. He'd turned out to be a superb rider and had obviously done some stock work in a previous life. Helen wondered what else there was to know about him since she'd found in the last couple of weeks that he was a dedicated skier and a talented horseman.

In the last couple of weeks, he'd kissed her a couple of times, friendly, undemanding kisses but nothing more. They'd shared dinner at home and partnered each other to a few early pre-Christmas functions but so far they had never talked about the relationship they had, even though other people were starting to see them as a couple and invite them together. Helen enjoyed David's company but she always had the feeling that there was a lot he wasn't sharing, especially since Liam had arrived. She wondered if it was just that she hadn't asked because she felt shy about it, that somehow she always let David enter in to her life so fully but never thought to ask him about his.

She and JJ fell in beside David on Superman, and followed the herd back toward the yards. Now that they were in the laneway, and Rhys was leading the mob on his whippy, little stockhorse, there wasn't much to do, just swallow dust and talk idly until they got to the yards closest to the homestead and the fun began. Jack, his tongue lolling, trotted along behind pretending he'd done all the work. It was lucky that Rhys loved dogs, because any training Jack had was due to the time he'd spent out with Rhys and Josie as an untrained pup. There was no way Helen could have kept the mad collie pup in town since he clearly felt he should be a working dog and lived for his expeditions to the farm.

David looked down at him, reading her mind as usual. 'You have to admit, he's done a pretty good job today, but it's just as well the day wasn't any longer. He's pretty tuckered.'

'If he didn't inhale his food the way he does and then look piteously for more, he's have a bit more chance of a long day's work,' laughed Helen. 'He has a pretty good life for a dog really. Lovely active farm holidays and plenty of rest in between. Not like a real working dog.'

'You hear that Jack,' said David with his eye on the dog, 'She said you are not a real dog.'

Jack tried to look intelligent, head on one side and one ear up, with his eyes fixed on David, but looking smart was hard when you owned the goofiest grin in the world. His bottom lip twisted sideways and a tooth caught one side of his top lip, not the best look if you were trying to project a brilliant mind.

On a big place like this, with huge yards, the cutting was done on horseback and everyone got to have a turn, picking out the animals big enough to go and putting them through the yards. Not all properties did it that way anymore, of course, but Rhys loved his horse work and reckoned that if they got too old for the horses, then he might as well take up pigeon breeding because all the fun would be gone from the cattle industry.

Camp-drafting was not just a hobby for these guys, but a social opportunity and a honing of skills that many of them preferred to keep, even though technology was creating tools which just about allowed the property owner to handle his cattle from the home computer. Camp-drafting was also a way to keep their good horses in working order and to network with other producers and breeders. Like many cattlemen, Rhys loved every aspect of the cattle, from the excitement and danger of a muster, to the careful thought and negotiation that produced the perfect generation of calves. He loved the smell and feel of the animals in the sun and the privilege of working with a good dog or a clever horse. He and Josie were also quite fond of the odd trip overseas to places like Argentina, Brazil and the USA, all in the name of breeding research and other places like Japan for market research.

Successful cattlemen had to be international businessmen as well these days.

He was not so keen on the paperwork though, and poor Josie usually dealt with the ever increasing requirements of the government, the public and the markets.

Helen often helped with some of the outside work on the week-ends and even occasionally during the week, which was one advantage of a flexible work schedule. Often she and Rhys got more landcare work done and problems solved on horseback, than they would have in the office or on the phone anyway. There was nothing like a day in the saddle for getting a bit of distance from office problems and a long sight view. It was obvious that Rhys liked David as well, and seemed to enjoy his company, and that David could become a valuable member of the property team. Both of the men had traveled extensively and seemed to have similar opinions on many issues, although David was regularly the butt of 'south of the border' jokes.

Watching them, Helen realised what a good looking man David was. At well over six foot, he needed a decent sized horse to carry him. He and Superman towered over Rhys on the bay pony. Not that it bothered Rhys- he'd won too many camp-drafts on that pony to be put in the shade by a bigger horse.

David turned and saw her studying them. 'Will I pass?' he asked. 'Do I get my pony club certificate?'

'No, you showed off too much and anyway Superman did all the work.'

Rhys laughed and turning to David he said, 'That's OK,

don't worry about her, she's too tough on the beginners but we'll still give you afternoon tea anyway.'

David glanced at her with a triumphant grin, 'At least some people appreciate my good looks and talent.'

'By the way, how's your friend getting along?' asked Rhys. 'I mean the chap who had the accident.'

'Slowly, and far too slow for him but I believe he's back at work. He's been finishing off his last job and, I believe doing some work for the new company he's contracted for. I'm going down to stay with him over Christmas so I'll find out more then. He just tells me it's an organization based in Riswell and he's still finding out what the job entails. I think there'll be a fair bit of traveling and work in the field so he just can't join them yet. There seems to be a problem on their end as well, something to do with the government so maybe it's just as well.'

'What does Liam do for a living?'

'He's a lawyer at the moment, although he worked as a power station chemist initially, then moved in to law. We lost touch a bit about that time so I don't know too much about it. He went off overseas and I only heard third hand through the family what he was up to until he came back.'

Helen could hear some old pain behind the words, and obviously Rhys could too since he let the subject drop.

'What are you up to over the Christmas break?' she asked Rhys.

'Josie and I are off to Sydney for a week or so. Her sister is down there and we haven't seen her for a year or two. How about you?'

'Oh, I'm not sure yet. Genevieve and I talked about meeting somewhere but we've been too slack to organize it.'

David volunteered that he was off to Brisbane, to visit Liam for a week or so and catch up with his sister Katie, who was passing through on her way to a skiing holiday in Canada. His brother Luke lived near the University at St Lucia, while teaching photographic courses and completing an Honours year., so he would see him as well.

She wondered if she'd miss David while he was away. They were not exactly living in each other's pockets but they had spent a fair bit of time together since David had bought Superman. What a name for a horse, but it suited him. His real name was SuperMax Eclipse but no one was likely to use that and besides, Superman suited him. He really was a super horse, a gentle chestnut giant with a lovely kind face showing his true nature.

In fact, David and the horse really had a lot in common, she realized. David was one of those gentle giants as well, with a real empathy for his patients and a way of listening to anything you told him that made you feel as if he was really interested. He always appeared to be turning over what you said in his mind, and asking questions that showed that he had really thought about it. Probably, this was one of the things about David that Helen admired most, and she wished that she had the ability to emulate it, but she felt it just wasn't in her nature. She couldn't help herself. When she heard a good idea, she just had to build on it, run with it and help to make it happen, jumping in boots and all with great enthusiasm. Sometimes, she felt that didn't really lend itself to empathy.

❦   ❦   ❦

CHAPTER 11

HELEN

Christmas was in full swing with parties, dinners and barbeques all crammed into the last four weeks of the year. Life in any country town becomes frenetic at certain times of the year and Christmas was one of the busiest. In the country, you don't just attend an event, you usually help organize it, fundraise for it, and drive to the nearest large town to shop for that special outfit for it. It all takes a lot more time than just turning up at an event in the city. The upside is that events are often nowhere near as expensive and because you know more people there, they can be a lot more fun.

Helen was pleased to have one night home at last, although it was a bit strange with her parents away overseas enjoying the snow and log fires. To tell the truth, she felt a little like an abandoned child and briefly wondered whether she might join them for a white Christmas. It sounded wonderful and while the north westerly blew and sucked the moisture out of everything at home and it was 45 deg in the shade, she thought longingly of the ski slopes. One thing about Carlisle, if you were trying to sell the idea of it to a Victorian, you could say it was similar to Melbourne. The climate showed huge variation; very hot, very cold, very humid or searing heat all in a week. Just last week, she'd had to slip home from an outdoor party and grab a jumper, when the evening temperature dropped dramatically from the day before.

She and David had had a good time in the last few weeks, although it had all been a little puzzling. The highlight was the Christmas Charity Ball and this was a once a year opportunity to see how all the farmers scrubbed up. It was a chance to wear a really glittering gown. Even some of the older men looked pretty good in dinner suits and without their ever-present scruffy old hats. This ball was the one where most people really went to town to dazzle, almost to the verge of bad taste, but all in good fun. 'Crossroads' were a great dance band with an enormous range of songs, in spite of the corny name. The organizing committee had excelled with the decorations, especially on the tables where bright bougainvillea vied with traditional Christmas decorations on crisp and snowy tablecloths.

The complimentary cabernet in her hand, she'd sniffed appreciatively at the rich, warm aromas of the meal being prepared by the local caterers. She hoped that they had included some of her favourite mango salad and the best caramel profiteroles in the state.

She felt good tonight, her dress an understated sheath in a deep turquoise with a heavy, self patterned woven neckline and extended shoulders which were not quite sleeves and a pair of high but extremely comfortable pewter sandals. David was so tall that she always felt comfortable beside him, her own considerable height a little less obvious than usual, and he sure looked good in evening dress. She caught his eye and they smiled warmly, just as Rhys and Josie moved up beside them. 'That looked like mischief brewing,' smiled Rhys 'or have we interrupted something private?'

'Leave them alone and get me a drink, you matchmaker,' responded Josie 'and go away so I can interrogate them in peace.'

Their group grew by the minute and by the time they moved in to the dining hall, they had collected a large group of their acquaintances, and raised speculation in quite a few households. David was a man who often touched people and his genuine warmth drew a crowd wherever they were. He had a great memory for faces and for the details that people told him of their own lives, an amazing skill that Helen admired enormously. In the short time David had lived in Carlisle, he seemed to have met and learned about, almost as many people as she knew. And she had been there all her life. She guessed that being a doctor did bring him in to contact with a great many people, and it was his job to keep track of their worries and woes, but he seemed to carry that ability with him wherever they were. She watched him now as he listened with his whole attention to whatever he was being told.

Helen herself could always remember what people told her about their property and the names of their dogs and horses, but wasn't so good on the personal details at times. The names of children and grandchildren often escaped her, and details of illnesses definitely disappeared a few minutes after she'd been told.

She'd had firsthand experience of David's empathy, the

day she took him out to visit her old home farm. It was meant to be a pleasant day, helping out the owners with a bit of mustering and then a ride down along the creek up to the boundary and back through the patch of scrub her father had been so proud of. Half-way up Rocky Creek, Jack had startled a big roo, who stood almost eye to eye with Helen as she sat on the horse.

Jack set off in pursuit with Helen desperately trying to call him off since a roo like that would make mincemeat of the dog if he was cornered. It was also quite capable of drowning Jack in the dam if he went in after it. They disappeared over the hill and into the bull paddock, the roo clearing the barbed wire with a flick of his tail and the dog slipping underneath. Helen knew it was at least a kilometer of rough country back to the gate and they'd both be long gone before they'd be back on the track of the dog. There was nothing else to do but wait close to where Jack disappeared through the fence and worry. The dog would tire long before the roo so she hoped he would come back before too long.

She and David found a tree, loosened the horse's girths and waited, but Helen was finding it hard. She'd lost a favourite dog this way before. Poor old Kipper was one of the fastest and smartest dogs they'd ever owned with a wonderful placid nature which changed to total business in a split second when he was after cattle. He'd been her constant companion on long holiday rides either alone or with her brother and sister. She remembered the sound of their voices echoing off the creek and campfires they'd had on wonderful treks on their own property, with Dad arriving with supplies in the ute wherever they had decided to camp for the night, sometimes with friends, sometimes with extended family or with just themselves.

'When they sold the farm' Helen told him, her face pensive, 'she had felt loosely tethered to the earth as if she could be shaken off at any moment. It was almost visceral and she felt its loss in every waking moment for a long, long time.'

'Sometimes I think I could understand some of the feelings of indigenous groups, only their occupation had a much longer and closer tie than mine.'

She resurfaced from her thoughts with David's arm around her and didn't need any words to know that he acknowledged the loneliness the loss of this place had left with her.

Her thoughtless dog returned at that moment, as pleased with the run as if he had caught the roo, and she and David had never talked about any of that again, although Helen was aware that David was one of the few people she could ever have expressed those thoughts to.

The Christmas Ball dinner was even better than other years, and the homemade ice cream and local strawberries with a maple syrup crisp was one of the most amazing desserts Helen had ever eaten, in spite of its simplicity.

After dinner, the band revved up a notch and like most country crowds, every age group hit the dance floor. Helen loved to dance and this band played a range of dance music that spanned the decades. There was an incredible variety of dance styles and rhythms to the same music. While some people jived, others attempted to waltz and still others were obviously fans of the dance video, knowing all the moves. The band played Shania Twain, Neil Diamond, Michael Jackson, Flashdance, Prince and a collection of other dance tunes and everyone, including the young ones had the time of their lives.

There was something about a country dance crowd, even at a formal occasion like this. Helen figured it was because people knew each other well and mixed easily that a lot of nonsense happened, or maybe it was because many of them worked in isolation, that they really celebrated at social occasions. There was something to be said for not seeing other people day in, day out but either way, it was enormous fun. She a David came in for their share of teasing.

David was a hilariously creative dancer and fooled along with the best of them, even kissing her passionately and very publicly as part of some silly party dare that had them all laughing uproariously.

'Are you sure you didn't mind Helen, it was all pretty silly really,' he apologized, as they sat in his lounge room later.

'I'd have felt worse if you hadn't,' she countered. 'It's just a part of the nonsense and if you don't give in graciously to what they want, the dares escalate.'

It didn't stop her hoping that there might be a repeat before they went home but, as usual he left her at the gate with a gentle, sweet kiss and waited until she'd gone in before he went home.

❧ ❧ ❧

CHAPTER 12

Helen was at home and the neighborhood seemed deserted. Everyone was away for Christmas and there were very few lights showing down the street.

She stared out the window and wondered what David was up to in Brisbane. He was probably shopping in air-conditioned luxury, going to concerts and dining out. 'Mmm….. eating out, was one thing she did love about the city, that and the excitement of this time of year with the lights, decorations and special family shows. Cheap and cheerful authentic ethnic restaurants were not plentiful in the country, although Carlisle had a good Chinese and one of the best gourmet pizza restaurants in Australia.

Helen thought of all the years she and her family had stayed in the Hilton for a couple of weeks during the holidays while Dad had been living there during the week and coming home on the weekends. He'd been on a contract for the company he worked for on and off even while they had the property. The energy in the mall had almost been palpable for country children who were used to a much quieter existence. There was music and there were buskers, fire-eaters, fashion shows and orchestras. Helen, her brother Damon and sister Lisa had learned to use public transport and to navigate their way around the city in their holidays, skills which were absolutely indispensable when they travelled later on. In fact, it left them with a real ability to travel in foreign cities as individuals rather than as tourists.

Later on, travelling with their parents had been a sort of examination, each child taking it in turns to negotiate the London Underground or the RER in France, following the maps and taking part in the decisions on where to go for the day. Suddenly, Helen missed her parents incredibly, but wishing they were home was not going to bring them back. There wasn't even any point to Christmas decorations since Damon and Lisa weren't coming home either. 'Poor little Helen,' she murmured to herself and then couldn't stop a giggle escaping. Last year it had been her who had escaped to England for the Christmas period, living it up with English relatives, and sharing a white Christmas while her parents missed her at home. 'Next year,' she vowed, 'I'll make sure we are all home for Christmas- Damon and Lisa too.' Although she wasn't sure how she was going to manage that.

Helen had a meeting to go to in Brisbane two days before Christmas and normally she would have driven to Riswell and caught the plane down, but that just seemed such a waste of a great opportunity for a bit of a holiday in the city.

Why not? she thought. *Why not book in and have a couple*

of days of city fun? Maybe she could talk Genevieve into meeting her there.

Genevieve was her best friend from boarding school, a petite blond where Helen was tall and definitely brunette with her naturally tanned skin and russet eyes. Dandy, grey, russet as Grandad had always said, which changed with the light and the colours she wore. Her mother was the same. With lovely olive skin, wide cheekbones and smooth, dark hair she never looked old enough to be a mother of three adult children, of which Helen was the youngest.

Picking up the phone she called Genevieve's parents number in Armidale. She was betting Genevieve would be at her parent's home rather than her own since it was school holidays. It was Genevieve's home town and where they'd met at the New England Boarding School they'd both attended. In those days they'd both been keen riders and the school had offered the only equitation program at a school in Eastern Australia. They'd been firm friends ever since, although Genevieve was much more of a party girl than Helen.

Ring Genevieve, book the Hilton, organize Maggie to look after the animals, fill the car, the list seemed endless just to get away for a couple of days but she knew it would be worth it.

'McGuires school for delinquent dogs, can I help you?' Genevieve's older brother was obviously staying with her and still hadn't grown up so Helen put on her best English Hooray Henry accent and enquired, 'I was wondering if I could speak to Miss Helen McGuire please. It's Lyndel

Jones-Smith here and my extremely valuable Pekinese, Juliet needs the services of Miss McGuire urgently."

'Ok, you win Helen,' laughed Alan. 'I'll get her for you.'

Helen could hear the scuffling in the background as Alan held the phone above his head and received a poke in the ribs for his troubles.

'Go and put the bins out, you ratbag, do something useful. Hi Helen, tell me you are going to come and rescue me from this madness.'

'Well, not exactly Gen, but I am having a couple of days in Brisbane over Christmas and maybe New Year. Are you interested?' She was sure that Genevieve would be wanting to stay home for Christmas with her parents, but maybe she could talk her in to coming up Boxing Day or a little after.

Instead, Genevieve was excited. 'Just what I would love.' She said. 'I am just so over Armidale at the moment and Mum and Dad have a McGuire family do lined up. I really don't want to go. Do you think I would be absolutely horrible if I didn't go this time?'

Helen hesitated. Nearly every Christmas, Genevieve's parents went to a huge family gathering on one of the local properties and it was an enormous amount of work and invariably ended up with the women washing up never ending loads of china plates. She could see why Genevieve felt the need to escape, just once.

'Tell your parents, I'm really lonely but I need to be in Brisbane for work,' suggested Helen. She knew if they thought she was lonely, they would insist on her coming to visit and she would end up washing up endless dishes on a stinking hot day. Brisbane, air conditioning and a little bit of spoiling was sounding better by the minute, much better than a ten hour drive each way. 'It is true, I'd be pushing it to make it to Armidale by the time I finish my meetings. It wouldn't be a great start to Christmas, but if you were in Brisbane with me, it would be amazing.'

'Done,' exalted Genevieve, 'I am practically on my way. I'll just throw the presents under the tree and I will be out that door so fast no McGuire will see me leave.'

❦ ❦ ❦

Jack watched with mournful eyes as she packed her bag and toted it out to the car. He trotted backwards and forwards to the car with her and sat at the tailgate as she loaded, just waiting for his travelling harness to appear. Sometimes, Helen couldn't wait for her parents to come home so that she didn't feel so damn guilty every time she left the dog on his own with someone coming in to feed him twice a day. If Rhys and Josie were home for Christmas, Helen knew he would be very welcome out there but there were just times when it didn't work out. He watched as she backed down the drive, then circled his bed twice and dropped with a grunt, following the car with his eyes all the way to the bottom of the street.

Helen knew there would be a little sulk when she got home. He was very good at pretending her didn't see her sometimes.

❦ ❦ ❦

When Helen reached Brisbane, she was horrified that she couldn't remember the trip down. She knew it was common with people who drove long distances regularly, but it never failed to scare her just a bit, that she couldn't remember most of the long drive. She enjoyed driving really, but her mind simply went on to auto-pilot when the road was familiar.

While the rest of Australia called Brisbane an overgrown country town, Helen knew that by world standards it was beautiful, with one of the best climates in the world. Brisbane was starting to develop a world class attitude, helped along by natural beauty, and a vastly improved transport system, particularly the ferry service. For some reason Helen just loved public transport. She assumed it was because she drove so much for her work and public transport just seemed like such an adventure and always reminded her of childhood when she and her parents caught the train in from Mayne to the Valley to go Christmas shopping, in the days before their city holidays.

She drove up to the back of the Hilton, cringing a little because her car was country-dirty as usual, and she always had the feeling that the car valet mightn't want to soil his uniform. She needn't have worried because the valet was as welcoming and friendly as always. That was what kept her coming back there, the friendly and comfortable atmosphere, plus being right in the city meant she didn't have to get in the car at all for the next couple of days. It was always a wonderful feeling to a country girl, accustomed to long distance driving. As her car disappeared into the carpark entrance, Helen silently wished it a Merry Christmas and turned to watch her bags being taken to the porter's desk. Assured of their prompt arrival in her room, she caught the lift to the reception area.

'Genevieve!' Isn't it amazing! We come six hundred

kilometers from each direction and meet as we're checking in. Look at you, a whole new outfit and we haven't even been to the shops yet.'

'And you. You're as brown as an Indian and your hair is fantastic. What have you done to it? Let me see.'

Helen spun around so Genevieve could see the tiny braids that swung in her shiny, dark mane. Just occasional little braids with tiny glittering beads, meant to sparkle in the light. As she turned they twinkled in the lights of the reception area, just like the small, Christmas lights they were meant to represent.

'Just like you, to celebrate Christmas in your own peculiar way,' said Genevieve. 'You always were a bit of a weirdo.'

'And I love you too. These are my Christmas decorations for this year. I couldn't be bothered decorating the house or a tree with just me there. What about you? You haven't grown at all.'

Genevieve's tiny size was the bane of her existence.

Each of the girls was enough to turn heads in their own way, but together they were stunning. Helen's long, smooth black hair and tall, slim figure was in complete contrast to Genevieve's true silver, blond cap and tiny bones. The happiness they wore at seeing each other again wrapped them in their own glow, and made other people in the reception area smile just to see them.

All the way up in the glass lift they chatted and laughed, each desperate to find out more of the other's doings. Not that they didn't keep in touch, but being together was different. It all came back to seventy percent of communication being body language, and the genuine joy they each felt in each other's company.

As they rode up in the glass lift, David and Liam watched in amazement from the Atrium Café.

'Helen didn't say anything about coming to Brisbane.'

'I wonder who the friend is?'

'Genevieve I guess, her old school friend. She's mentioned her a few times but I didn't get a description, apart from that she is an amazing rider and up for any adventure, I gather.'

'What a contrast.' said Liam.

At that moment Helen was laughing at something the tiny blonde had said. On a floor, way above the café, the girls stepped out and turned right toward the Queen Street side of the building, moving along among the balcony planter boxes to a room halfway along the corridor. 'Well, we know where they are if we want them,' remarked Liam, lifting one eyebrow at David.

'Is that what you want?' asked David with an edge in his voice that Liam was not slow to recognize.

'Not tonight obviously, and not tomorrow, because I've got that meeting in town with some of the people I'll be working with, both here and up north. It looks like there might be a bit of a situation with this job, some little regional jealousies and I'm going to have to tread a bit carefully. And, we're going to Luke's in the evening remember so maybe the day after tomorrow.'

'Which is Christmas Eve,' said David 'so they might have other things to do.'

'Oh well, we'll just have to see. Maybe we can just catch up for dinner or lunch.'

'Right, well, I might leave it until tomorrow morning to ring Helen since they'll be busy settling in and catching up tonight.'

The girls' version of settling in consisted of a great deal of information exchange, a meal at the Italian place in Albert Street and some serious late night shopping. Helen had a real belief in shopping locally as much as she could but there were some things it was very hard to buy in a small town and a visit to the brightly lit shops of the city was always exciting and extremely detrimental to her budget.

Both the girls admired the same sapphire, body contouring cocktail dress in Myers but the only one left fitted Genevieve's size ten frame perfectly. 'That's the worst of being a size twelve,' mourned Helen, 'so is everyone else. I'm sure most of the world is a twelve.'

'Yes, but they aren't as tall as you so you look better in a twelve than anyone else I know,' comforted Genevieve.

'Well, at least I got the last pair of those black trousers and that gorgeous red Basque top.'

'Ah yes, but I got the swimmers from heaven.'

When the shops shut at midnight the girls were carrying a multitude of bags from shops from one end of Queen Street to the other and still talking, twenty to the dozen.

They fell in to bed, falling asleep as soon as the lights were out, in spite of several cups of coffee and far too much rich chocolate dessert in the beautiful dessert shop in Albert Street down the road from the Myer Centre.

When the mobile rang at eight the next morning, Helen and Genevieve were breakfasting at the Atrium and watching the yuppies in their business suits at executive breakfasts. Part of the breakfast game between them was to spot the occasional property owner, in Brisbane for a conference or meeting, although there probably wouldn't be too many at this time of year. It was strange how even in business dress, the country men and women could be picked out from the rest of the diners. Helen herself was wearing her version of the business uniform, a neat tailored denim skirt, colored top and light jacket and her shoes were reasonably low heeled.

'Hi David.' She automatically glanced at the screen as the phone rang and saw his name appear. 'You know, I was just thinking about you and wondering what you were up to. Have you had a good week?' She held her hand over her other ear as a noisy aircrew walked past on their way to their transport to the airport.

'Yes, they've been missing you up home. Poor old Dr. Jason was nearly frantic but the locum is starting to get the hang of things now.' 'How's Liam getting along?' Her left hand fiddled with one of the small braids.

'Good, he'll be pleased.'… 'So how did you know I was here?'

Genevieve gave her a curious look that clearly asked who Liam was, but Helen lifted her shoulders in a shrug which indicated 'no one important'.

'Spying on us were you. And I thought small towns were bad.'

'Well, I'll just check with Genevieve but I would think so.'

'Putting her hand over the phone, Helen asked quietly. 'Are you interested in meeting David and Liam for breakfast tomorrow and maybe going over to Southbank?'

'Genevieve looked a little puzzled but nodded her head anyway. She had heard quite a bit about David over the last couple of months but Liam had never been mentioned.

'She says, fine. See you at eight o'clock.'

'Look Genevieve, I don't know much about Liam but you'd remember David. You know, I was telling you about him last night and the horse he bought. She frowned a little, 'He and Liam have been friends for a long time and he seems like a pretty interesting chap, but he was a bit edgy when he was up with David, so I didn't exactly chase after him to get to know him better.' She thought for a moment. 'Maybe he had a few things to work out with this accident he had and I guess a wheelchair can't have been much fun. David says he's on crutches now, although I guess he'll be back in the chair tomorrow or we won't be going too far.'

'So what's the story with you and David? I'm getting some funny sorts of vibes here.'

'To tell the truth, I'm not really sure. Just friends really but you know what small towns are like, and how after a while you start believing what everybody is saying about you.'

'Well you hang in there and let them talk.'

'Oh, it's not malicious talk, just an assumption really that we'll go places together, and it's made worse by the fact that we do enjoy each other's company and like many of the same things and live next door to each other. Plenty of ammunition there.'

'So what's he like.'

'Well, he's reasonably attractive and I really like that he's very caring of everybody. He also has this incredible ability to remember just about everything you've ever told him about yourself and treat it like it's important. I could learn a lot from that I think.'

'Helen, you always put yourself down. You are about the most caring person I know.'

'Yes, I care a lot, if only I can remember the name of the person I happen to be talking to. I hate that I often just plain don't recognize people.'

'I think we all do that, but some people are really good at hiding it.'

'Well I'd like to know David's secret then, because he never seems to forget a thing.'

'I'll have to be careful what I tell him then, won't I?' said Genevieve with a laugh.

'Oh, and Norm hates him. In fact Norm has decided that David is batting for the other side as his rumour mill puts it, and won't have him on his place and has done his best to get him kicked out of the practice. Especially after Liam came to stay with him. That vindicated Norm ten times over.' Helen pulled a face, her skin crawling at the thought of Norm.

'And is he?'

'Is he what? Getting kicked out?'

'No, is he gay?'

'Well, I wouldn't think so but maybe you have a better chance of finding out, especially when you wear those sexy new togs.'

Genevieve looked thoughtful, 'He couldn't just be using you as a cover could he?'

Helen was shocked. That thought went against everything she thought she knew about David. She knew she might have been a bit confused about where they were heading, but she'd always felt that he was a very straightforward sort of person. She was sure he would have mentioned if he was.

She shook her head emphatically.

Helen had a work meeting soon after breakfast with some of her contacts in Brisbane and the people she worked with in Riswell. She thought Genevieve was going to visit an old friend of her parents who lived in a retirement home, but when they parted in Queen Street, Genevieve was warming up her credit card with the purchase of a pair of leather sandals. 'Yet another pair of shoes to add to your extensive collection.' Helen told her.

There were two meetings lined up for the day, the first concerned with the submission that had been written earlier as part of a larger submission from the Regional Group. The whole document had been put together in a hell of a hurry because of the Government's initial procrastination in getting it out to the regions and their insistence that it still should be submitted within the original timeframe.

The second meeting was particularly important as funding for their next round of projects could depend on how well they talked today and if they managed to convince the various Government bodies that their region was vitally important and that their organisation would be able to monitor the projects effectively. This was a lot of 'ifs' for the reasonably small amount of funding they were asking for, for a project that could kick-start a niche market and potentially vital small industry for properties in the area.

They met on the third floor of the St George building in a small room overlooking the river and out toward the Riverside Plaza and Stamford Hotel. Helen watched the graceful City Cat ferries sweep up and down the river as they waited for everyone to settle with their paperwork and cups of coffee. For a moment she wished that she was there on the water. Anywhere but in the room having to explain the project yet again, to people who didn't really have an understanding of her area, of the distances and driving that was required just to obtain signatures. They didn't understand the relative unimportance of the paperwork required compared to the everyday battle of a farmers work week. Then she thought of the group of enthusiasts and committed property owners she was representing and her generous spirit and genuine belief in the project slipped back in to perspective. *A couple of hours of good solid discussion, doing the absolute best she could do and she would be a free woman for a week with the added knowledge that she had done the most she could for this year.* She smiled her warm and compelling smile and plunged in to the introductions and small talk that accompany any meeting.

At the last minute, as the meeting came to order the door opened and a man on crutches came into the room. *Liam! What was he doing here?*

Helen darted a puzzled glance and half smile his way, then sat up as the meeting opened.

Sitting on her left was Brian, the bean counter who was very far from being easy-going Rhys's favourite person, an officious and pushy head office administrative type with a prominent bottom lip, which Helen often had a great desire to flatten for him. Brian fussed over every detail, seemingly unnecessarily and although they represented the same regional organization he would often correct small details as she spoke, interrupting everyone's train of thought. It made it very difficult to function well in meetings and Rhys had often come head to head with him, but Brian was good at his job. His penchant for detail kept his paperwork meticulous and their projects well accounted for, even though that level of detail was not needed during this initial discussion of major project concepts. In reality, Brian who was not a conceptual person at all was there so that he could get an understanding of the framework of this type of project. He had no patience for or sense of a concept or any understanding of the meaning of 'DRAFT ONLY.' He was the only person she knew, who would correct spelling mistakes on a brainstorm document.

Helen smiled at the chairman, a cattleman from beyond the Darling Downs, who had been extremely informative and helpful when she and Rhys had approached him for advice on a project idea earlier in the year.

'Good morning everyone, welcome to Brisbane and what I hope will be a most productive meeting. This morning I'd like to introduce a couple of people to you. Firstly, on my left is Janice Monogan of the Murray Darling Basin Group who is going to update us a little later on some of the developments out there. With us also, is Liam Graham, who has just recently returned from Vietnam where he was working with the Mekong Project. Liam will be working with the Jabina Basin Regional Group and in particular, fairly closely with Helen's Carlisle Group. Later on, Liam might give us a run down on some of the work in the Mekong, but for the moment let's get this submission out of the way and then talk about money matters.'

'Mark, I think I'd like to comment here...'

'It couldn't possibly be done in that time frame...'

'Well the Jabina Basin Group did come up with something... Liam, your comments?'

'It was well put together, but I feel that some of the more controversial issues were not covered as completely as possible.'

'For lack of scientific evidence,' parried Helen.

'For lack of investigation, I think.'

'Well, there was not a lot of time, and volunteers can only contribute so much,' she defended.

'Then, I'm sorry but the organization needs to become more professional if they want to have a worthwhile say in Government policy.'

Helen tensed. *How could anyone be so critical of a group of volunteers who worked so hard? Liam was just another of those armchair professionals who never came out to see the way things really operated. Well, he'd find out if he ever made it on to the job and wasn't scared off by their unprofessionalism at the beginning.*

On one hand, ten professionals were needed to collect the evidence needed to convince the government that even two professional people were necessary. On the other, the whole organization was based around volunteer landowners and the specific and unrecognized professional knowledge that they brought to the organization. *'back to the grass roots',* it was referred to it in patronizing, city-slicker jargon.

The meeting ground on, and although the Jabina Basin submission was passed for inclusion in the major submission, Helen was left with a hollow feeling of incompletion and more than a little helplessness and frustration.

Liam spoke well. The politics involved in the handling of the Mekong issue were complex, with five countries involved, and the immediate survival of a huge population living on the fishing industry of a delta affected by upstream damming and the needs of a landlocked population.

As he spoke, the basic differences between his glamorous seeming international problem and the seemingly, less interesting domestic problems became obvious to Helen.

In Australia, many of the property owners were as well educated as the designated professionals and able to observe and put into words the needs of their region. There should not have been the need for as many professionals as in the third world countries Liam had worked in. Mind you, it would not have hurt them to have listened to the locals just a little more in the Mekong. She could feel resentment building up again. *How dare he come back here, and criticize something he could have little knowledge about, before even poking his nose in to the region and meeting the real people.* To add fuel to the fire, she remembered that he was a qualified lawyer, so what was he doing here applying for a lowly paid field position, then putting his lawyer skills to work. Her thoughts by this time were going round in circles and she caught herself before they circled off the planet.

This was not a good start to Christmas and a long working relationship, Helen thought with her dry humour. *I do not like this man and I have just agreed to spend time with him tomorrow. Oh well, tomorrow is another day*, she thought philosophically, not being the type of person who held a grudge.

By the time the meeting broke for lunch, Helen was looking for a little pleasant diversion and feeling the need to walk off some of the irritation of the morning. Mark joined her as the lift dropped to the ground floor and automatically turned toward the river walk with her at a brisk pace.

'So, how's the world been treating you?'

'Fine, how about you?'

'Well, we did have enough rain to be a nuisance, but basically it's dry although Christmas is coming up and they reckon there'll be good rain. I could handle Christmas day in bed, listening to the rain.' 'They', the weather bureau were the gods of the farmer and regularly predicted rain, but someone else always seemed to get it.

'Ours has been mixed. We had a lot early on, enough to stop some of our monitoring but since then it's been pretty dry. I'm hoping for rain as soon as I get home so I have an excuse to do absolutely nothing as a start to the New Year.'

'How's the education project going?'

'Really well! You know, I really enjoy that part of it. I wouldn't want to be a teacher, but going in as a guest and curriculum planner is just great.'

'You know, it will probably work out fine with Liam, if you give it a chance.'

Helen gave a sideways glance and listened carefully. Mark was usually worth listening to and now she'd cooled down a bit, she did feel as if she had been a bit quick off the mark.

'Just at the moment he can only do the paperwork and get a feel for it all through that. We do know he's good at the political stuff and negotiating although you might have to educate him a bit in local politics and possibly some basic lessons in tact. I think it can all work in well, with a bit of effort on everyone's part.

Including Liam's, thought Helen, but she asked 'Was it really that obvious that I was a bit disturbed?'

'Only to someone who knows you well and cares,' answered Mark.

CHAPTER 13

LIAM

Lunch was the usual sandwiches and grainy coffee.

It didn't change wherever you were in the world, thought Liam.

John Topliss walked over and put his hand on Liam's shoulder.

'Well done,' he said 'I thought that went pretty well.'

'Yes, well, I'm still a bit in the dark as to who everyone is,' said Liam 'and I think I may have upset the Jabina Basin people a bit just when I didn't need to. That Brian chap was on my case right from the start about some of the details he wasn't happy with. I haven't sorted it out yet but there seems to be some problem there and he took every comment I made and enlarged it ten times. I'm sure the authors of that submission would like to shoot me on sight.'

'Quite likely. Helen wasn't her usual chirpy self and she walked out in a bit of a hurry too. Normally, she would have been over here giving you a big welcome, especially since you'll be working so closely.' John wondered then whether he had let the cat out of the bag a bit since Liam's face showed firstly surprise and then considerable chagrin.

'Oh hell, that wasn't a good start them was it? I was hoping to live in Carslisle to work and Helen would be my next door neighbor.'

'Why Carslisle? Surely that will make it all a bit harder for you won't it, especially for travel to Brisbane and meeting with the Jabina Group.'

'Yes, but the job is really mostly with the Carslisle Group and besides, one of my best mates lives there so I'd move in with him. He's practically family.'

'I also think I'd like to be right in the community and get to really know what is happening there.'

'Well, you'd better make it up with Helen then. If anyone has a finger on the community pulse it is her. They think the world of her up there.'

It would have been good if I had thought a little more about where that paper came from then, Liam decided giving himself a mental kick for carelessness. He would never have gone to a meeting so unprepared during any of his overseas jobs. Obviously, he had relaxed too much back in Australia.

'Could you give me some inside information on the group? I gather that I may not be quite what they're expecting or something.'

Liam kept his eye on the door as John outlined some of the achievements and the problems facing the Carlisle committee of the Jabina Basin.

His eyes lifted as Mark and Helen came back in to the room, laughing together and totally at ease. He immediately noted what a difference it made to see the frown lines smooth away. Here, was the gorgeous girl of the evening before and his heart did an uncharacteristic flip as she turned and touched Mark's arm, smiling up at him. Momentarily, Liam felt that touch on his own arm, warm and teasing through the material of his work shirt.

CHAPTER 14

HELEN

Helen caught sight of Liam and tensed. *Why was it he immediately made her feel out-of-place and gauche, as if she were the new recruit to the team and had committed a social error by entering the room laughing.* As she watched, he turned to the man beside him, smiled an apology then made his way across the room toward Helen and Mark, with an obvious purpose in mind. Half-way across, a blonde with elegant features and a determined look stepped in front of him and introduced herself.

Right thought Helen, *Brenda is always first in with every new face in the work arena, especially if the face was attached to an attractive male body.* Until now, Helen had only seen Liam in a wheelchair and had not realised how well built he was. Broad shoulders and firmly sculpted arms filled the short sleeved work shirt to perfection, and even with the crutches she could see that he had long, sportsman's legs and narrow hips. Helen was used to the fit, lean horseman and hardworking property owners that she worked with but Liam looked even better. It was the old story reversed, 'clothes do maketh the man.' She had to admit, those same farmers she worked with regularly and never gave a thought to, looked great in evening dress-most of them scrubbed up pretty well. She wondered how Liam would look in dress clothes. Mmmmm! Her thoughts may have betrayed her, as Liam glanced across the room with a rueful half smile, indicating that he couldn't leave Brenda without rudeness, and the meeting was about to begin again.

As usual, everyone still needed to finish networking or whatever it was they were doing during the lunch break and if Liam felt any frustration at having had no chance to speak to Helen when he had been on his way across to her, he managed to hide it well, listening carefully to Brenda as they moved toward the table.

Not that she felt interested in acknowledging that she even knew him, Helen told herself trying not to remember that oddly speculative little glance as he was accosted by Brenda.

Helen was feeling guilty. She should have been adult enough to bypass her prejudices and introduce Liam around. After all, she did know him and really, when it all boiled down, had had a great evening in his company. Mark had helped to give her some perspective on the submission and how it had ended up with Liam. *But*, she consoled herself, *Brenda had seen to that good resolution by planting herself firmly as close to Liam as she could.*

And time, as it always was, was against them and she didn't get a chance to catch up at all. At the end of the meeting, Liam, looking tired and withdrawn accompanied John and Brian down in the lift and hailed a taxi, just as Helen managed to make it out of the building.

❧   ❧   ❧

CHAPTER 15

GENEVIEVE

'Mrs Latcham,' repeated the lass at the front desk 'that'll be room 212. The lift is just around the corner, take it to the second floor, room twelve.'

'No, I mean Ivy Latcham, she'll be in one of those houses as you drive in. I'm sure my parents said No 6 was hers.'

Genevieve was becoming very concerned. She'd decided to visit an old friend of her family's, an old lady who had been wonderful to her when she was a child. Ivy was a Quaker, or at least that was what everyone had assumed as she followed a religion which discouraged the borrowing of money, or conspicuous consumption and encouraged very old fashioned values. She was an old country woman who had lived near Genevieve's parents and occasionally, when Gen's parents had to go somewhere, Ivy had babysat.

Genevieve still remembered the old house, and the taste of green cordial or the smell of Anzac biscuits brought back the mysteries of her childhood and the wonders of the dim, cool verandah and the old dolls and children's clothes kept in a camphor chest. Mrs Latcham had made her own soap and Genevieve could still smell the lavender and powder smell of it. It was such a peaceful memory that it chilled her to realise how old her childhood mentor had become. Sure, the address was for Chartwell Retirement Village but Genevieve hadn't given it much thought, her parents having assured her that Ivy lived in one of those pleasant little detached homes that left her free to travel.

As she had walked in to the reception building she had looked around with interest, sure that she'd be given directions to one of one of the lovely little homes she'd noticed on the drive in. But she hadn't, and sure enough Ivy was in one of the upstairs rooms, sharing a bathroom with one other poor old lady who was so gaunt and pale that Genevieve shuddered. As a primary school teacher she was used to the other end of the age scale and sometimes the emotions and smells associated with that was enough to make her uncomfortable, but this was worse. The heavy smell of a commercial disinfectant permeated even the walls and the sound of weak coughs and distressed throat clearings reached out to smother her in their intensity. She drew in her shoulders as if the wall were moving in to touch her as she walked through the halls.

Why do we do this to our old people, she was thinking. *This is not where any of us would choose to live and especially beautiful Ivy.* It was so hard to associate her with the smells and noises that gave the home the feeling of a hospital.

Ivy's room contained all that was left of her most precious possessions and Genevieve smiled as she spotted the lovely bay stallion ornament that she'd insisted on buying for Ivy one Christmas. Here was some part of the white haired old woman in the bed that she could relate to.

Just a couple of minutes in to the visit Genevieve realized that Ivy hadn't changed. She still radiated peace, even in the midst of the activity and noise that was a cross between a hospital ward and a madhouse She was so pleased to see Genevieve that it was hard to leave at the end of the day. Instead of a lovely cup of tea and a cosy chat, and maybe taking Ivy out to lunch, Genevieve ate in the home dining room and looked after all the other oldies at Ivy's table. There were some wonderful stories, but the pleasure of brightening the day of so many old people didn't compensate for finally realizing that this was everyday life for the home loving, hospitable and active person that Ivy had always been. Genevieve kept thinking that there had to be another way and it was in a thoughtful mood that she reached the reception area in the Hilton and sat down in the deep, comfortable blue chairs to wait for Helen. Her gaze roved idly around the room people watching, and snagged on an attractive man who seemed to be watching her. She was quite surprised when he rose and came across to introduce himself.

'I know you don't know me,' he said' but I'm David Temple, Helen's neighbour.'

'Genevieve,' she said as she held out her hand 'Helen has mentioned you.'

'Well, I do have an advantage. I was here with a friend last night when you both arrived, and we watched you go up in the lift.' David didn't add that they had also watched half the restaurant watching them go up in the lift. He felt it may have been bit early in their friendship to embarrass her with this information.

'Why didn't you come over?'

'You looked so happy to see each other that we didn't want to intrude and also Helen hadn't mentioned that she was coming down to Brisbane so I felt a bit hesitant about butting in.'

'Thank you, you're probably right. It was so good to get together again. Helen is the closest I have to a sister. It always feels like years between catch-ups.'

'Have you had a good day, you and Helen?'

'Oh, we weren't together. Helen had a meeting and I went to visit an old friend. What about you?

'Pretty quiet day really. I went to visit one of my patients at the hospital, an eight year old boy who ended up there as a complete shock to everybody. Such a great kid too.'

'What about your friend from last night. Is he staying here too?'

'No, no, Liam and I are staying at his unit just up the road.'

'I assume that's he Liam that we are meeting up with tomorrow? Is he here?'

'He had a meeting too. Something to do with his new job and I think he was a bit nervous about it, which is really weird for Liam. He can usually handle just about anything and he has been doing much more high powered work overseas I gather. This seems to be really important to him.'

'Liam is the man that Helen met at your place isn't he?'

'Mmm, he stayed with me for a week or two after his

accident and Helen met him then. I'm not sure they were very impressed with each other and they only met once or twice. Liam was pretty intense at the time, a bit unsure about his treatment and Helen had had a really bad meeting the one night we really got together. It turned out a great evening in the end although I'm not sure I did the right thing, introducing them that particular night.'

'I'm not sure you can take responsibility for the way other people feel all the time. We do our best and sometimes it just doesn't work out.'

'So true, but I can't help but worry, and feel I should do something about it. They are two of my favourite people and they didn't get off to a great start.'

'That's true, well at least I know that Helen is great, but as I don't know Liam I'll take your word for it. In that sort of situation, I always feel there's more I should be doing then it all becomes too much and I do nothing.'

'That sounds like a very recent experience you're thinking off and a bit of depression coming on. Did something happen today?'

David could have bitten out his tongue, asking such a question in the first few moments of their acquaintance, but Genevieve didn't seem concerned.

'The old friend I visited today shook me completely. Last I knew she'd come up here to stay in a retirement village near her family. Today, I found out her son and his wife were killed in a road accident and she has gone so far downhill that she's in the nursing home part and has no one to visit her because she doesn't know many people here. She didn't write to tell anyone because she didn't want them to worry.' Genevieve paused to smile unhappily at David, then continued 'Last time I saw her she was driving her own car and helping at the school, now she's an old lady. I feel I should do something, but what? Mum and Dad will be so shocked and I feel terrible. I can hardly take her back with me. There's no home in Middleton where I live, although there is in Armidale and I couldn't leave her at home while I work even if she did come home with me. It's horrible.'

David was a sympathetic listener and by the time Liam and Helen turned up, almost simultaneously, Genevieve was feeling more positive about being able to help Ivy with regular visits, letters and phone calls and David had helped her to realize that lots of people from Armidale came to Brisbane. She would mount a 'Visit Ivy 'campaign when she went back home. Meanwhile she and Helen would go out to see her again before they left to go home. Seeing Helen would brighten Ivy's day as well. David even promised to pay an occasional visit when he came to Brisbane, especially since Ivy sounded very much like someone his sister Katie would love to know. Katie was a writer and always had an ear out for a good story from different areas of Australia. 'Maybe we could visit together during the week,' he suggested.

Helen and Liam entered the waiting area at the same time, both lifts disgorging passengers simultaneously, Helen from the car park where she'd gone to retrieve a Christmas list from the glove box, and Liam from the ground floor Taxi entrance.

Liam looked tired.

Genevieve soon saw David jump in to caring mode although she wasn't sure Liam was as appreciative as she would have been.

David rose and took his friend by the elbow, helping him to ease himself into an armchair.

She could see Liam think about objecting and then relax but it was David who explained.

'This was his first day out without the wheelchair and crutches are so tiring.'

'Liam, we needn't go out to Luke's if you aren't up to it.'

'I would think he'll be pretty disappointed, wouldn't you. After all, it's two years since I've been back and I didn't see him for more than a couple of minutes then and I don't think you've caught up with him much either. Besides I'd like to see how he's getting on.'

'Well what if I go and get the car and bring it around through the driveway now and you can have a nap in the chair while you are waiting.'

Liam started to insist that he was fine and would be able to make it back to the unit, then seemed to realise how ungracious he was being, not to mention impossible it would be. He eased back into the chair. 'Tell me again why I met you here instead of at the unit.'

David looked a little abashed. 'Because it was easy for the taxi to drop you off here where you could get a seat easily and where I could pick you up easily. Less walking for you. It's just that I was running late so I dropped in to see if you were early. I was going to race back and get the car and be back to get you but Genevieve and I got talking.'

Liam looked at him expectantly.

'And I forgot that was what I was going to do so I'm still here. Maybe we can go out and stay the night and talk in the morning. I don't think Luke has to work in the morning.'

'Sounds good, but we were coming here for breakfast, remember.'

'Don't worry on our account,' said Helen quietly 'we could both do with a sleep in anyway.'

Genevieve looked at her. It was unusual for Helen to sound so ungracious.

❧   ❧   ❧

CHAPTER 16

HELEN

In spite of her promise to sleep in, Helen was awake bright and early and to avoid waking Genevieve who always slept in, she dressed in the bathroom and then let herself out of the room. It was quite possible Genevieve would sleep in till nine o'clock if no one woke her, so Helen had a couple of hours to indulge in a peaceful walk down near the river. She wandered up the mall toward Victoria Bridge, admiring the Cultural Centre and museum across the river. In the middle of the bridge she stopped to look back and glance at the Old Treasury Building and the Conrad Hilton, which was the old Lands Department building.

'I must go out to the University this time,' she thought. It's so beautiful and there won't be many students around. I'm sure Genevieve has never seen it. Of course, coming from Armidale, Genevieve thought that the University of New England campus with its beautiful avenue of Autumn trees and vine covered pathways was the most beautiful in Australia, especially since she had done her teaching degree there. Helen had done part of her degree at Armidale then moved up to the University of Queensland, at St Lucia, for the remainder, and for her post-graduate as well. Some of her degree work had also been out at the Gatton Campus and she was pleased that she'd had the opportunity to go to all three even if it had taken a little longer. As she walked along the river path, she watched the bike-riders on their way to work and wished she had her push-bike with her. It really was the best way to get around Brisbane, especially if you were working or studying at any of the many campus's close to the River. *It was strange how important the River had become in the last twenty years or so, she thought. I remember Mum and Dad saying that when they lived here as young people, no one but a couple of old cross-river ferries used it.* Now, there were bike paths from Riverside to St Lucia Campus, which must have been about 15 km, on both sides of the river, and the Rivercats cruised up and down the river from below Newfarm to St Lucia. It was a shame the beautiful floating river walks further down the river had been washed away during the floods in 2010 but she'd heard that the Council were looking at building new ones. 'What an amazing and inexpensive way for tourists to see our city,' she thought as she watched the city cats.

As she rounded the University of Technology, she caught sight of the Kangaroo Point cliffs across the river. There were abseilers there, even this early in the morning she noted, and a group of people having a picnic breakfast below the cliffs. There were walkers and joggers and push-bikers competing for the tracks below the cliffs and all along the Southbank boulevards. There was a group of kayakers and even a stand up paddler getting his feet wet to get across the river to work. She would like to have stayed see where he stored the boat, or did you call it a ski, but decided she's better keep walking instead. She turned and watched him every now and again but he disappeared before pulling in to the banks so she still didn't learn his secret.

She decided she'd walk as far as the Marina, check out all the boats to see what countries they'd sailed from and then head up to the hotel. If Genevieve wasn't awake by then, then she'd just have to wake up. Suddenly, Helen was in a hurry to begin her holiday.

'Come on, I'm starving.'

'All right for you, you've probably worked up an appetite, but I need more sleep.' Genevieve was not a morning person and Helen often wondered how she made it to work each day.

'Half the day will be gone by the time we have breakfast and those dratted men will be here before we've even seen a shop if you don't get out now.'

Having got her own way Helen leafed through the brochures in the room to see what free entertainment was organized in the city area, while Genevieve was dressing.

'Hey Gen, there's a Christmas performance at Southbank this afternoon, featuring that singer from Bardot. You know, the blonde one that's gone out on her own.'

Through the bathroom door Helen heard 'You mean Sophie Monk and her new single. I liked that.'

'Yeah, I liked it too, so maybe she's worth a look.'

'You are so hopeless with names. I don't know how you ever do a job where you have to network all the time.'

'I just remember what property they come from or where they work. Easy! Even easier if they have horses or dogs.'

'So how was the meeting yesterday, did you get it all off your conscience before Christmas?'

'Not too bad but it started off a bit rocky. You know I told you about the chap that's eventually coming to work with me? Well, he was there yesterday and as it turns out its Liam and he came on a bit strong for a newcomer I thought. He was a bit critical.'

'What happened?'

Helen explained the misunderstanding if you could call it that, and as she did she could see that her own discomfort with the submission process had coloured her perception of Liam's contributions to the meeting. It was strange how telling someone else gave it a completely different perspective.

Genevieve looked a little surprised and said without hesitation, 'Do you think your reaction was obvious to everyone else?'

'Well, I know Mark realized because we talked a bit about it at lunch.'

'It sure doesn't sound like you at all.'

'I know, I really don't know what it was. Maybe I just need a holiday.'

'Well then, let's go shopping and let the holiday begin,' called Genevieve as she exited the room quickly, last up but first to the shops.

Just then, the phone rang and David's warm voice came on. 'Helen, would you like to meet over at Southbank at around eleven thirty? I think Liam will be fine by then and Luke will have had enough of us. He starts work at twelve so we'll just be in the way shortly.'

Luke was David's younger brother and a keen footballer. He didn't have a lot of room in the unit he shared with a young chap from Darwin and Helen imagined Liam and David and Luke who was at least their size, plus another footballer rattling around in a small apartment. She couldn't help but smile at the picture it made.

'What about we meet you at the Deckhouse then? I feel like a leisurely lunch and maybe a peek at the show afterwards.'

'What's on.'

'Just a Christmas performance with a few different singers and one of them is that Sophie Monk from Bardot, and also the choir and orchestra from the Bayside Girls College. They're always good.'

'That sounds like a good line-up and I'm sure Liam will enjoy it as well so we'll see you there then,' agreed David.

❦   ❦   ❦

Helen amazed herself at how easily she could bury differences and feel comfortable with someone she had had a disagreement with not long before. She often wondered if she was a bit wishy- washy in her dealings or if there was something ambivalent in her personality that allowed her to dissimulate so easily. In spite of the fact that she felt she had a million reasons not to look forward to seeing Liam again, and part of that was guilt over her own rude behavior, they'd had a great afternoon.

David and Genevieve were both peacemakers in their different ways, and had greased the wheels of conversation excellently. No work talk was allowed, which was one of Genevieve's rules. As a teacher in a small town, she often found herself with parents of children she taught or with other teachers socially and she had decided early in her career that there was a time and place for social talk and a time for work. It didn't always work with child obsessed or aggrieved parents but Liam and Helen managed it with good grace.

A beautiful day, near Christmas at Southbank wasn't a time to work and Helen was pleased that Genevieve had tactfully mentioned her preference to both the men. They just concentrated on being themselves on a fine sunny day near the river.

There was plenty to see. Wandering buskers and semi-circus performers appeared during the school holidays and there were children's shows and Christmas shows, but the best bit was the food. Helen hit the noodle bar and later on, the Mediterranean Café with an appetite starved for Japanese and Greek food. That was the one thing she didn't have in common with the older beef farmers in her area. Many of them were great believers in using the home product, preferably as steak or roast and the obligatory but reviled three vegetables that went with them. Some of the younger farmers were notable foodies though, and the odd work jaunt became an exploration of food and wine when they got together, paid for from their own private purses and very much enjoyed.

Helen was thinking of one trip to the Barossa Valley in particular, where she's gone some of the younger farmers in her area to meet with Jim Lester a man who was doing some very proactive water conservation work on his property.

'Ah, guys….there's this great Lebanese restaurant not far from here and I was wondering…..who'd be interested in

Lebanese tomorrow night. Honestly, it's the best in Brisbane everyone says and I'd like to see if it's true.'

Liam took the challenge. 'I'd be interested, I've heard about it before and I've been told it's as good as you'll get anywhere in the world. Well, apart from Lebanon and a few close neighbours maybe'. Helen knew that Liam had spent some time in Lebanon, although with the ban on work talk, the only detail they learned was about the people and the food and some of the political nuances. Helen would have loved to sit down and pump him for geographical information and find out what it was like to really live and work in a country like Lebanon but that would have to wait for another day.

Genevieve groaned. She'd forgotten Helen's obsession with different foods, the wider the variety the better. Helen reminded her of some horses that could never seem to graze peacefully, but were continually on the move to search out different plant varieties. Fortunately, like Genevieve herself, Helen never seemed to fatten either. 'OK, but I bags we eat at the Hilton the next night. I just love their desserts and that buffet of entrées is almost as perfect as the dessert bar. I don't need a main meal at all.'

This was another of the mysteries of life. Just where did Genevieve pack all the dessert she ate?

Helen was perfectly happy to eat at the Hilton on Christmas Day and both the young men were agreeable so the group broke up at last to arrangements for Christmas dinner and various entertainments proposed for the next couple of days.

❦ ❦ ❦

The girls elected to walk over the bridge home to the Hilton, vowing they would be absolutely safe with the Christmas crowds moving around, while David drove Liam back to his unit.

The walk over the river on Victoria Bridge was incredible at that time of night and there were still a lot of people around, enough that the girls felt perfectly at ease. Helen thought back to when she came to Brisbane with her parents and the stories they'd told about Brisbane at night when they were younger. Not that Brisbane was a rough place, but with the whole of the city-centre shutting down at night and the industrial and boat building areas on the south bank, it wasn't a place that you walked around at night. Now, there were even families returning to the units in the city and a multitude of Asian students, many of whom lived in the same sort of units that Liam was currently occupying.

Helen knew, that as you got out of the lift in Liam's building the smell of Indian or Chinese cooking would be drifting around the hall like a tasty soup and she mentally followed the men, wondering what it would be like to be going home to an apartment rather than a motel room. Her family had always stayed in apartments when they travelled, except in Brisbane, and she had fond memories of shopping for groceries in England and France or any country they stayed in. Her parents always said it was half the fun of travelling, seeing what was for sale in other supermarkets and stores.

Genevieve studied her as they leaned on the rail of the bridge looking at the water 'You are thinking very deeply and I have a sneaky feeling I know what of,' she said.

Helen turned to look at her 'Well, share the secret so we both know.'

'Well, he's been to Lebanon, loves food from all sorts of places and will be working in your office.'

'What on earth made you think that?' demanded Helen. 'It so happens I wasn't, I was thinking of Mum and Dad and wondering how they were travelling.'

Genevieve didn't look at all convinced and shook her head, 'Then how is it that suddenly our week for two has become a week for four?'

'Oh Gen, I'm sorry. I'm not sure how that happened. Do you want me to ring and back out, maybe tell them we've decided to go up the coast instead?'

'No, of course not. I'm just not sure which of us agreed to it, but I'm very happy if you are. Besides, they've both promised to come and visit Ivy and I absolutely know that will be the high point of her year, so I couldn't back out and deprive her of that, even if she doesn't know about it yet.'

The next few days were spent mostly with David and Liam, Christmas dinner was a huge success, as were the dinners they teamed up to cook in Liam's apartment. All of them visited Ivy together to her great delight and her prophecies of romance were not only confided to her roommate but provided food for gossip for the whole home. Ivy was thrilled to receive so many visitors and she and David hit it off straight away. Of course, David was a doctor and was very easy around an old and bedridden lady but Liam was obviously not quite as comfortable. Helen was pleased to see Ivy but shocked by the change in her and her circumstances. Last time Helen had seen her, Ivy had bustled around her kitchen, preparing tea and biscuits for Helen and Genevieve and Helen's parents, talking about her son and his wife and how she was going to live near them and making all sorts of plans for trips away and visits to Helen's parents. *How could this happen, how could things change so quickly,* thought Helen *and we didn't even know about it.* Genevieve's parents were going to be horrified that Ivy had not told them, but as Ivy explained, she hadn't wanted to burden them and she was not their responsibility so she had asked the home not to tell anyone about her move into the home itself. 'Everyone in Armidale knew that Ivy's son and daughter-in-law had been killed in an accident soon after Ivy moved to Brisbane but her occasional letters had said nothing about her own change in circumstances, except little observations of the other residents and the staff that had made her life seem quite full and pleasant.

'Fibbing by omission' as Genevieve told her forcefully. 'You needn't think you'll get out of visits from us this way, and maybe you'll be able to visit us sometimes. I'm sure we can find a way.'

On the way back to the city, when David and Genevieve stopped off at a small supermarket in Milton, to pick up some little necessities for Ivy, and a few extra's such as the chocolates Genevieve knew she loved, Liam and Helen wandered down to the river.

'You know I have decided to move in with David when I start work. I'm sure I can work as well in Carlisle as in Riswell. 'Will that worry you?'

Helen was immediately on the defensive 'Is there any reason why it should?'

'Well I felt we didn't start very well and I don't want to

make it hard, but I think David needs me at the moment, with Jonathon and everything.'

Helen stepped back. *Why is Jonathon so important?* she thought. *He keeps coming up but no-one is saying why, except that he's decided to stay overseas.* She tried to look as if she knew what Liam was talking about, but he was continuing on.

'Helen, I'm sure we can work this out.' He looked at her seriously 'I would like to...' and reached out toward her as David and Genevieve caught up with them.

'I bought Ivy a little gift for her birthday on the10th, so I thought we'd put all our names on it.'

Genevieve looked from Helen to Liam and Helen knew there was going to be a question and answers session when they got back to the hotel room.

CHAPTER 17

'Rhys, you'll never guess who our newest staff member is!' Helen thought she'd get in first to tell everyone so there wouldn't be any inadvertent rehashing of the submission process and reference to earlier conversations about it, especially in front of David.

'Remember David's friend Liam? Yeah, well I met him at that meeting just before Christmas and there were a few sparks flying. He and Brian didn't hit it off real well so that should recommend him to you.' Helen didn't bother to tell Rhys that she'd practically spent the holiday in Liam's pocket.

'What did you think of him, young Helen?'

'He's very professional... I'm not sure, very different from David, but as for the rest I guess I'll just have to wait and see.' She could see Rhys trying to picture Liam, whom he'd seen once, in the role of an employee. It was rather like catching a lizard and finding you had an alligator.

'Did you find out what the holdup was besides him being hospitalized?'

'I think it was to do with the fact that he's got more than

just science qualifications, and they kind of rewrote the job description, which changed the funding a little bit.'

'So what's so good about him?

'He's studied law and specialized in environmental issues but he wants to work in country Australia. He's tired of being overseas and doesn't want to live in the city. So, we're the lucky ones.' Rhys shuffled the papers he was holding and glanced over, a little surprised by the tone of her voice.

'That sounds a bit reserved for you, just a tad ungrateful.'

Helen thought she had managed to get her voice quite neutral but obviously there was no fooling Rhys, who had known her most of her life.

'Not at all, I just hope he lasts a while. I get a bit tired of people coming in and telling us how to do the job then moving on. He's already decided that we're unprofessional, no…I shouldn't say that, he took it back when he realized the timeframe we'd been given and here you go, that was very unprofessional of me to prejudice you before the poor guy's even started. Forget I said all that, he's a lovely man and we're lucky to get him. There you are.' She knew it sounded childish, even as she said but sometimes it was impossible to get the right words when you wanted them.

'Helen this doesn't sound like you at all. You're usually so upbeat about new people and changes.'

'Hmmm… you're right. I don't know, I just don't feel comfortable with it all. You know, change imposed from above and all that, but I'll be right once we work out a relationship.'

What that relationship was likely to be, puzzled her. What was it he had been going to say on the riverbank? Surely he wouldn't come on to David's girlfriend. Or was she David's girlfriend? There seemed no proof of that either. In Brisbane he had made no special effort to be near her. In fact, he and Genevieve seemed to peel off as a couple more often than she and David did so maybe her relationship with David only existed in the minds of the people of Carlisle. *Small towns and all that goes with them,* she thought.

'You know David doesn't seem his usual self either, now that I come to think of it, you two haven't had a falling out have you?' Rhys said thoughtfully.

'No, I think it would be impossible to fall out with David but you're right and I can't help you, I don't know what it is. Maybe, he doesn't really want Liam to move in or something.'

Helen wondered if it was that or the mysterious Jonathon, making David more serious than usual. Perhaps, she should just bite the bullet and ask him, but somehow Jonathon just seemed like a closed subject. She wondered if she had a touch of Norm's belief about David, but shook her head in denial. That didn't seem right to her either.

'Josie was wondering if you and David would like to come out to tea sometime this week since we didn't see you over Christmas. You could bring Liam too if you like, and introduce him to local high society.'

'Lowlifes, more likely, but I'm sure he'll be happy to come. It'll depend on David's schedule but I haven't got any meetings this week so I suppose Liam hasn't either. We're sort of on the same meeting schedule at the moment but that will change as we decide which projects we are going to take individual responsibility for. You might even like the guy, he's been around a fair bit and kept his eyes open, so he's extremely interesting to talk with.'

'I sense a mystery here. How come you know all this on the basis of one hurried meeting?'

Caught out, Helen had to laugh and wonder why she'd avoided the subject so far.

'Well, it just so happens Genevieve and I met David and Liam in Brisbane and spent a bit of time together, and before you ask, the subject of work did not come up. We let that one lie by common consent.'

Rhys gave her a thoughtful look. Why on earth hadn't Helen mentioned it? She would normally have been keen to tell him all about the new team member and full of plans on how to include them socially, especially since Liam was coming to live in Carlisle. Come to think of it, she'd been pretty quiet about this chap all around. Maybe she really didn't like him at all, and was going to let everyone find out for themselves, but she had slipped up on the charge of unprofessionalism. Well, time would tell and Rhys was not going to worry about it till it happened. If he worried about every little thing he would have had no hair a long time ago, instead of the little he did have left.

'So you'll organize these two neighbours of yours for one evening the week after next, will you.'

'I'll do my best. Liam gets pretty tired still and I'm not sure how he'll go after a week at work, but he's a big boy and can make up his own mind about that.'

Privately, she also thought a night out at Rhys and Josie' might rally David a little as well.

❦   ❦   ❦

By the time the dinner date rolled around, Liam had been ensconced in the office for a week and a half. They'd found him somewhere to sit, a computer to work at when he wasn't working in Riswell, and introduced him to some of the volunteers. Thankfully, he hadn't had to face Norm yet, although Helen suspected that Liam would make mincemeat of Norm, at least she hoped so and she secretly looked forward to it.

Liam had turned on the charm with all the ladies, and talked seriously to all those who wished to be serious and generally started to make himself indispensable, all within the first week. He had proved himself as an easy officemate, as prepared to make the coffee or lend a hand to scan or photocopy, as to get out in the field and take samples. In fact, he really seemed to enjoy some of the more mundane tasks and Helen really hoped that it was not just a settling in phase.

Some of the tension that Helen had noticed in him at odd times, seemed to have disappeared, although she couldn't help but be aware that Liam and David seemed to have something very tense between them at times. It was so unlike easygoing David, that Helen found herself watching them. It was as though there was something unsaid between them all the time they were together, a waiting and expectancy that she found it hard to put her finger on.

Liam seemed to watch David with a cross between puzzlement and frustration while David seemed undecided and nervous at times. She'd come upon them a couple of times exchanging heated words and Liam seemed to be pressuring David at some times and comforting him at others. Helen was occasionally aware of long silences when she was with David that before had been filled with easy conversation, so that he seemed to be making an effort to be social, even with others besides Helen rather than the chap who had just plain enjoyed every event.

Their conversations over the fence became awkward and forced, each avoiding topics that they felt the other one might not be comfortable with. Helen wished she could just ask David flat out about Jonathon and Liam and where they all fitted in, but the topic seemed off limits. She did wonder how much of that was in her own head.

Helen had worked with a girl once who would have asked David and Liam for every intimate detail of their lives as easily as asking a child its name. Leanne could say the most outrageous things to people and no one ever seemed to take it the wrong way. Helen wished desperately that she could take a leaf from Leanne's book and just come straight out with a few questions that she would love to know the answer to, but it just wasn't in her makeup to race in and ask personal questions, no matter how much she wanted to know.

'Liam, you know Rhys, and this is Josie, his long suffering business partner and wife.'

'Not so much of that, we know who suffers around here.' The women smirked at each other, Josie raising a quizzical eyebrow. Helen's mother always said that Josie was probably the kindest person she had ever met, with a heart that had room for everybody and Helen had to agree. There was something about Josie that made you warm to her the minute you met her and Helen wondered if it was something to do with the way her smile turned up at the corners of both her mouth and her eyes.

There were several others in the room when they arrived, just a little bit late. David, being a doctor, didn't often manage to get anywhere on time.

'This is Jess and Fiona and that old bloke in the corner is Owen, who's been allowed out on his own.'

Liam nodded to them all and looked enquiringly at David.

'It's Ok, I know everyone. It doesn't take long in a place like this, and besides if you hang around with Helen for a while, you'll get to know the whole town.'

Rhys and Josie's house was unusual, shaped like a 'c' with a large open area in the middle that was like a room without the wall to the outside. Here, Rhys and Josie even had a proper lounge and close to the internal walls a piano. Helen had often wondered what would happen in one of the violent windstorms that occasionally swept Carlisle, but Rhys claimed that it faced the right way and never got the storm blows. Since the house was over eighty years old and had been in Rhys's family since it was built, she guessed he would know.

'Everyone coming tonight is part of the Landcare Group so you'll see quite a bit of most of them in the future,' said Josie. 'I even thought of inviting Norm, but that thought didn't last long.'

'Well, I'm glad of that then' David grimaced.' I'm surprised you even thought it briefly.'

'Who is Norm?' asked Liam. 'I keep hearing funny little bits.'

'Ask David, he's his special friend,' said Rhys, with a teasing look in David's direction.

Liam looked at David and opened his mouth to ask, but

David, looking uncomfortable and muttering about hearing another car, had moved toward the door.

Helen rushed in, 'Norm is a cross old man who likes to make everyone miserable,' she said. Instead of adding that Norm had as much as accused David of being a homosexual, in the nastiest and most public way he could think of, Helen continued, 'He knocked every single thing David tried to do to help the group on the grounds that he was a city boy and wouldn't know how to do anything properly, just because David had a different way of doing things, like tying off wire and moving posts. Now, wouldn't Norm get a shock if he saw how our 'city boy' can ride a horse and cut out stock?' she asked Rhys.

Rhys nodded. 'That's some horse he's got though. He's taken to the stock work like a duck to water.'

Liam looked interested and commented to David when he came back 'If you'd like that horse ridden anytime, you know who to ask.'

'That'd be right' thought Helen 'I'll bet he can ride as well as he does everything else.'

What was it about Liam that made her so defensive, she immediately wondered but said out loud 'I imagine you won't be riding for a little while Liam. Maybe by then we'll have found you a great horse of your own.' There that sounded friendlier, didn't it?

As the conversation roamed from horses to cattle, the weather and new beef management technology, Helen watched as David came back into the room again, this time with Liz and Michael. David did not look toward Liam at all, but devoted himself to helping Liz stow away the desserts she'd brought with her to help Josie out. Just what was wrong with David? The slightest mention of Norm had him running and there was some connection with Liam that she was completely missing. She wondered if she dared to ask Liam the question that was burning in her mind. Was David really gay, and was that who Jonathon was? A lot of funny little things were beginning to make sense if that was the case. Not that it would bother her in the slightest although the town grapevine would have a field day since they'd practically married her and David off. And where did Liam stand in all of this? Was he a part of the problem with Jonathon or just trying to help?

Helen really had to do some thinking about how she felt about all of this, if it was true.

Even though she had no problems with it on principle, it was different if you weren't being told the truth and the truth was a hard thing to ask for. She wasn't sure if she even had the right to ask for the truth. Should she put some pressure on David to make him tell her, or should she sit tight and be just a sympathetic friend? Was David simply using her as a shield? She hoped that their friendship was a true friendship whatever happened, since she was really very fond of him, but not she had suddenly realized recently fond enough to become a lover, whichever way their relationship went.

At least that realization did make her life a little easier, but she found herself unable to be comfortable just the same.

Just then, David came over and sat down beside her, closer than he usually did. She saw Liam frown as their shoulders touched and David's hand closed over hers with a convulsive movement. A perverse streak made her turn to David and smile, and a warm and genuine smile lit his face as if she were a haven in a hostile world, although the room was filled with uncritical and genuinely caring people. Helen let her hand lie there. One of these days she was going to have to have this out with David, but for the moment it was enough that he seemed to need her support.

The evening turned out to be enormous fun as it always did at Rhys and Josie's. After dinner, the group broke into teams to play Pictionary, a ridiculous game where a team member drew a picture representing a word on a card picked at random, and there was a race between teams to guess the word.

Josie, Michael and Liz competed outrageously as the red team while Liam, Fiona and Jess became the green team. Rhys and David chose Helen as their first pictorialist by common consent, both of them denying any ability to draw, while Owen elected to be impartial witness.

'Impartial, my foot. You know which side your bread's buttered on old man.'

'That is definitely not a dinosaur. Looks more like a duck.'

The game ran hot and wild, with accusations, laughter and insults flying.

'What's that? A sausage dog?'

'It looks like a martian.'

'It's a what?'

'Here give me that pencil, even a broken down old farmer can draw better than that.'

Helen made a grab for the pencil Rhys had filched and held out of her reach, laughing at the absurd claim. The hand she supported herself with on the table slipped and as she fell she threw herself sideways to avoid the tray of coffee cups on her left. A yelp of pain surprised her as she landed heavily in Liam's lap, knocking his crutches flying with a deafening clatter. Amongst the concerned voices she could hear Liam's pained breathing and jumped horrified to her feet. His face was white and strained with the effort to control his pain and David was already steadying him with professional concern and gentle voice.

'Look, I think Liam should stay here tonight if that's OK with you and Rhys, Josie.

I don't think there's any major damage done but there does seem to be a strong shock reaction and I've no doubt he'll be sore for a while. Do you mind if I stay too, and that way I can keep a check tonight and drive him home in the morning.'

'Well that was a heck of a way to break the party up.' Helen was numb as she drove home with Michael and Liz. David had assured her that it could have happened any time and that he had told Liam over and over, and the physiotherapist had told Liam, that he was doing too much, but it wasn't easy to get him to rest.

At least, Helen told herself, *that explained some of the tension between David and Liam*, but that didn't help to erase the anguished look on David's face when it had first happened or the fact that he didn't want to drive Liam home in the same car as Helen. Surely it wouldn't have hurt to bring him home, closer to the clinic and the hospital if they were needed. There were so many things Helen found it hard to understand and she was not used to the feeling of being an outsider. She found it hard to understand herself, and why she just couldn't seem to ask the right questions.

For some reason, nothing seemed easy for her around David and Liam most of the time.

❦   ❦   ❦

'Could you do me a big favor, Helen?' pleaded David the following Wednesday afternoon, 'I have to go to Brisbane for a couple of days, and for the weekend, and Liam is not as good as he thinks he is. He has strict instructions for bed rest for this week and I wondered if you could pop over and take him some meals, so he doesn't have to move around more than necessary.'

'Sure David, I can manage that,' agreed Helen 'I don't have a lot of travel in the next couple of days and I'm home all week-end, so it'll be fine.'

'I'll warn you, he is not a good patient. A bear with a sore head has nothing on him and he probably won't be terribly grateful.'

'Does he blame me for putting him back on the bed, you know by falling on him the other night?'

'No, I don't think so. He knew he had it coming. He's been doing too much, and anyway I don't blame you, and I'm the doctor around here. Probably the best thing for him anyway, he needs the rest.

Helen wondered if Liam saw it that way but she felt a lot better about the whole episode and she was pleased that David had turned to her. She'd thought things seemed a little strained the last couple of days, even more than in the previous weeks, although they had hardly seen each other except passing in the drive way.

Probably, just my eternal guilty conscience and overdeveloped sense of responsibility, again, she thought.

She promised herself that when David came home, she would ask him straight out who Jonathon was and what relationship he had to everybody including Liam. It always seemed to Helen that Liam was a bit protective of David where Jonathon was concerned. It was an odd sort of triangle.

Thursday lunchtime, she headed home from the office for lunch, bringing a Donar kebab from the shopping center for Liam as well. The smell as she drove home woke her stomach to the fact that she hadn't eaten since an early breakfast.

'Well come in, I'm not getting up to open the door for you,' shouted the voice from within David's house when she knocked to let him know she was there.

'Didn't expect you to,' she muttered 'but hello would be nice.'

'But you already know what a bear I am. I'm sure David told you not to come any closer than I can reach,' he growled, 'I eat little girls for breakfast.'

'Well, I think you'd find me pretty tough and anyway, what's your problem? I can say I'm sorry that I hurt you when I fell but somehow I don't think it will make any difference.'

'No, it won't. Look, I'm sorry if you feel bad about it but don't expect any more than that.'

'I don't expect anything and I don't want anything but for you to eat your lunch. That way you'll please David, too. I'll see you at tea tonight.' And Helen walked out. How was she going to put up with several days of this? She hadn't even asked him how he felt.

CHAPTER 18

LIAM

Liam scowled after her *Please David…. is that all she was worried about? She hadn't even asked how he felt.*

By the time Helen returned with dinner, Liam had convinced himself she was not coming back and to tell the truth, he didn't really see why she should. He decided he would apologise properly the minute she walked through the door. If she walked through the door, that was.

It seemed to take ages from when the car pulled up in the garage next door till the kitchen window lit up. Helen hadn't drawn the blind and Liam could see her moving around from where he sat in the lounge. She moved in and out of view and the light was swallowed by her dark hair, leaving her lovely face in bright relief. Every expression showed as she listened to Enya's haunting voice and occasionally sang parts of the melody, fading in and out of range as she moved around the house. Liam wished he could hear her more clearly. He'd been told she had a lovely singing voice by more than one person and David had said she occasionally sang with him while he played the guitar. His fingers itched for his piano and he could feel the notes vibrating in them. His piano was the one thing he really missed when he traveled.

Just then, Enya was turned off and a simple piano rendering of 'Blue Lake' floated through the twilight. Helen played it well and it was obviously one that she played often. Liam smiled as she jumped straight from the watery pensiveness of 'Blue Lake' to a lively rendition of 'Baby Elephant Walk' and then 'Grandma's Feather Bed.' Like himself, Helen had a broad range of interests and that included her taste in music.

He thought about what he knew of her.

David had told him quite a bit about her work and her family and how close they were, even though they apparently didn't always agree. He had mentioned some pretty lively dinnertime conversations, which usually but not always, ended in laughter.

She'd been an A student at school and excelled at University. She rode well and enjoyed the lifestyle in the country and her work with property owners and in the field. She played piano and sang and put a lot of time and effort into both instructing at the local pony club and supporting any musical or theatrical activity that happened in town. Helen and her parents had also traveled when she was a teenager and later on she'd gone overseas herself, living in England part of the year and Canada the rest. He wondered why a girl with all her talents chose to work in a small country town, when job opportunities were so much greater in larger towns and cities or even overseas. He didn't think it was just to be with her parents or even not wanting to leave her hometown.

He'd discovered there was a whole raft of talented young

women in the country who wanted to stay there. Most of them came from properties, went on to Agricultural College and university and then what? Very few girls were encouraged or even allowed to stay on the family property. That was a right reserved for boys and the only other work available for many was the life of a nanny or general hand with maybe some bookkeeping or cooking thrown in, none of which would satisfy an ambitious person for long. If a girl was really fortunate she might be lucky enough to meet the son of the property and be allowed to be an unpaid hand until Dad and Mum retired and they were allowed to buy out the lease and live in debt for the rest of their lives. Either way, they were not in charge of their own destiny although they were in environment of their own choice.

Some of the lucky ones became country radio or television reporters and traveled throughout the rural areas covering a whole range of issues and events. Others were able to find jobs in the diminishing government offices and research stations dealing with primary producers or as consultants in Agricultural businesses. The other rising profession in rural areas was a position with Landcare and other environmental organizations. These were definitely not highly paid and were often fairly contentious. One thing they had in common was that the hours were reasonably flexible and definitely self- managed, at least until the Government managed to stifle the movement with paperwork and regulations. But there were a lot of hours and many of them were voluntary and the rest poorly paid. Driving a truck at the mines or cleaning the loos there netted at least three times the money.

A knock on the door broke into his thoughts and Helen's head appeared around the door frame. 'Would you like to eat in here, or will you come out to the kitchen?'

'The kitchen's fine, I'll be there in a minute.'

Liam was aware of a sense of excitement. This was the first time he'd ever had a chance to have Helen to himself and he meant to make the most of it, now that he was over his little tantrum of the lunch hour. He had even confused himself with that reaction and he was so relieved at her appearance and cheerful greeting, that he promptly forgot that he was ever doubtful, resentful or even completely puzzled by her relationship with David.

She'd changed her clothes to a lightweight summer dress, old but flowing and soft, and she'd put up her hair, leaving soft tendrils escaping to curl around her nape. Liam marveled again at how she managed to look fit and sporting but exotic at the same time. She had an indefinable look that held his eye every time she entered the room and he couldn't put his finger on what it was that made him want to watch her.

CHAPTER 19

HELEN

Helen took in Liam's eager expression and smiled 'You look like you're starving, must be all that thinking you've been doing, staring out the window.'

Liam felt the colour rising from the nape of his neck. She must have caught him watching her out the window.

'I have been working today, you know, and I'm entitled to a little thought break, now and then. Besides, I was enjoying the view.'

Helen couldn't help smiling back, recognizing a compliment when she received one. Obviously whatever had bothered him earlier was over and this Liam was hard to resist, so she didn't try. It was pleasant to sit and talk without sparring and they did have a lot in common.

They never lacked for conversation.

Helen had been to the Serengeti, one of her treasured memories being of the helicopter flight down into the Ngorongoro Crater. Liam had been to Hawaii and spent some time on the cattle properties there, even competing in the rodeo events. The thought that there were large cattle properties in Hawaii had always fascinated Helen, and although she was a bit disappointed by Liam's disclosure that there was really only one large ranch. Parker Ranch, she was interested to learn, had some of the most progressive cattle ranching techniques in the Unites States in spite of being owned by a cooperative. There was so much to talk about and so much more that they would both like to do. The Grand Canyon, the most trite destination in the world was on top of the both their wish lists, along with the highlands of Scotland. It was amazing when two minds considered it together, how many exciting things there were to do in the world, foods to try and shows to see, mountains to climb and animals to train. The list was never ending.

At last Helen felt she should leave and let Liam get the rest he so badly needed.

'Look, Liam, I am dreadfully sorry about falling on you the other night. It was thoughtless of me and to tell the truth, I'd forgotten you were still…' she searched frantically for a word.

'….fragile? Is that what you're looking for?' supplied Liam.

'Not really, that's about the last way I'd describe you,' answered Helen.

'How would you describe me then?' asked Liam. 'Sexy, good looking, charming? Any of those will do for a start.'

'Big headed.'

'Ah, that's the Helen I know and love. No beating about the bush for you.'

She smiled at him and the look held. 'Yes, well, we

didn't start off very well did we? Maybe, I was just a little bit touchy.'

At last she reluctantly got up and began to clear the dishes. She was careful not to reach across Liam, not wishing to risk hurting him again but her mind was clearly telling her not to brush up against him and it had nothing to do with causing him pain again, but all to do with how conscious she was of his large, warm presence in her immediate vicinity.

As she washed up in the kitchen she heard him get to his feet heavily next door and the tap of the crutches as he moved toward the door. She turned as he came into the kitchen. 'Liam, there's no need, I can do these few dishes.'

'There's every need,' he answered from directly behind as his arms came around her waist. She turned to find his face close to hers and he lowered his head in a gentle questioning kiss, as if to ask her permission. Not game to move in case she knocked Liam off balance, Helen stood against him, her wet hands held high against his shoulders. Of its own accord, her body responded and she kissed him back, too stunned by her own reaction to think clearly. Liam sagged and reached for his crutches. 'I'm sorry, I really will have to make it back to bed for a while.'

'Helen reacted quickly and supported his weight as he maneuvered the crutches back under his arms, then escorted him back in to the bedroom. Once on the bed, Liam lay there for a moment to get his breath, then looked up at her impishly. 'You could always join me here and we could start off where we finished before.'

Helen had had time to remember that she was in David's house. How could she have done this to David? No, she really needed to sort out how they felt about each other before contemplating any other involvement. The town was too small and gossip too rampant, to play the field, especially with the small problem of Norm's campaign against David. And it had become a campaign, no doubt about that. Norm was desperately trying to raise a petition to have David removed on the grounds of homosexuality and his unsuitability to be a doctor. Sensible people were taking no notice of course, but there were some very biased people out there, who weren't even worried whether it was true or not. *Frustrated drama queens, all of them, who just liked a little excitement in their own boring lives,* she thought, *the more vicious the better.*

'So,' Liam interrupted her thoughts 'not such a good idea, huh.'

'Oh, Liam, I wasn't thinking about that, but about David.' She wondered if she should ask Liam about David.

'About David…,' she began.

'What's he got to do with this?' Helen recognized the antagonism in his voice with concerned surprise.

'Doesn't matter. It was just something I wondered, but I'd better ask him myself. You have a good night. I'll see you at breakfast.'

CHAPTER 20

LIAM

No mention of how she felt about their kiss, nothing. Liam lay there and cursed his leg and he cursed David and also that he never seemed to be able to talk clearly to Helen. There always seemed to be something in the way, like talking through water. What was her interest in David anyway? He thought she and David were good friends but was there more that he didn't know about? They had spent a lot of time together, and seemed to have an incredible number of friends and interests in common, as well as being a mutual admiration society. In fact, the whole town seemed to assume they were a couple. Was there more to it, than he had observed? It wasn't like David to be secretive. David was going to be on the receiving end of quite a few questions when he eventually made it home.

CHAPTER 21

HELEN

'*Oh damn*, another project planning day'

Helen woke early next morning. She always did on the days that the group had meetings and she hated the fact that she couldn't seem to control her nerves on these days. It had become so bad that she wondered if she should give up the job but she knew that the only real problem was Norm and the unpleasantness that he brought to every meeting. It felt like entering a war zone at every meeting and more often than not, she felt like the target. It was only the support and genuine friendship of the other group members who tried to protect her from Norm's barbed tongue and constant negativity that kept her going. One minute she had decided she had had enough and that no one should have to work like that, and the next, her stubbornness kicked in and she couldn't see why she should give in to his bullying. It all depended how tired she was and if they had had any recent triumphs or failures.

It was rapidly getting to the stage that the group were going to have to ban Norm from meetings, and then no doubt, there would be petitions and rabid articles in the paper for them to deal with. *Some people were just determined to make life hard for others,* she decided.

It was strange how some people spent their lives building things and working for others and other people spent just as much effort trying to knock it down.

Owen had even found training courses for committee members to help them deal with the kind of interference and bullying that Norm specialized in, and they had tried listening and focusing on what Norm was trying to achieve with his behavior, they had tried deflecting it and also tried asking him to clarify his thoughts for them. Nothing he did made sense to anyone. His behavior was inconsistent and obstructive rather like a bouncing, weaving jump on a cross-country course.

Even before David had arrived as another personal affront to Norm's worldview, he had targeted Helen. It was obvious that he had only one place for women and everyone agreed that his wife had to be a saint. He seemed to find everything Helen said a major irritation, and tried to cut her off or denigrate her at every turn of the topic during the meetings. *The problem with a character like that,* she thought *was that everyone else was too polite and were prepared to let each person have their say.* Norm took advantage of this and unless he was cut short by the chairman, he had his say loudly and long. Meetings became marathons of unpleasant encounters.

Breakfast, lunch and dinner with Liam were silent affairs as Helen brooded and worried and Liam wondered what he had done this time. Helen didn't want to share her problems feeling it was unfair to prejudice Liam from the start as he had barely met Norm. Besides that, it was possible that Liam's strong and assertive manner, not to mention that he was obviously in a more senior position could make Norm listen to him. One thing Helen was certain of, Liam would not tolerate too much of Norm's nonsense when he got back on his feet and in some ways she was looking forward to that. She was pretty sure, based on last night's encounter that Liam wouldn't be listening quietly to Norm's homophobic accusations, snide as they were likely to be. It was unclear to her how she knew that about Liam but she hoped that she was going to be proved right. Meanwhile, there was tonight's meeting to live through.

'The important issue for this area has always been water, and as a founding member of this group I made sure that the Carlisle and Archer dams were built.' Norm always made it sound as if he had wielded the shovels to dig the dams himself. 'They were the solutions and it's these irrigators who are causing all the problems now. It doesn't matter, what you all think and what funny little projects you come up with, we have to cut those irrigation licenses. Even if we get good rain, and this is not an unusual cycle… I know I've been here all my life….. you are never going to do any good until you beat the irrigators. If nothing is done….'

'Norm, I think we'd better get back on to project planning don't you?'

'Get that girl to do it, that's what she's here for. Seems to lead you mob around by the nose.' It's time you got that new man on to the job. What's his problem anyway?'

'Thank you Norm. Liam is still recovering from his accident. He had a bit of a relapse last week but he is doing some work from home.'

'Sooner the better. Mind you he's probably no better than that other fella he's living with. Probably about as much use as whistle in a windstorm as well- birds of a feather, from what I've heard.'

Helen wondered what Norm had heard and who he could possibly have heard anything negative from. He must have had more friends than she gave him credit for, if anything he said was true.

'If we can convince this group along the creek to …' and Rhys continued with the meeting in spite of further protests and jibes from Norm.

As she drove up the slight hill home, Helen debated what she should pass on to Liam about the meeting. *Maybe, she could leave thinking about it until tomorrow morning when it would all seem a little less important.* But like all the 'best laid plans of mice and men' this one went astray. Liam must have heard the car from miles away, and was at his door as she came out of her garage.

'Like a coffee?'

Of course she would, but Helen wasn't sure if she needed a replay of the night's events to go with the evening coffee, but as usual she wasn't exactly going to sleep early anyway.

She also had her doubts about the wisdom of being alone with Liam again.

'Yeah, guess so,' she answered.

'Well, don't sound so keen,' huffed Liam, but with a smile in his voice that Helen didn't hear.

'I see you are still alive, even if just barely. How did it go?' asked Liam 'Norm hasn't eaten you yet?'

'No...oo, but it wasn't for lack of trying,' she replied.

She wondered how much David had told Liam about how truly awful the meetings could be. She'd been reasonably careful herself not to prejudice Liam, but obviously he knew a lot more than she had told him. It was possible Mark had boned him up on it while he was in Brisbane, although he didn't tend to be much of a gossip.

'Do you want to talk about it, or would you rather debrief formally tomorrow and relax this evening?'

Helen glanced at him in surprise at his insight, 'Tomorrow would be great,' she said. 'I'll have it all back in perspective by them and give you a much more balanced view, but I will tell you this- Rhys ran a good meeting and it was constructive…in the end.'

Liam nodded, 'That's all I need to know for the moment then,' and hit the remote for the CD player.

Music from the Coffee Lands' was just what the doctor prescribed, thought Helen.

'One coffee coming up!'

'Liam, no', Helen jumped up guiltily 'I'll get them. You shouldn't be on your feet.'

'Don't fuss. I'm a lot better than I was, you know. Just needed a little bit of rest for a day or two and I'll be fine for work again by next Monday. I even did a bit today.'

'You know what David said.'

Helen seemed to bring David's name in to every conversation, and Liam reacted automatically. 'Look, David doesn't own me and he doesn't own you, yet. Just forget him for a moment will you.'

Puzzled, Helen took her coffee, wondering what she had

said this time to upset the fragile peace, and too tired and drained to pursue the matter.

Silently she drank her coffee, her mind leaping from one issue to another as parts of the meeting replayed.

'.........mind seeing that new movie with Tom Hanks'. Helen tuned in dazedly to realise that Liam had been speaking to her.

'You mean the one with Leonardo Di Capprio? That's on in Riswell at the moment and it sounds pretty funny.' Helen liked funny movies. *After all, what was the point of deliberately setting out to frighten or horrify yourself, since you could do that for free watching the news.*

Suddenly, she realised what Liam was asking. 'You want me to come with you to Riswell?' she asked.

'Welcome back,' came the sarcastic reply, 'I was looking for a chauffeur since I'm not allowed to drive at the moment, and we both have meetings there next week. Thinking about someone else were we?'

Helen snapped, 'Look, I was thinking about Norm, if you must know and I think I've had enough of this.' She picked up her coffee cup and made for the kitchen.

'Good night, I'll see you in the morning' she called as she marched out the door.

'What was his problem anyway? How could anyone who instinctively knew what music to put on and that she didn't need to talk about the meeting, then go and spoil the evening like that?'

CHAPTER 22

This time of the morning is the best time of day, thought Helen. *I should be up at this time every day to ride.* It was hard to get up at four in the morning, especially if you had waited all night for the phone call that the dew was coming in, but it was a lot better than getting up at one or two am in the full dark. The time at which lucerne is baled depends entirely on the moisture in the air. On nights when the dew doesn't fall at all and the phone call to come out to the farm might never happen, but it was easier for Helen than for James and Roseanne, the farmers. They had to be up every hour or so to check the moisture in the hay, and as special as it was at night in the hay paddock, getting up every hour, even taking it in turns, became less pleasant on the second or third night without dew. And they did this for each of their four paddocks, every month. *Lucerne farming is probably even more demanding than dairy farming,* thought Helen.

The morning star shone in front of her as she aimed the tractor down the middle row in the paddock, and glanced across, automatically counting the rows and calculating which row was next, to maximize the turning radius needed to steer the unwieldy tractor, baler and trailer assembly on to the remainder of the rows. She loved the mathematical precision with which she had to calculate the next line of hay to pick up with the baler, she loved the rocking motion of the tractor, and the ozone smell of fresh lucerne as it was compressed in the baler chamber.

Even at this time of the morning, the birds were down in their hundreds, picking over the newly exposed ground for a morning feast. As she often did, she counted the species of birds on the paddock, amused by the number of black or black and white ones.

At least seven of the species fitted in to that category, with the ever-present crows and magpies dominating the count. This time of year brought the stately bustards, and more often than not, they were joined by egrets and straw necked ibis, while the white cockatoos screamed and stripped the trees down in the creek paddock. Even over the noise of the tractor, she could hear the lorrikeets quarreling in the grevilleas around the house yard.

Everyone was waking up, especially the corellas in the trees near the small gully. Every now and then they rose in an enormous, screaming, white cloud, only to resettle a few minutes later a couple of trees away.

As the tractor moved up and down the rows the birds on the ground flipped up and moved, swooping straight down again after the tractor passed.

Part of her glance took in the men on the trailer, checking that they were keeping up with the constant flow of bales and that no bales were broken. *Sometimes,* she thought *it's just a constant monitoring job-* listening for the revs of the tractor and baler, watching the amount the baler took in and adjusting the tractor speed and watching the men to make sure they were coping and hadn't fallen off the stack. David grinned as he saw her glance his way, and indicated for her to turn off the back light of the tractor. It was light enough now for them to see without lights. She could see he was enjoying the work, but then David always seemed to enjoy any of the farm work, and he fitted so well in to the farming community that she found herself wondering about him all over again. What was it about him that had Norm so upset? It sure didn't seem to bother anyone else but Norm and his mates.

They'd finished in good time this morning, no hiccups, no broken strings and James thanked them with a very early barbeque breakfast, in plenty of time for both Helen and David to go home before setting off to work.

'Well that's something I haven't done before,' remarked David, 'and I enjoyed it much better than a work out at the gym. I have to say the smell of fresh Lucerne is a lot better than sweaty armpits and sodden towels.'

'Well, I'll tell you what…I'll save you the gym fees anytime you like,' laughed James. 'This happens regularly and I'm always short of workers. I don't have any trouble getting the blokes to work when it's an evening baling, but no one enjoys being rung at two in the morning, even in summer and even with double pay. Only this young lady here will come and help when she can, and generally my wife, Roseanne.'

'Then we fight as to who gets to drive and who gets to stack,' added Helen. 'Roseanne doesn't like me to stack but she's only tiny so it's more sensible for me to do it.'

'At the risk of seeming chauvinist, it's not good for either of you, even though you do it as well as any of the men,' said James 'but sometimes there's no choice.'

Helen knew it was true and she was secretly relieved on the nights when she didn't have to stack. Stacking the bales higher than her head was just too hard. Although she could move 600 or so without a worry at any level below her neck, once she had to lift them high it became extraordinarily hard. Even giving them a heft with her knee didn't lift them high enough or fast enough to stack more than 4 high easily. She hadn't minded the sight of the men stacking though. After a short while David made it look just as easy as James did, but the sight was much prettier. *Not a good choice of word*, Helen grinned to herself.

'Well, I'd like to come when I can, I really like being up at this time of the morning but I just don't usually have a reason to unless there's a baby involved and that is becoming less and less often as more people have caesareans,' said David. 'Unfortunately, I won't always be able to help since I may be on call but you can always try me. I will if I can.'

'I'd like to offer to pay you, but the hourly rate for farm workers wouldn't impress you and Helen seemed to think you would probably refuse. I can give it to you in hay for your nag though. That's what Helen and I do, and it means when the price of hay goes up, you don't have to worry about that, because you'll have a little stockpile and lots of brownie points with me.'

'Suits me fine. Just think of all the money I'll save on gym fees, and hay as well.'

The night had well and truly gone and cars were beginning to move as David and Helen headed back toward town. Once, this road had been a quiet little dirt track, but since the council had sealed it, all the mine workers realized it was a quicker route to work. It was as busy as Queen Street and the fact that they were heading east, straight in to the rising sun made driving very tricky.

'David, thank you for helping out this morning. Are you sure you don't mind going back?'

'No, I enjoyed being there and seeing how it was done. James is a great bloke, but what a life. Lucerne growing must be just as binding as dairy farming or owning a small shop, and the hours are worse. You'd just have to want the lifestyle to do it.'

'There are compensations' said Helen. 'It is mainly organic for a start, not a lot in the way of fertilizers and sprays and there's something wonderful about the smell and the time of day you have to work with it, as long as you are only helping and not responsible. The days when you try to bale between rain showers are the worst, or trying to get it in before a storm. I've seen James and Roseanne trying to finish as the lightening flashed all around them.'

David pulled the car up into his driveway as she spoke, and they glanced at each other. 'Liam's still home, I wonder what the problem is.'

Helen felt concern flood over her. Surely, he hadn't had a relapse. 'No he wouldn't be home if that was the case, he'd be in hospital somewhere. Surely, he'd be smart enough to ring the hospital if he'd needed to.'

She got out of the car and walked up the path as a raging Liam shot out the door, anger in every line.

'Where have you two been?'

Looking horrified at his own question, Liam backed in to the house and David and Helen followed, puzzled, curious and totally confused.

'What on earth could that be about?' thought Helen. 'Hadn't David mentioned the possibility that he would be out baling to Liam.'

David recognized jealousy when he saw it but was overwhelmed as soon as he walked in the door. On his lounge sat a young man, very obviously nervous and extremely unkempt.

'Jonathon'! David's voice held a wealth of emotion and Jonathon's weary and defensive eyes turned toward the older man.

Helen, feeling like the third wheel, retreated to the doorway and vanished into her own house.

❤ ❤ ❤

CHAPTER 23

Ivy was pleased to see Helen, and had a pile of news from Armidale to share. True to her promise, Genevieve had organized people to visit her and Ivy appeared to be a lot better for it. Some of her frailty had disappeared, replaced by an eagerness for news and pleasure in being able to impart her own.

First she asked after Helen and Helen's parents, who had put off their return from overseas yet again. They were certainly making the most of the airfares they'd paid and kept finding more and more, old friends to see and places to visit. While Helen missed them, she was also enjoying the freedom of the house and developing her own routine.

Sometimes she had the very real desire to move in to a rental when her parents returned home, but for the moment she would stay where she was. She'd lived away from home while she was at boarding school and while she was at university, but it had been so easy just to slot back in to the old home life as if she had never left. It was a slippery slide to becoming dependent on the company of her parents and lazy about her own social life.

'And how are you getting on with that lovely young

man of yours?' Ivy enquired. 'He'll be a pretty good catch if you can get him.'

'There is no young man' replied Helen, a little sadly, thinking of her last view of David, with Jonathon's face between his hands. She'd left that morning, without going back to bed. She knew it had been irresponsible to drive five hundred kilometres with little sleep the evening before, but she needed to be in Brisbane for the next day's meeting and she wasn't going to sleep then anyway and she certainly couldn't have concentrated on work. Were all Norm's barbs true? Had she been just the blind for David, someone to make him more easily accepted in a small community? *It wasn't really necessary*, she thought *people loved David for who he was.* All except Norm, but while that was annoying, it wasn't really a serious problem.

Ivy shook her head thoughtfully. There had been sparks there if ever she'd seen them, she thought, but she didn't persist. Instead she told Helen about the lovely day when Genevieve had taken her out to see 'Mama Mia', as if Helen had known about the treat all along. It had been arranged the month before, she revealed, when David had been down for a conference and popped in to see her. They'd rung Genevieve too, since Ivy was sure that Genevieve would love to see it, and it was a long week-end they were getting the tickets for. Helen nodded and only half-listened, not letting Ivy in on her hurt surprise, since she didn't want to distress the old lady. Helen had been vaguely aware that David had been away a couple of times but he hadn't mentioned Ivy, or for that matter Genevieve. It seemed very strange and she was hurt in an indefinable way, more by the fact that

Genevieve hadn't mentioned her visit to Brisbane. But then, they hadn't really phoned in the last couple of weeks, since Genevieve was up to her neck in exam papers at this time of year but obviously, not that deeply that she couldn't take a week-end trip to Brisbane. She hadn't really seen David a great deal either, and their discussions over the fence had been brief and businesslike as they both came and went for various out of town excursions.

"I'm going to be away for a couple of days, will you keep an eye on Superman, please?' had been about the extent of their communication, until they both got the call up to go baling last night.

As she left, Ivy persisted, 'Now you bring your young man to see me next time you're down' she said. Why on earth did Ivy insist on calling David 'her young man'?

Helen knew it was not going to be a happy day, as soon as she walked in the door of the meeting. Professional as he was, Liam still did not manage to completely hide his anger from her and she found it hard to concentrate with the confusion that his attitude was engendering in her. She prickled with a mixture of annoyance and frustration, not knowing what she had done to create this atmosphere of tension between them. For some reason, the fact that she had driven down and Liam had flown the night before prickled her with annoyance every time she thought about it.

The meeting ran smoothly enough, but by lunchtime Helen felt she needed to escape from the disapproval, and her need to avoid any contact with Liam, led her to disappear with a hasty aside of 'shopping' to Mark.

As the afternoon meeting wore on, she realized with horror that an after work dinner was being arranged and that she could hardly avoid it, without appearing rude and missing social opportunities that she once would have embraced wholeheartedly. After all, these trips to the big smoke were about networking as much as about the content of the meeting, and some interesting people were invited to the dinner. Helen was popular and it would be seen as seriously odd if she didn't turn up for a social function like this without a good excuse. There would be concern that she was sick or teasing that she had better options and Helen would find it very hard to lie. It just wasn't something she could do convincingly, so she decided she would just have to go and make the best of it.

Luckily, she had brought a decent dress with her, the warm beige soft against her olive skin and the gold chain she always carried with her giving it just enough glamour for the restaurant chosen. Generally, she favored very simple clothes, usually pants, but this dress hung in soft folds and had felt so good when she'd tried it on, that she would have bought it anyway, even it had not looked as fabulous as it felt. She was a sucker for materials and designs that felt sensuous.

Liam and Mark stopped in mid conversation as she entered the restaurant and at her warm greeting to Mark, Liam's eyes snapped. Stepping up beside her, he took her arm in a firm grasp and whispered in her ear, 'I need to talk to you...Don't leave without me,' and he moved off into the crowd. Mark turned a puzzled look to her 'So what have you done to provoke Mr. Graham? I thought things were OK up that end.'

'I don't really know, 'replied Helen 'I haven't seen Liam to talk with since last week and everything was fine then as far as I know. We got the funding, the project planning is on schedule and all seems Ok.' She wasn't about to tell Mark about David and all the funny, confusing little incidents of their neighbourhood life. *I guess I'll find out later.* She tried to put Liam out of her mind and concentrate on the company at her table but every time she looked up, there he was, watching her in case she left early. *He can't be very good company for the poor woman next to him,* she thought wryly, unaware that her own preoccupation was quite as obvious.

Prawn cocktail was followed by Lamb Roulade, Pecan Tart and then the speeches.

Why is it politicians feel the need to make a speech at every occasion? she wondered. *As if we hadn't just spent all day listening to each other.* And really, nothing was said that meant anything. All that had already been covered and it was really just a politicians opportunity grabbing. Her mind wandered, flicking over the possibilities for escaping the current situation without encountering Liam. Making a sudden decision, she got up during the applause for the speech and gathered her bag, heading for the ladies, taking out her mobile phone to call a taxi while she was in the corridor. A large hand came over her shoulder and took the phone, pressing the red button before she could get it back. 'I'll come with you', Liam growled 'so you can't escape me yet again.'

'Escape was the last thing on my mind,' she countered' now if you don't mind,' and she brushed past Liam, entering the ladies minus her phone. *Could she do without her phone for the rest of the evening, and would she be able to evade Liam if she exited through the door into the other function room?* It seemed a bit childish and melodramatic and she was just a bit curious as to what Liam had to say to her that was so important. In the end, curiosity and dignity won out, and she entered the hall through the same door, expecting Liam to be lounging against the opposite wall. He was gone.

Mark's voice came from the end of the corridor. 'Liam had to go, but he left you this,' and he held up the mobile. 'He muttered something about "stupid young bastards" and disappeared.'

Not entirely unaccountably, Helen was angry. 'I'm tired of not knowing,' she stormed at Mark. 'I feel I am missing the point and the bus on every turn with David and Liam.' Leaving a surprised, confused and amused Mark behind, she turned on her heel and pelted out of the building. "I am going to get to the bottom of this with both of them' she muttered to the taxi driver, 'and Genevieve too, for that matter. Why am I the only one that doesn't seem to know what's happening?'

CHAPTER 24

LIAM

Liam slid into the hospital ward as quietly as possible, trying not to disturb David, who seemed to be asleep in the chair beside the bed. Jonathon lay there, attached to tubes and monitors, looking almost as small and as defenseless as he had as a child. Liam knew that he wasn't defenseless, not really, nor harmless. He just looked that way and David had always been a sucker for it. In fact, Jonathon was pure trouble but David could never see that defending him against any accusation, always championing him no matter what dirty deeds the child had performed. Liam never quite understood the link between the two, it seemed to be buried in some past that he was not a part of, even as David's best friend for so long. This time, Jonathon had almost gone too far, according to the nurses.

He'd been found down near the bike-path in Carslisle and brought in almost comatose, with occasional lucid moments of sheer anger and rage. As usual, he wasn't wearing his bracelet, and there was no medical information in his wallet. Liam wondered what it was that made Jonathon neglect himself so badly. The only way the doctors knew what was wrong were the needle marks on his stomach and there were nowhere near as many of them as there should be. They were far outnumbered by those on his arms that were nothing to do with prescribed medication. At that moment, he looked up and the sheer misery in his eyes almost threw Liam off his feet.

'Why can't you all just leave me alone and let me get it over with?' he rasped. 'Just let me go'. He closed his eyes again and when Liam asked what time David had arrived, there was no response. Liam debated whether to wake David but elected to steal the chair from next to the empty bed next door and try to get his thoughts together.

In Canada, where Jonathon had fled to after his last trouble, he had quickly found more strife for himself and by the time Liam himself had gone to the rescue, on his way home from Vietnam via the ski fields of Montana Jonathon was in deep. He had a drug addiction, diabetes, no money and an out of date visa, so Liam had lent him the money for a fare and bundled him in the car to drive to the embassy and the airport. He'd intended to stay with Jonathon and take him to a hospital on the way to sort out his medication but Jonathon suddenly had had other ideas and they had ended up upside down on a snowy mountain road hanging below the guard rail. While Jonathon walked out in one piece, Liam ended up in a wheel chair, a long way from home and his new job prospect. Jonathon never reappeared to come home, just leaving a note to say he was sorry and that he would never trouble them again and that no one was to look for him or try to contact him.

'*So much the better if he had kept his word*,' thought Liam as he gazed at the angelic face before him and wondered what had prompted him to come home after all. He was back in Australia less than three days and already he had David's life on hold again, and not just David's this time. Liam nursed his own store of resentment, even though he had never really held him to blame for the accident that had put him in hospital. That had been black ice and drug or diabetes induced strength but Liam was sorry that he had never finished telling Jonathon what he thought of him for disturbing David and David's family the way he did.

At that moment, Jonathon's eyes opened again and he smiled wryly. 'I guess I didn't succeed again,' he said, 'but at least I didn't take you with me this time.' Liam's anger melted, pity for the damaged personality before him softening the edges.

'Why?' he pleaded 'Why, when you know that it causes everyone else so much pain?'

'I really didn't' mean to this time,' Jonathon surprised him. 'You see there was this party.'

CHAPTER 25

HELEN

The freeway was choked and drivers impatient. Not a good start to a long drive. Although she was a very confident driver, Helen was did not feel up to the amount of energy that was required to concentrate on the freeway and to tolerate and avoid the sheer stupidity of some of the drivers.

The city itself was a mecca of good driving manners compared to the freeway and every time she drove down to Brisbane she wondered why she didn't fly, at about this point. *Imagine having to drive to work every day in that,'* she thought *you'd be tired by the time you got there every day, all day. No wonder road rage is such a problem.*

A hundred and fifty kilometers up the road she no longer wondered why she drove. The countryside opened up into farming land and the traffic reduced to a level and behavior standard at which you could actually enjoy the response of the car and sometimes the scenery. Each property was one she had been familiar with for years. She noted every change, the condition of the paddocks and even the acquisition of new machinery on farms. She smiled to herself as she thought *you can always tell a farmer driving- the car and his hat weave from side to side as they check out every property and the cows.*

There was a need to see everything that was happening in their world, she decided. She did a fair bit of that herself, at least mentally. Helen enjoyed the sweep of the corners on this section of the road, and the way the scenery rose in front of her as she topped the undulating rises. It always felt as if there was a new world over each hill and occasionally she occupied herself with imagining what she might see if the universe were suddenly to change just before she hit the top. Shaking her head at her own imagination, her mind turned to the mystery of David and Jonathon. What did she know?

Well,   One: David was a kind and warm hearted person. Two: He and Liam were purely friends she had decided. She was pretty certain Liam was heterosexual from the very few and far between personal encounters she had had with him. Three: On brief acquaintance, Jonathon looked like trouble no matter which side he batted for. No, that was unfair and maybe it was only her own annoyance speaking. Four: Why was Ivy scheming with David & Genevieve if she thought she and David were a pair? What 'romance' had Ivy seen? The only sparks around were the ones she and Liam struck just about every time they clashed- which was pretty frequently, come to think of it.

Four hundred and fifty kilometers later, Helen was still puzzling over her points list and no closer to an answer. On one hand, David was warm with everyone but they had spent a huge amount of time together and everyone saw them as a couple. To tell the truth, she often felt like an old married couple when she was out with David. Her unruly mind turned to Liam, hearing his deeper voice, his genuine grunt of laughter at a joke Mark had told him yesterday and seeing his way of tilting his head to listen to tiny Genevieve as she talked about her students. His presence seemed so real in her car, that she felt if she turned around, he might be in the passenger seat, but she knew he was still in Brisbane for a specialist appointment and flying home on Thursday. Forcing her mind back to her list, she tried to make some decisions which would help to sort her thoughts out.

She decided a phone call to Genevieve was her first move, closely followed by finding out whatever information she could about Jonathon from either David or Liam, whoever she saw first.

❦　❦　❦

'Teacher's conference' she said 'in the Hilton.

'So what are you doing at a Queensland Conference?' asked Helen.

'Presenting a paper called 'Community Volunteering for Schools,' responded Genevieve, 'something our schools have been doing for ages.'

'It's amazing. I've only just left and there you are, just about staying in my room. You know, both Liam and David are down there at the moment. Apparently, the mysterious Jonathon decided to overdose and they flew him down yesterday. David went down on last night's plane, so I'm guessing that's why Liam ran out on the work dinner last night.'

'Yes, I saw Liam this morning. I think he'd come looking for you but he wasn't letting on.'

Helen wondered how to introduce the subject of 'Mamma Mia' and decided the quickest way was just to ask.

'So how was Mamma Mia.'

Genevieve gave a blow by blow description of the stage show, without mentioning either Ivy or David.

'Yes, Ivy told me she enjoyed it too. What about David, I've barely seen him to talk to since then?"

'David?'

'Yes, Ivy told me David organized the tickets.'

'No…"

'Now why would Genevieve fib to her,' wondered Helen. 'It was Liam.'

A pain knifed straight through Helen, from front to back. It had never occurred to her that Ivy meant Liam. In fact, she was sure that Ivy had definitely said David. Maybe she had them mixed up. She didn't think Liam qualified as 'a lovely young man' but then to an old lady, maybe he was.

Why did Liam ring Genevieve? He had hardly spoken to her at Christmas time and he wasn't a soft touch like David. She knew David would continue to call on Ivy but hadn't realized that Liam would. She was also reasonably certain that Liam had only been down to Brisbane once in the last month or so although it was on a long weekend, come to think of it.

Unwelcome thoughts chased Helen to bed that night, and she tossed and turned, and finally awoke early and angry. Work, was about the last thing she felt like, but the world waits for no man and Helen was no exception. At seven am the phone rang. An unidentified caller complained about a weed in an upstream neighbor's waterhole. Could she come out and identify it? She arranged to drive the thirty two kilometres there and back, before her meeting with the council at 9am.

At ten thirty am, she taught a local high school group water testing techniques down at the creek and then after a late morning tea finally settled to her emails.

Liam walked in just before lunch, and she just managed to ask him how Jonathon was getting on and get a hurried, 'fine' before he was out the door again on the way to a workshop he was running for one of the grain-grower groups. Since she had a another farm visit herself in the afternoon, Helen packed up at lunch time, putting her laptop in the car and headed off to the next valley where she spent the afternoon bumping around the farmer's back paddock in the farm ute, with a drooling dog leaning in the open window every time they stopped to talk about the fence line he was putting in, and his two children clamouring for lessons in using the GPS. They got out at the end of the gorge to mark some water-points and traverse the difficult parts of the fence line. *'At least with the kids there, I don't have to get out and open the gates,'* she congratulated herself. They and the dog swarmed off the back of the ute like great spiders, opening the gate even when the ute had barely stopped.

Driving home into the afternoon sun, she could feel a headache starting in the base of her neck and the tension in her shoulders made her hold the steering wheel as if it were trying to escape. She drove straight home and even though she knew she would be best to have a break before settling down to the computer, she attempted to enter up the information she'd collected during the afternoon but it was as if her computer had taken on a life of its own. Microsoft Word was possessed by a demon, and had decided that every second letter she typed should be in the wrong place or the wrong letter, and every time she went to fix it, the program came up with its own offbeat solutions. Deciding that it was probably more to do with her poor coordination and woeful concentration than a willful computer she eventually gave up and wandered outside with no fixed destination in mind. Although it was close to dinnertime, she decided to go for a walk and Jack, realizing a walk was in the offing, bounded over with a huge grin and ecstatic wriggles of his whole body. Nothing was more guaranteed to immediately make Helen feel way better, at least momentarily.

David turned up at six thirty pm, at the same time as Liam drove in, and they seemed to take forever banging car doors and talking before they went in to the house. By this time, Helen's headache had reached gigantic proportions, in spite of her walk, and she had given up trying to do anything remotely constructive in the garden that she'd retired to afterwards. She was sitting on the ground next to the wooden part of the fence near the swing, idly pulling at weeds in the shade of the tree while Jack slept a contented sleep beside her, snuffling and snoring and chasing imaginary roos.

'David, it's time you gave up on him, he breaks your heart every time. All you do is hurt yourself when you try to help him, and he uses you. He always has.'

'Liam, you will never understand. There will always be a connection and I can't help it if he is not able to care for himself. It's not his fault he's the way he is. Blame his parents or even blame me. We created him between us, and they're not here to live with that anymore.'

'Well, this may be for the rest of your life, David. Have you thought of that?'

'Yes, well, it's the rest of his life too.'

Helen listened in growing horror. Maybe Norm wasn't so far wrong, but in spite of all she'd heard, it just didn't seem to add up, a small section of her mind repeated.

'And did you see Helen while you were down,' asked David 'and did you ask her why?'

'Almost,' replied Liam 'but she escaped just before you rang from the airport, and I couldn't chase her down.'

Unfair, thought Helen. *I did no such thing.* Suddenly she felt virtuous. *Well if that's your story, you stick to it,* she muttered crankily. *I know the truth.*

She got up suddenly and popped her head over the fence. 'Liam,' she said 'Don't forget the meeting tomorrow night. I'll see you then.' She went inside, turned the music up loud and got into the shower. Fortunately, she was going out and wouldn't have to face them while she was still angry if they decided to come across. She definitely did not want to discuss what she had overheard, or even let them know that she had overheard it now she had cooled down a little. Miserably, she decided she really didn't want the truth anymore. They could both go and jump in the lake as far as she was concerned and in spite of her headache she went out determined to put it all out of her mind. She hoped that the friends she knew all about, since she'd known most of them since she was a teenager, would help her feel back in step with her own life

❦   ❦   ❦

'Just what is your problem?' Liam hissed the next

evening. Probably he was peeved that he hadn't been able to catch her all that day. He pinned a smile on his face as more members of the Landcare group filed through the door.

'Concentrate,' she muttered 'you mightn't have to live here but I would like to, at least for a while.'

And I really don't need a reputation as a street fighter. It's hard enough to do what I do anyway without a public spectacle, she thought.

Liam turned away and moved toward a group of members chatting pleasantly, but his eyes followed her wherever she went.

'So what is his beef?' Owen asked her 'I'll bet he's giving David a run for his money and losing, at the moment. That's my guess.'

Aghast at Owen's powers of observation, Helen retreated into efficiency and organization.

'Coffee before we start the meeting, anyone?' she offered.

There was a general rush toward the coffee pot, and in the confusion Helen managed to place her folders on the big table as far from Liam's as possible. Usually Helen chose her position at the meeting table carefully, try to minimize the impact that Norm could make on the group. She generally placed herself where she could communicate with Owen as chairman, but with Norm between them. She and Owen had worked out that while they needed to be able to communicate, they also needed to be spread far enough apart that one of other of them could be heard by all members if possible, when presenting factual information. It remained to be seen where Liam would fit in the meeting grouping, but Helen was professional enough to acknowledge that he had a very good grasp of facts and information and would not be swayed by pure rhetoric and hearsay. She was confident that although they might not always agree, Liam would not allow personal feelings to influence his decisions or his presentations to the group. Helen thought about this for a moment, realizing that this was a significant relief to her as far as meetings were concerned and that she should give this the appreciation it deserved. She straightened her shoulders, realizing that the formal part of the meeting was over before she had managed to stop her thoughts from simmering and truly concentrate on the business at hand. Then she almost wished she hadn't.

'There's a chance for a couple of us to catch-up with the Broken River Group in Victoria. They have invited us to a two day combined workshop on identifying paleochannels using radiometrics and geomagnetic sensing,' the secretary informed them excitely. 'Arrangements have been made for accommodation for four people from our group who would like to work with them.'

'That could be just what we need at the moment,' enthused Owen 'since they are bit further forward than we are.'

'Yes, but we have some extra data sets that they don't and our analysis techniques are a bit different,' put in Liam.

'And who do you think will pay for this rubbish?' asked Norm in his best offensive manner.

'According to this, sharing the information with other groups throughout Australia, and also helping to coordinate and standardize data sharing with other groups doing similar work, is a part of their funding agreement. As far as I can see, this means all costs will be covered,' replied the Secretary.

'Bloody Government money, you'd think our tax money could be put to better use than flying you lot around the country. I'll say no more.'

Good, thought Helen. *That would have to be a first,* but of course Norm had a lot more to say but was given less time than usual to say it as Owen called, first for a vote on whether they should take part and then for a discussion on who should go.

'It's really more of a data sharing and technique swapping session by the look of it and could be really useful. I move that we send at least Liam and Helen, and it would be good if a couple of others from the group took the opportunity as well.'

Helen's heart sank. The last thing she needed at this moment, was a trip away with Liam. Just now, her confusion and discomfort with both David and Liam made her feel like leaving town, but not in their company. She didn't even want to be with Genevieve and that was worse since there had never been a moment from the time they met that they hadn't been best friends. There was no way she would refuse this opportunity though. It would be totally unprofessional, and why should she disadvantage herself just because of Liam. She raised her chin and looked at him. 'Yes, sounds like an amazing opportunity,' she smiled. 'Since the flights and accommodation will be looked after by the Broken River Group maybe any incidentals can be taken care of by the salinity project or the workshop budget. Who else is going to come?'

When dates were finally worked out and discussion covering technical abilities, communication skills, time constraints and possible contributions had been covered, it was decided that Owen and Josie should accompany Liam and Helen, the mix of skills in the group giving the greatest advantage possible. Amid much laughter Josie and Owen were cautioned to behave by their respective partners and let the 'singles' play up. Helen took it all in good part but knew that Owen had cast her a few concerned glances as the good-natured teasing became more pointed and David's name was mentioned in passing.

'Next item on the agenda,' Rhys announced at last and let the noise die down before proceeding with the meeting.

Josie was obviously looking forward to this trip. She and Rhys were true partners in the property business and Josie's training as an accountant was an essential part of running both the cattle and crop marketing components of the farms, but occasionally she felt she needed a change and her expertise in project and financial management was essential to the group. The opportunities this trip offered the organization would possibly include negotiations for flying of their own imagery and costing of interpretation and production of data from it.

Helen really was very pleased with the group who were going on the trip, even if there were personal concerns. She knew the expertise and concentration that Josie would bring along with her experience as an irrigation and dryland farmer, and Owen was always good value for his practical and technical on-ground knowledge as much as his common sense, charm and warmth. If anyone could impress potential project partners, it would be Owen.

She knew that Liam had great project management and negotiation skills as well as amazing technical expertise, and for herself she was excited to be able to relate this exciting new field of knowledge to her specific local area, using the knowledge she gained daily from a network of landowners and to learn new techniques for interpretation of the field work they'd already done. She always looked forward to meeting new contacts and enlarging her network of knowledge. She felt she was bringing a gift back to her local community each time she came home with new expertise.

By the time the plane left the ground, Helen was completely reconciled to the trip and looking forward immensely to the two days of intense work.

Even the sight of Liam with his bag in his hands did not dampen her enthusiasm at all. They'd managed to work cooperatively for the last couple of weeks and were generally in good accord. Helen had to admit that Liam had some skills that she could definitely learn from and provided she concentrated on that, she was fine. She made sure that they were not alone and there was little opportunity for personal talk and that way managed to ignore any discomfort. David had been extremely busy as well, with regular flights to Brisbane on his days off and it seemed that by common consent they could all ignore each other indefinitely.

Helen had spoken to David a couple of times and asked how Jonathon was getting along, but apart from saying that he was progressing, David didn't seem to want to communicate too much more. Once or twice he mentioned Genevieve, since he still visited Ivy when he was down and Ivy apparently talked about Genevieve constantly, but that was all. Any closeness he and Helen had developed seemed to have disappeared and with it, his interest in poor Superman. The horse was agisted with JJ and Helen was out there most weekends and occasionally in the evening but never saw David there. Obviously he just visited to check on the horse occasionally but very little else. If Helen had been better friends with Liam, she would have suggested he ride the horse, since it seemed such a waste but she felt so out of step with both men that she hesitated even to do that.

CHAPTER 26

The Kinambla Motel was not luxurious but it was very friendly and the room Helen and Josie shared had a good view of the mountains. Helen was excited to realize that the hills she was looking at were some that she had seen on the imagery they'd been studying before they left home.

It was cool but not particularly cold, just crisp enough that the mountains called to Helen, saying *You would like to climb me, come on, there's still lots of surprises up here for explorers.* At times like these, Helen envied the first explorers of Australia, heading off to find what they could in a land that no one knew anything about. *What an incredible world it must have seemed to them.*

Members of the Broken River Group met them at the airport to bring them to the motel and dinner was at a nearby member's house that night, so there was no need for a hire car. It felt strange to country people, used to always needing a car, to have no form of transport. Helen and Josie decided to go for a walk down along the river, another novelty for people from their part of the world - the river had water in it.

The men had elected to stay back at the motel and have a

beer and watch a part of the Bronco's vs Cowboys game and Helen was not sorry. Strangely, for the first time in weeks she felt unwatched. At home, there was always someone next door when she was home and she was always a little on edge that either Liam or David would decide to visit or she would run in to one or the other. At least this way, she knew exactly where Liam was and David was nowhere in sight. She heaved a sigh and Josie looked at her curiously.

'Pining for a lost love' she enquired.

'No, just the opposite' responded Helen. 'Must be the peaceful effect of that flowing water but I feel relaxed for the first time in weeks.' Suddenly, it occurred to her that she could talk to Josie about the whole mixed up business and maybe Josie would make some sense of it.

'Rhys and I did wonder' replied Josie when the story was told. 'There certainly seemed to be something three-cornered as soon as Liam came to town.'

'No, that wasn't what I meant, I didn't say that' stressed Helen, 'Liam has nothing to do with David's problem. I mean the Jonathon problem.' Helen hoped she was not letting out any secrets that David would rather she didn't, but she also knew that Josie was not likely to spread gossip of any sort. Rhys was the only other person likely to find out this information from Josie.

It was obvious that Josie was seeing a lot more than she was supposed to and Helen wondered how many other people in Carlisle were just as observant.

'I don't think David is the problem' commented Josie, 'I think that you and Liam have some sorting out to do that has nothing to do with David. David is a big boy and can look after himself, and I don't think there is anything we can say or do which will improve things. He obviously has a long standing obligation of some sort that is not going to be helped by us making our opinions known.'

'And as for worrying about letting David down yourself, he's had plenty of chances to make any advance he wanted to, so I wouldn't worry about that.'

'Well' thought Helen 'that's telling me.' But probably Josie was right and she did have no obligation to help David except as a friend. He was old enough to sort out his own problems and repair his own image if that was what was needed. It was just that sometimes she felt that everything had been really comfortable and pleasant until Liam hit town, in spite of niggly old Norm already being there. He was starting to feel like a minor menace beside Liam and Jonathon though.

'You grimaced, I'll bet Norm crossed your mind,' laughed Josie.

Together the two women walked back toward the motel, both with a great deal to think about. Helen knew that Josie would talk with Rhys. There was not much they didn't share and Helen would always appreciate his commonsense approach to the problems of their friends- all three of them. It hadn't taken Josie and Rhys long to take Liam on as part of their extended care group, which included a great many friends and relatives including David and Helen.

For her part, Helen felt marginally better, although how long that would last was anybody's guess. At other times she had managed to talk herself in to believing that all this was not really her concern but her mind just could not work that way for long. She was too involved no matter what she told herself.

Dinner was an exciting affair with a great deal of technical discussion and comparison of projects and operating circumstances. Helen tried to keep her observations as impartial as possible, especially with Liam seated right across the table and mostly she succeeded.

She tuned in to other conversations at one time to hear Josie telling a dinner companion some of the 'Norm' stories and in this setting they made a funny story. *Not so funny though, when you were right there on the receiving end,* thought Helen and smiled slightly to herself. Liam caught her eye and grinned conspiratorially, and for a moment Helen had the feeling that everything was OK. It didn't last long. In fact, with dessert she realized that Liam was beginning to look extremely tired. It was the first time for a long time that she had seen that brand of fatigue on his face and she realized what long hours he had been putting in. They both had, which was part of the reason they hardly saw each other, even though they lived next door and shared an office. *Liam has spent a lot of time driving to Brisbane with David as well,* thought Helen. Funny how it never occurred to her until tonight, what long hours both the young men had been putting in to support Jonathon in hospital.

Helen felt slightly ashamed of herself for some of the thoughts she'd had about the two of them lately and leaned across the table toward Liam.

'Are you ready to catch a taxi back?' she asked.

He looked at her in surprise but made no objection when she excused them both to their hosts and steered him toward the door.

'You look like you are about to collapse any minute,' she

muttered 'and to tell the truth, I'm not a lot better. I need get my beauty sleep so I can make the most of tomorrow.'

'Stay for a drink, please Helen. I'd like to talk to you, see if we can work some of this out,' Liam pleaded.

'Ten minutes but that's all,' she conceded, 'or you'll probably pass out on me anyway.'

'You know we've just given Rhys and Josie something to talk about,' he said.

'I have no secrets from either,' countered Helen, 'and they will understand that you needed to rest.'

'Well let's make ourselves a secret then,' he whispered as he turned and encircled her in his arms as she entered the door.

'What on earth are you up to? I feel like the proverbial mushroom,' she said angrily 'kept in the dark. One minute you are so angry with me you can barely talk, the next you're like this. I don't understand and everyone else seems to be in on some wavelength except me. So this had better be good. Her voice grew deeper and quieter as her anger rose. 'So now tell me…Who is Jonathon?' Why are you making love to me and buying tickets to Mamma Mia for Genevieve. What is going on?' Helen had completely shocked herself at her unguarded reaction and knew that at any moment, terrible embarrassment would set in. She just hoped she got some answers for the awkwardness she was going to suffer for the next few weeks.

Liam reared back. 'Well, maybe you can answer some questions too- like what were you and David doing out all night the other night? He's not saying.'

'What right do you have to know? David and I have been friends for a long time'

'Well maybe there's some things you need to ask David then before I give you any answers'

'Goodnight!' Helen left, her body stiff with anger and no answers.

❦ ❦ ❦

CHAPTER 27

At least someone is pleased to see me, thought Helen as she came up her driveway. There was no mistaking Jack's ecstasy as he ran circles dementedly in the back yard. She felt some of her grumpiness lift as she ran her hand over his shiny skull and caressed the silky ears. *There is no mistaking when a dog loves you, that's for sure,* she thought. Sometimes though he'd given her the cold shoulder, especially when he had been out with Rhys and Josie, so this greeting lifted her heart.

An email from her parents, currently in Denmark, distracted her for a while as well, and her reply was full of the real achievements of the trip to Broken River. She had learned so much and come up with so many ideas herself, that her other considerations took a back seat for a while.

She sat at the computer and drafted a complete project in less than two hours, binding together all the good ideas and research their group had done in the last couple of years. It was amazing how a welcome from the dog and an interesting email from her family could lift her spirits and make work such a breeze.

'Spring in Denmark,' wrote her parents 'was the most

amazing experience. After a winter inside, with rain and short days, everyone was outside. There were apple festivals and maritime festivals and all the build up to a huge, summer beach holiday where populations of seaside towns could swell from five thousand to fifty thousand in a matter of weeks.

Funny, Helen had never realized that Denmark had a beach culture. She was amused by her parent's descriptions of the German tourists who came to the town they were staying in, many of whom had never seen the beach before just like many children from the inland of Australia. Helen's parents had decided to stay a bit longer and help with some of the festivals that their friends were involved with, and although Helen was pleased that they were enjoying the time away, just at the moment she would have given a lot to be able to talk to her Mum. But they deserved this time away and their support and caring flowed through every word in the email.

Suddenly feeling lonely and at odds with the world, Helen decided to go for a run. *Given two seconds to think about it, I wouldn't even manage that* she thought. She knew, though, that she would feel better afterwards.

It was a dark night and Jack was frisky, since he'd been mostly on his own while she was away and had no cattle work to do either. Like all Collies, Jack needed to be kept busy. Like a bright and active child, either his mind or his body needed to be working most of the time and just like any child, he needed company and routine and when that had been disturbed, he welcomed it back with enthusiasm although sometimes he had been known to have a little sulk.

It was Jack's enthusiasm that helped Helen to make it out in to the night, running.

The roads were dark, but once her eyes accustomed, there was an incredible pleasure in the flow of soft, not yet cool, autumn air and the brilliant stars in a dark sky. *One of the great joys of living in the country,* she thought *those amazing stars, when I take the time to look.* The road looped in front of her, down over the gully and across the park, each garden up the next hill lit by solar garden lights. Street light hadn't quite made it this far yet and she could hear voices and smell dinner in most of the houses she passed but very few barking dogs. Most of these people were retired farmers and if they had dogs, they were very well trained and managed.

Closer in to town, she and Jack left a trail of barking dogs and yelling owners, much to her amusement. Bored animals with indifferent owners left the whole block in uproar, which Jack ignored with his usual gentlemanly aplomb. By the time she reached home Helen felt so much better that even cooking dinner seemed a reasonable task instead of the necessary evil it had seemed before. After a quick shower, she wandered out in to the garden with a torch to see what was available in the vegetable garden for dinner.

A quick scan picked out the Chinese cabbage, spring onions, chili bush, coriander and some small limes that had fallen off the tree so Helen took a small packet of chicken from the freezer and quickly put together a Thai chicken recipe she'd downloaded from Taste.com.

Suddenly, the week that had seemed never ending and out of whack, became a raft of possibilities and exciting future activities, if only Helen could get her mind together long enough to appreciate the opportunities. One of them may have had an infrequent but heart stopping smile and definite attitude problems. She smiled to herself. Suddenly all things seemed possible.

❦ ❦ ❦

CHAPTER 28

'There's another way to look at it.' Rhys was juggling his coffee and a pile of flyers as he spoke. 'We've had a fair bit of rain so you can't get on the properties for the field day, but we can still have the speakers earlier in the day. The hall is booked and the catering organized. We could go home straight after lunch and come back some other time for the farm visits.' Rhys was always so optimistic and positive, but there were times when Helen really felt the strain of organising an event like the one on Monday. The last week or so always felt like being sucked down the plug hole as events built to a climax and arrangements changed by the minute. There was always a speaker who pulled out, or it threatened rain without actually doing it or she felt she hadn't done enough to ensure success. The whole world knew that Helen would have a contingency plan for everything but she never, ever felt that she had done enough for success herself.

In her saner moments, Helen knew that what she was forgetting was that these field days were a social outing as well as a learning opportunity for many farmers, where they could rub shoulders with neighbours and other people who spoke their agricultural language. What the group was offering was really a free conference, a 'free lunch', a social occasion and good information all packaged up and offered for nothing but the investment of a little time on the part of the landowner. It was the indecision that was killing her this time as it always did when rain hung around. She almost wished it would just flood and get it over with, but once they made the decision to go ahead regardless, she felt much better. By that stage it was 'Que sera sera,' in the words of Doris Day.

Monday though, dawned clear and bright after a warm, wet weekend and arriving at the hall Helen was pleasantly surprised to find a number of group members there early and a cup of tea already on offer.

It seemed the farmers were out for a holiday and the hall already had a festive feel.

As she moved around, putting up displays, supervising speakers and their presentations, the thousand and one tasks an event organizer has to do, she could hear more people arriving and a buzz of conversation and social chat at a level she really didn't expect.

Neal came in and reported that his property was dry enough after the weekend to at least enter the paddocks near the road and that there would be no problem with Joe's place, since he'd re-graveled the road and also missed most of the rain. Helen heaved a great sigh of relief, and looking out the window, she was astounded to see car after car driving in.

It was one of those days where everything went perfectly and each speaker followed the previous one seamlessly and logically. The paddocks dried enough to see what they wanted to see- the huge equipment that had been cut in half and re-welded to make all the wheels tracks on the same width. Helen was continually amazed by the ingenuity of the farmers who had no problem with chopping a 10 ton planter in half and remodeling it. It was about four hundred thousand dollars' worth of equipment and the grey paint showed where it had been sliced in half and pieces added in the middle. Many of the farmers did this work themselves or helped each other to do it.

One of the reasons for the success of the day had become clear as time progressed. The farmers couldn't get on the paddocks to plant, as they were still too wet, so many of them had taken the opportunity offered to share successes and learn what was happening around them and have a great old chin-wag while they did it. The other reason was a complete surprise. Rhys took the stage at the end, even though he was not on the agenda.

A pleasant buzz of conversation had started up, but there was immediate silence as he started to speak.

'Now ladies and gentlemen I have an announcement that I know you will all be pleased to hear.'

Rhys went on to talk about some of the group projects over the last couple of years, the amount of funding and support that the group had managed to organize for conservation projects and all the other achievements of their organisation. He went on to say, 'I know that Helen has been paid in her position to achieve all these results but we all know as well, the amount of time that she has put in out of work hours. We all know the passion and expertise she has brought to her job and to her volunteer work. We know the commitment she has made to her community, as a young person who could easily have pursued better paid employment in some other lucky community. I am pleased to announce that we have nominated Helen for the State Landcare Facilitator's Award and she is a finalist. Please join me in wishing her all the best at the State Awards.'

A sense of unreality hit Helen, and also the certainty that Liam was behind the nomination in some way. While Rhys and Owen were good friends and definitely extremely supportive, she didn't think it would have occurred to them to seek recognition for the group in this way.

That was so cynical, she chided herself. *They would have done it to reward her, if they'd thought of it,* she knew. She also knew that Liam would be aware of the advantages for the group as well.

A win for herself also meant that the group projects got positive exposure at the State level and possibly even Federal as she would be asked to speak at conferences and forums if she won.

The thought still lurked in the back of her mind even as she made a quick speech thanking them all for their support and cooperation for so long. She thanked them wholeheartedly for the nomination, even as she pushed the cynical thought so far back in her mind that there were tears in the corner of her eyes. A ripple of spontaneous applause startled her halfway through her speech and goosebumps sprang out on her arms. There was so much genuine pleasure in the room that all her doubts and insecurities faded away and she simply enjoyed the moment, and 'who' had actually suggested the nomination became unimportant beside the genuine support that emanated from so many people in the room.

Helen knew her parents would be far more excited than she felt herself to be but all the same she found it hard to conceal her smile as everyone wanted to speak to her and give her a hug, wish her good luck or tell her that she would be the obvious winner for the State and would definitely go on to the next level.

It became clear to Helen, that whoever had put forward the nomination had also given a new life and purpose to the group itself and that there were many more people than just herself going home feeling a part of something truly good that night.

Liam, of course flatly denied the charge and put the blame squarely on the shoulders of Rhys and Owen, but Helen still had the feeling that there had been some of his influence at work. 'You deserved it you know. Look at how the whole of the two groups were behind you.' And for the first time, Helen sensed the warmth of his regard and his pleasure at being able to be a part of a wonderful moment for her.

CHAPTER 29

One of the things that Helen had always wanted to try was Endurance Riding, a sport where all that matters is getting to the end of the ride with a healthy horse. As beginners are only allowed on the twenty kilometre rides, even if their horse is vetted as fit, they have to notch up a lot of kilometers before being allowed to compete in the long rides. Helen's first ride had the best twenty kilometres of the ride right at the beginning so she didn't feel she was missing out on too much by not covering one hundred and sixty grueling kilometres on her first attempt.

They were starting near the top of an escarpment in the forestry country west of Kingaroy, and following fire and logging trails most of the way past a set of waterfalls, dry at this time of year but whose cliff faces in the distance were quite spectacular. Since the logging trails weren't normally open to anyone but walkers, Helen was really looking forward to the ride. This was all part of one of the biggest State Forests in the southern hemisphere and the trip down off the escarpment included some rolling hills with great opportunities for long views and feeling on top of the world.

Helen left Carlisle early on a Friday evening with JJ in the float and Shania Twain on the CD player. There were no towns with takeaway between Carlisle and the start point so she had packed cheese and salami sandwiches for dinner and high carb snacks to keep her going for the next day.

As soon as she had settled JJ in his camp for the night, Helen was supposed to attend a briefing, essential information for the ride the next day and then it was lights out for the whole camp, except for one horse in the distance who let everyone know he was not happy to be away from his stablemates. Fortunately he was far enough away that Helen could tune him out although the mosquitos which buzzed all night were a little harder to ignore. Eventually the close sound of dozens of horses tearing at the grass and stomping at the mozzies lulled her to sleep. The alarm woke her early, very early.

Like any horse event, it was controlled bedlam at the starting point. After the first few kilometres everyone settled to a steady pace, each horse and rider sticking strictly to their individual controlled and comfortable long distance rhythm.

Most of the time, Helen could see another rider up ahead and could hear others behind her but their voices came and went between the corners and the steep hills, swallowed up by the trees on either side of the road. The odd rider had passed her and she passed one or two herself, as they all took rests at different times, easing from a canter to a trot or a trot to a walk, depending on their maximum pace allowed on the training ride. Some of them rode as a pair or as small groups but she felt fine by herself, although when another rider tracked alongside for a little while she quite enjoyed the company. The tracks were firm underfoot from a light rain a day or so before and ran south in front of her, in huge undulations like a razor cut through jungle, generally following a power line of striding triffods. As JJ settled in to an easy swinging trot, Helen relaxed and her mind wound back a couple of days to the weekend before.

David had been away again, this time picking up Jonathon and taking him back down to the family in Byron Bay. It did occur to Helen to wonder why he needed a chaperone- after all he was in his twenties and had been travelling overseas by himself. She told herself it was David's business if he wanted to drive two and a half thousand kilometres in one weekend to look after a spoilt and angry young man.

Saturday morning, Liam knocked on the door and putting on an apologetic face, held out his hand with an invitation for her to smack it.

'What for,' Helen wanted to know.

'In case I do anything wrong today,' he responded. 'I wondered if you'd like to come to Riswell with me and maybe go down to the beach for a swim since its pretty warm at the moment. You know I'm not allowed out on my own yet.'

'Since when.'

'Since I thought I'd like some company,' he answered 'and you are better company than Norm would be.'

'Well that wouldn't be hard.'

Helen thought for a minute. It really did suit her to go to Riswell. There were a couple of things she would like to pick up in Target and a swim sounded amazing. In spite of approaching winter, they had been having a warm spell and a dip in the middle of the day in the bright blue sea appealed to her as a fitting end to the summer and a suitable shortening of the winter months. On a day like today, King's Beach and the islands off it were spectacular and it was only another half hour drive from Riswell. The longer she thought about it, the more a day out appealed. Helen felt like she had been offered a holiday.

'Ok, I'll just be ten minutes. Can we drop in to Target for five minutes while we're up there?'

'Of course, what would a trip to the big smoke be without a visit to Target.'

They'd had a wonderful day, with all irritations deliberately buried and magic weather.

The movie they'd decided to see turned out to be just as good as promised and the fish and chips they'd bought to eat in the park was piping hot and crisp, just the way it should be.

The water was the perfect temperature, so that floating around in the swell was a pleasure rather than the disappointment a minimal surf usually was.

Helen found herself thinking about Liam and their relationship during the day and it was on the tip of her tongue a couple of times to try to discuss their differences with him and to find out more about Jonathon, but the day was too comfortable and pleasant to bring up what she knew would be a touchy subject. There was so much she wanted to know but now just didn't seem to be the time.

So even when the day ended, she was no wiser. She and Liam had avoided any controversial topics by common consent all day and at the end of it she knew no more than she had in the morning, at least about those subjects. They had managed to cover a lot of other topics though and the kiss Liam dropped on her forehead as he thanked her for her company was sweet and pleasant and demanded nothing. Altogether, it was a day to be treasured, a glowing, restful spot in a busy life.

At the moment she hardly saw David, with all the running he was doing for Jonathon and trying to catch up on some of his own work and she realized that it didn't bother her like it should if there had been any real feeling on her part toward him. It was almost with a sigh of relief that she realized that she now knew how she felt but she did wonder how she would convey that to David when the time came to sort it all out with him. If, in fact there was anything to sort out.

JJ's pace changed, his head suddenly high and tight and his hooves on springs. Helen realized with a start that just at this moment there was no one else in sight except a herd of brumbies, standing alert and watchful about two hundred metres away. At the back of the group she could see the young ones milling and bucking, picking up on the tension of the older horses. Her stomach contracted with fear and she thanked her lucky stars that JJ was a gelding and generally fairly placid, but even the gentlest horse could be railroaded by a whole mob. Helen brought him to a walk and considered her options, realizing that they were governed by whoever was behind her and where the brumbies were headed to after they crossed the road. Going on, just at that moment was out of the question and she sure didn't feel like turning her back on them, especially if they were headed in her direction. As best she could, she judged that she was probably close to the path they wished to be on, probably between the brumbies and the waterhole, if she was reading the slope of the country properly. She looked around and decided that she probably was best on the same side of the road and further back up the hill so they could cross in to what looked like a clear area. She backed JJ up with as little fuss as possible, thanking her father for the time he had spent helping her to train him to respond gently to her commands. Keeping a wary eye on the brumbies, she turned him and crossed the road at an angle back up the hill, not quite turning her back on them, and moved in to the trees about 100m from where she hoped they would cross the road and enter the forest on the other side. JJ stood quietly but watchfully as the mob started to step out and move up the road at the sort of angle Helen had hoped they would, obviously seeing her but not too concerned.

Helen held her breath and hoped that the horses were thirsty enough to ignore her but she heard a scream and watched in horror as a riderless horse careered around the corner towards her, straight in to the middle of the herd. She could see the animal rearing, its bridle flying out around its head and watched as the others turned on it in a vicious, milling pack. Helen vaguely realized that it was a huge chestnut that she had noticed in the yards earlier that morning, one of the horses which had been completely unsettled and yelling for its mates most of the night.

JJ backed and snorted as the brumbies swirled closer, swinging his quarters into a tree as he tried to dodge away from the mob. Helen had no idea what to do, but swung him across the road to the other side with the idea of skirting the mob and heading off while they were distracted by the chestnut who was snorting and squealing, stretching out with his great teeth bared and the muscles standing out aggressively in his neck and his feet striking out. Her plan would have succeeded except for the flying hooves of the chestnut as he turned in a circle of churning hooves and accidentally caught JJ on the shoulder, hitting Helen's knee like a hammer blow. The chestnut went down to one knee as Helen and JJ backed off, Helen falling forward and striking her nose on JJ's poll as he threw his head back and ran backwards, before swinging around to make a limping escape, Helen clinging in desperation as she fought from blacking out completely with the pain of her abused knee and cracked nose and forehead.

Through her own gasping pain, she felt the stumble and hesitation in JJ's step, felt it in every part of her damaged knee and pulled joints, but there was an urgent need to get as far away as they could before either she or the horse could give up. She made herself go on, agonizing for JJ every step of the way but a couple of hundred yards down the road, her head filled suddenly with a black cloud of cotton wool and she slid off. Poor JJ was suffering badly. With her own control slipping she just had enough presence of mind to loosen the girth and untie the reins so they wouldn't catch his legs if he did run off, before she leant back against a tree and gave in to the gathering blackness, hoping that she was well off the path of the brumbies, and that other riders would come along soon.

She was still slumped there, JJ patiently beside her when the next group clattered around the corner, having seen nothing of the brumbies or the chestnut. There was immediate consternation and cursing of poor mobile phone coverage, then the group abruptly separated, two to stay with her and the rest to head on to the closest post for help.

Gradually, Helen became aware of voices and people as other horses and vehicles arrived and the group swelled to what seemed like hundreds, all speaking at once. She cast around anxiously to find JJ and spotted him with a vet in attendance being loaded on to a large float, hastily padded and set up to carry the injured horse. As the dark reclaimed her she could hear a distant throbbing, the sound at once the savior and the dread of rural Australians. Her heart racing to the beat of the blades she was at the same time, oddly reassured that help was near, coming down somewhere close.

She came to as urgent voices drew closer, enough to know that unless there was more wrong with her than she thought, the chopper was probably not really necessary for her. She wriggled her hands and feet and moved her head experimentally, thinking she might be able to get up, only to be sharply told to stay still and keep out of trouble.

The chopper landed further down the road, and it seemed to take forever before a vehicle turned up with a paramedic on board.

'Can you tell me your name.? How old are you? They asked all the standard questions and by this stage Helen was able to answer them all, since people had been asking her the same stupid things since they first arrived. In an odd pocket of her mind she knew the questions weren't stupid, but she had already given the answers at least ten times. If only they would leave her alone to get herself together. Next, they checked her over very thoroughly and stabilized her knee then maneuvered her on to a stretcher and in to the back of a vehicle for the trip down to the helicopter. Helen gave up protesting and started to worry about JJ, but anyone associated with the horses had left by this time and no-one could answer her. She had vague memories of a horse float in the road and tried to comfort herself with the only bit of knowledge she felt she had.

As they pulled the stretcher out near the helicopter, it became clear why it had landed where it had. The rider of the chestnut horse had not been so lucky, and was still unconscious and hooked up to various machines looking deathly pale. It was a girl Helen had been briefly introduced to named Janice, and Janice was the main reason for the chopper. Helen felt she was really just hitching a ride.

She tried to turn and watch what was happening as the chopper lifted with a swing of the body and thrumming of the blades, but it was impossible strapped in as she was and with every movement sending pain shooting straight from her knee to her hip and back, which pulsated with spasms in sympathy. Briefly she wondered if they had found the chestnut and if he would be alright before the pain killers kicked in and she dozed the rest of the way to the hospital in Riswell.

❦ ❦ ❦

CHAPTER 30

LIAM

David was just dishing out dinner when the phone rang. 'Yep, that's always the way', he grumbled, 'the minute I put the dinner out, it's guaranteed to ring.'

'Evening, David Temple speaking.'

The voice on the other end of the line sounded anxious, even from where Liam stood.

'No that's terrible, is she OK, where is she?' David listened. 'Yes, I'm sure I can organize both, I'll talk to Josie and we'll figure it out between us'

'And what about the horse? What will happen there?'

'Oh, Ok, well, we'll make sure someone is there and I'll come down myself, as soon as I've organized some gear.'

'Thanks so much, yes will do, thank you.'

David put down the phone and turned. 'Helen has had an accident and they've taken her to Riswell and poor old JJ is on his way home. He's on his feet but they're not sure what will happen, he's so badly bruised.'

Liam felt the blow in the pit of his stomach. 'Is she OK, what's wrong?'

'Mainly just a blow to the knee as far as they can make out, but she wasn't fully conscious at all before the flight left, so they don't know if there's other damage or not and the emergency guys weren't giving out too much information. They don't think she fell off at all, so it's a bit confused. But she was conscious enough to worry about the horse.'

'I've offered to go up to Riswell and take what she needs, since I know where the spare key is, but I wondered if you would mind helping out with the horse. I know she is going to be incredibly anxious about him?'

Liam knew it was logical for him to stay and look after the horse since David was Helen's friend and also a doctor, but every part of him rebelled at that. He considered objecting but then thought better of it. Now, was not the time but he decided at that moment that the time would come to try and sort out where he stood with David and Helen. At this moment he was just plain worried about Helen and so he figured the best he could do would be to see to the horse and make sure there was least amount of worry possible for her while she was in hospital. With the thought in mind that it could be a long and draining night with a badly injured horse, he packed himself some overnight gear and a couple of sandwiches, bolted his dinner, made sure his phone was charged and headed out to the vets to wait for the truck.

❦   ❦   ❦

JJ was suffering and it was excruciating to watch. Even with the pain killers he'd been given he shifted around in the stall, stretching out his neck to shake his head in distress and Liam felt totally useless. All he could do for Helen was to use his voice to soothe the troubled horse and try to ensure that he didn't injure himself anymore. JJ had been placed in a large and luxurious stall at the vets but it was clear that the trip home had been hard on him and during the long agonizing night, Liam began to wonder if they should have brought him home after all. It was difficult to remember the big, gentle-eyed giant that was JJ when faced with the twitching, stomping and head shaking behavior of this animal.

By eight the next morning, he was exhausted and the horse seemed no better in spite of another painkiller needle at about five am. At last the vet on duty, who had been out to see to an urgent case, came back in and sent Liam off home for some breakfast, although he knew he would be back for another long stint within an hour or so. The phone rang as he entered the house and it's normally bell like tones sent hot knives of anxiety through his body.

'David, what's the news, is she OK?'

'Well firstly, she will be OK but she's in a lot of pain. Evidently there was a runaway horse from one of the competitors, and a mob of brumbies and they all got mixed up and Helen and JJ ended up in the way and one of them has kicked out at her, injuring both her and JJ. She has a pretty nasty leg injury and she banged her head on his poll they think. But it looks like she didn't pass out until after she managed to ride a safe distance away. She even managed to dismount and do her best for the horse. They found her sitting up against a tree, still holding the reins. Since she didn't fall off and she's conscious enough to ask questions, they're assuming it's only the injury to her leg, some pulled muscles and a bump on her face that they're watching her for.'

'She's pretty groggy and likely to be in here for a while, but she is desperate to find out how JJ is. What can you tell me? Is he OK?'

Liam hesitated, unsure how to answer. 'He's in a lot of pain, but they don't think anything is broken, just extremely badly bruised probably.'

'Probably?'

They'll X-Ray this morning and then we should know some more. Look I've got to get back so I can see what happens and believe me I'll let you know as soon as I know something. Just tell Helen, he is being looked after and is not in too much pain. Liam crossed his fingers when he passed on this bit of prevarication, but he just didn't know enough at the moment to give any false hope and it was the best he could come up with.

When he arrived back at the vet's, Doug came out looking harassed. 'I just don't know what to make of it. There doesn't seem to be anything broken but I can't get him at all comfortable, in spite of giving him an even bigger dose. It is like there is something else wrong but I just can't place it and I've been all over him.'

'I need to go out to 'Blythedale' to a couple of beasts they have down out there. I'll be a couple of hours- can you spare that to spend a bit of time with him?'

Liam nodded.

JJ was moving around the stall, obviously in a great deal of discomfort but totally doped as well. It was as if he was moving in his sleep and Liam found it distressing just to watch him. He spoke calmly to the horse, dropping his voice to a murmur and putting his hand on his poll to rub it with gentle finger. JJ submitted and settled for a minute or two and then began to shuffle again, lifting one foot and then the other, occasionally stomping with a back foot as if angry at an annoying fly.

By the time, Doug returned Liam was exhausted and extremely concerned that the horse would need to be put out to it altogether or perhaps even put down.

Doug looked over the stall door with Liam and grunted. 'Only thing I can see for it is to put him out altogether or use a sling. I've looked in his feet but there is nothing obvious and nothing showed up on the x-ray either. I assume Helen would want me to do whatever we can for him.'

'I have no doubt she would, 'said Liam 'but I'll guarantee it myself. Just go ahead and try whatever we need to and I will fix it up. I really don't want to worry Helen at the moment. To tell the truth, I haven't even heard if she is fully conscious yet, so she doesn't need to be making decisions.'

Decision made, the vet team flew in to action and it was not long before poor JJ swung from the rafters with a support under his neck and his eyes closed.

'At least he looked moderately peaceful that way' thought Liam as he left to find some lunch and to catch up on the sleep he'd missed the night before. Just an hour or two and then he would ring David again before going back out to the vets.

CHAPTER 31

David picked up his mobile, and visibly winced as he caught Helen watching him anxiously.

'I'll have to go outside to ring him' he said, 'there's no reception in here and I don't want to use the hospital phone to ring his mobile.'

Helen knew it was only an excuse in case of bad news but didn't feel up to arguing about it. In spite of being desperately worried, somewhere inside, the medication appeared to be taking the immediacy from her anxiety. She lay there in a fog of pain and desperate grief somewhere deep in her mind, but couldn't seem to utter the words to bring it to reality.

'If I don't cry' her body seemed to say 'then it will all be OK.'

Somewhere, David and Liam were talking about her poor damaged horse, but Helen couldn't seem to keep her mind on what it was she was worrying about for long enough to really worry. It seemed like years before David came back in to the room and she could see he had deliberately erased all anxiety from his smile. It didn't fool her for a moment but she couldn't string the words together to ask.

'He's doing OK, Liam says, but there seems to be something else bothering him besides the bruising from where he was kicked, so they've got him doped and strung up in a sling to investigate. There're no bones broken according to the X-Rays, so it is just a matter of having a closer look and a lot of wait and see, I suspect.'

'Liam is still out there with him, and there's no one better with a horse than Liam, so you can relax. He is getting the best care they can possibly give him.'

'Thank you.' Helen struggled even to get that one word out but in her foggy mind she knew there was something odd about that statement about Liam and horses. And drifting through her mind to confuse her thoughts was something she should know, but just couldn't catch, something important, that she was sure she should tell David. She couldn't picture Liam and horses at all and vaguely wondered if he had even been out to see Superman with David. Odd that! She was trying hard to remember what else she knew that was important but it kept getting mixed up with thoughts of Liam.

Helen guessed he was probably not supposed to ride yet. It was the only answer she could come up with. She thought Liam had implied that he came from a family that was nowhere near as wealthy as David's family, but had gone to the expensive Sydney school on a scholarship. For some reason, Helen had assumed he was a city boy, since she was sure that he said David had boarded and he hadn't. She drifted off to sleep without even giving a thought to the location of her vehicle and float and what arrangements had been made to bring them back.

Helen came to with a start in the middle of the night, a

slight erratic snoring from beside the bed bringing her fully awake. David lay sprawled in a chair beside the bed looking extremely uncomfortable and with one arm across the side of her pillow and his head resting on it. She opened her eyes and turned very gingerly to look at him fully, although the support on her leg made it hard to move quietly. For the first time since the accident she felt as if she could more or less think through what had happened and start to make some sense of what David had told her. Somewhere in her memory, there was something she thought she should remember about JJ, but it just wouldn't come to her.

She struggled to remember the sequence of events and saw again the great big chestnut as he spun with his hind feet extended to connect with her knee and JJ's shoulder with a sharp crack that swung her leg back and almost over the back of the saddle.

She remembered scrambling to regain her seat and seeing the indent in the front of the saddle flap where the horses shoe had clipped a piece from the leather.

That could so easily have been her leg hammered in to the saddle rather than shot backwards, she remembered thinking, before the pain hit her, surprising her that she really had been hurt after all.

She'd hauled JJ around the mob and headed off down the road, although neither of them were in any condition to be moving far. They needed to get enough distance from the brumbies, so that she could get off and check him over.

JJ had been limping but a hundred yards down the road, he went completely lame, and she couldn't think why. There must have been something, but once again she drifted off before she could sort out what she was thinking at the time, apart from needing to get away.

'No, Mum, there is no need to come home.'

'But how are you going to manage, once they do let you home?' Helen could hear the concern in her mother's voice and her need to be home to care for Helen.

'By the time you get here, I'll be on crutches I'm sure, and I do live next door to a doctor. Besides, it's holidays and maybe Genevieve will come up or I'm sure I could go and stay with Rhys and Josie. You know how Josie loves to look after people.'

Helen knew, that of all the people in the world, her Mum would trust only Josie to look after her. Sometimes she wished that her Mum would let go just a little bit more, but then she remembered just how lucky she was.

Mum was unconvinced but Helen was confident that her father would sort it out, once she convinced him she would be OK. 'Just put Dad on please Mum, I'm sure he'll say the same as I do. If you like, I'll ring Josie soon and then let her talk to you. You'll see, there will be no reason at all to come home. I will be fine.'

'Ok, love you too.'

Helen put the phone down and looked up as Dr James entered the room.

'So how's the knee today, have they been in to check your dressing and support yet?' He held the chart in his hand and looked over the rims of his glasses at her, his head held slightly on one side and an amiable smile on his face.

For all the world like Jack the dog, thought Helen with a little rush of homesickness.

Helen shook her head, 'No,' and the doctor frowned. 'I'm sorry about that then, but they must come along soon. Apart from that, how are you feeling this afternoon? You were pretty out of it last night and we were a bit concerned,' he continued.

'I'm not too bad' she answered 'but I still feel pretty confused and I had some pretty strange dreams. At least I think they were. She looked puzzled and upset, so Dr James sat down on the chair near the window and waited patiently as she thought for a moment.

'You know I'm sure there's something I should remember to tell David about JJ but I just can't seem to think straight.'

'I'm sure it will come eventually, when your body settles down a bit,' comforted the doctor.

'Yes, but that feels wrong, I need to know now. David isn't saying much and it's what he isn't telling me that makes me worry. I'm sure there's more wrong than just some bruising. I remember him going completely lame, I'm sure.'

'I wonder if a talk with Vivienne, the girl who came in at the same time, would help at all?' he suggested. 'You never know.'

'I didn't even remember she was here.' Helen felt terrible and felt she should have known that the rider of the huge chestnut would be in the hospital as well. 'Is she OK? Obviously she can talk or you wouldn't have suggested I meet her, but is she very hurt?'

He looked a bit sheepish. 'She's in better condition than you are, that's for sure, but a lot worse temper.'

Helen was taken aback. 'Do you think she will talk to me, then?'

'Well, I hope so, since I hope it might help you, but she blames everyone but herself for the fact that they haven't found that horse yet. He was worth over twenty thousand dollars apparently and they were going to win for sure.'

He looked at her. 'Probably, I shouldn't have said that, in fact I know I shouldn't have, but she truly was not that injured, she just put on a tantrum and passed out apparently, so they assumed the worst and hooked her up, but it was only more or less from her holding her breath in anger that caused all the fuss. She does have a sore foot though, where she kicked a rock or something in temper.'

He scratched just above his right eye and looked at her speculatively, drawing in his breath.

'But I hope it helps you find the information you need somewhere in that head of yours.'

'Thank you doctor, I'll try and be very sympathetic,' said Helen, 'just send her around.'

CHAPTER 32

Vivienne was a tall girl and she came into the room tempestuously, in spite of a pronounced limp.

'Thanks for coming in to see me,' started Helen but she was interrupted before she could continue on to ask how Vivienne was feeling.

'Oh, you're the girl who saw Lister, just before he disappeared aren't you? I would have thought you'd have made an attempt to catch him for me, he isn't vicious you know.'

Helen looked at the girl and realized from her uncompromising stance that Vivienne had no idea what had really happened, but was desperately trying to find someone to blame. It occurred to her, that probably no-one really knew what had happened since she'd been by herself at the time and not able to talk much since she'd been in hospital. In fact, she had no idea what she'd managed to tell anyone. She rubbed her cheek with the gesture she'd had since she was a child and listened as Vivienne continued.

'It was that stupid girl I was with. We heard some horses calling out behind us, I guess it was yours, but she insisted it was brumbies and that we should hurry to get away. Her horse broke in to a canter but she decided to pull him up suddenly, I don't know why, but she didn't bother telling me before she did. She said it was because they would hear the hoof beats, get excited and chase us. Silly cow. Lister tried to avoid her horse but we hit his hindquarters and that stupid animal of hers kicked out and knocked my foot out of the stirrup. And she didn't even chase him, when she managed to pull her horse up and turn around.'

Well that had explained the sore foot. Perhaps Dr. James had exaggerated just a little.

Helen listened in disbelief as she went on and on. 'She probably couldn't have caught him anyway, he's very fast, but you could have. You were behind me.' As she drew in her breath to start all over again, Helen managed to get in first.

'There were brumbies.'

Vivienne gave her a sideways look that clearly said 'I don't think so, Dodo,' and said, 'there are no brumbies up here in Queensland.'

'Weren't you listening at the briefing when they told us to what to do if we ran in to a mob?' countered Helen, 'and there are brumbies everywhere in Southern Queensland, even in some of the coastal forests.'

'I had an interview with the local paper while that was on. I couldn't possibly have gone to it.'

'But you're not supposed to ride unless you do,' said Helen, 'and surely you saw the piles of horse manure along the roads. Great big piles, where did you think they came from?'

'Well we weren't the first horses on the ride to go through,' said Vivienne, 'Where else would it come from?'

It was clear that Vivienne had no idea about the

territorial habits of brumbies and Helen gave a fleeting smile which lit her eyes momentarily as she had visions of lines of endurance horses filing through one at a time and carefully placing manure on the same pile before they moved on.

Vivienne eyed her narrowly, 'You wouldn't think it was so funny if it was your horse.'

Helen gave up and lost her temper, 'For your information, there was a mob crossed the road just behind you and that is where your horse went. He got caught in the mob and when he tried to get out and join me, they chased him and he kicked me as he went to chase them off. You'll be lucky if he doesn't break his leg, running around with those hooked together reins he had and his stirrups flapping- all because you weren't prepared to listen to your riding companion or attend the briefing.'

'I suppose you think you are going to make a story out of that so no one thinks it's your fault,' suggested Vivienne.

It hadn't occurred to Helen, but she wasn't going to say so just at that moment. 'I think I'd rather you left, you know,' she flung at Vivienne.

She was still shaking with disbelief and anger when Dr James returned, popping his head around the corner of the doorway and asking how the interview had gone.

'Not well.' Helen gave a rueful shrug. 'Anyone would think I deliberately lost her horse for her. Except for the fact that I feel sorry for the horse, I'd hope he's gone forever, but I do hope they do find him and at least get the saddle and bridle off before he kills himself.'

'So, I don't suppose you remembered anything then.'

Helen looked up. 'Well yes I did in spite of all that. It helped me visualize where we were and exactly what happened and I know we were near the old oil drilling rig from the 50's. I'll bet there was something like a nail or old glass that he's picked up when we took the path out through the bush to get to the road. It's probably only a small piece or the vet would have found it earlier. There're some nasty prickly vines in there as well with decent sized thorns so it could be either. I definitely remember seeing old glass bottles around there, when I was there ages ago having a look around. I'm sure I also remember them the other day.'

'Well that's good then, I'll go away so you can ring the boyfriend to let him know.'

It wasn't David but Liam who answered the phone when Helen rang the house and she was aware of a little lift of pleasure that curled through her chest when she heard his voice on the other end.

'Helen it's so good to hear you, how are you feeling?' Liam sounded genuinely concerned and pleased, his voice dropping intimately a note or two deeper.

'I'm getting there,' replied Helen, 'at least I can think straight now that they've cut back on the painkillers. I really appreciate what you and David have been doing for me.'

'Helen, don't even think of it. We just wish we could do more but Doug has been over him really carefully and there's nothing broken.'

'I don't think it's that Liam. I think he probably has something like glass in his foot. There was a lot of old debris lying around from the old mine and I wouldn't be surprised if we ended up in the middle of it. Will you ask Doug to check for me? It'll probably mean an extra X-ray I imagine.'

'Well he has done one and they didn't find anything, but maybe it's a long thin sliver and it might show up from another angle. I'll talk to him about it, as long as you don't mind the vet's bill.'

'Oh no Liam, whatever it takes. Doug tries to be reasonable.'

'I'll do that Helen. It is so good to hear you sounding like yourself but take it easy and don't worry about things here. We'll sort it out.'

'Liam, you don't know how much that means to me. Thank you so much and I will owe you and David big time.'

'You just get better and then I'll come and pick you up, that's a promise,' said Liam, 'and then you can make it up to me, I'll find a way.'

Helen could hear the sincerity of the promise in his voice.

CHAPTER 33

Looking forward to a much better night's sleep, Helen settled down with a book in the evening. David had brought up her current selection which included a novel by Agatha Christie. Helen had spent years avoiding Agatha Christie, as she told herself and everyone else that she really wasn't interested in murder mysteries. Then one day it occurred to her that a couple of her favourite authors did in fact write crime fiction and that that was what she had been reading without realizing it. She enjoyed them because of the humour so she decided then that she really should not limit herself and at least should read the recognized doyen of the genre. To her surprise she thoroughly enjoyed most of the stories and had even sought out more every now and then, thoroughly enjoying the dry humour and tongue in cheek characterisations as well as the strong minded female lead characters of many of them.

'Murder in Mesopotamia' was the choice for tonight and Helen had reached the point where the second victim had just died, when the whump of the helicopter landing on the pad outside the window disturbed her concentration. There was no reason, except it was late in the evening and the scene had been set in Mesopotamia, that Helen should feel a premonition that would have done Agatha proud. She listened intently, wishing that she could get out of bed and peer out of the window.

When the nurse came in to the room fifteen minutes later to help her settle for the night, Helen was still on edge, over stimulated and jittery like a cat near a snake track.

'That was a late run for the helicopter,' Helen ventured. 'I thought they didn't run after eight o'clock.'

'It was a young bloke that someone found on the highway, way out at whoop whoop and the helicopter was in the area, doing a return so they took him on as an emergency.'

'Any idea what's wrong or who he is?'

'Not at the moment but they're working on it. I shouldn't tell you this but it looked like he was dead drunk. Out to it completely and seems to have run the car off the road, but not too much physical damage though.'

'Silly young fellow, I hope he's better in the morning then.'

'You just worry about yourself so you can go home,' said the nurse firmly 'and we'll worry about silly beggars who have too much to drink.'

In spite of these everyday comments, Helen still felt a connection, a feeling of urgency and responsibility that she couldn't account for. She eventually went to sleep, but only by convincing herself that her disturbance was due to a combination of the sleeping medication and her own recent experiences in the helicopter. She drifted in and out of sleep convinced she could hear urgent voices and quick footsteps coming and going, but next morning when she woke, everything seemed so calm and normal that she knew she had dreamed it all.

Breakfast came at the same time as a phone call from David with the wonderful news that they had found the problem with JJ. Helen had been right. JJ had a tiny sliver of old green glass lodged up the side of the frog and once this was removed had promptly demanded his breakfast and generally behaved about one thousand percent happier. It also appeared that there was very little of the infection normally expected with that type of injury and very little heat.

'Now, we'll just have to concentrate on getting you home,' was David's response to her genuine and heartfelt thanks.

'So what has been happening there?' Now that JJ was on the mend, Helen found she was suddenly interested in other things and would love to have talked to Liam about some of the unfinished work on her desk. She hoped that someone had thought to look in her diary and decided that her first action after breakfast would be to ring the office. It was amazing how much clearer her mind was now.

'What's that David, I'm sorry, I was just making a mental note to ring the office?'

'Did you say Jonathon has disappeared?' 'Again?'

Last Helen had heard, David had driven Jonathon down to David's parents in Byron Bay but here he was telling her that Jonathon had been taken to a mental health assessment unit later on, where they were trying to decide if he genuinely was trying to harm himself, and attempting to inspire him to look after his diabetes and kick his drug habit at the same time. 'Somewhat of a long term project, according to Liam,' said David, and one they had been through with him before apparently.

It turned out, Jonathon had simply walked out of the hospital, hired a car and headed off and nobody knew which direction he had taken. That was yesterday morning and there was nothing the police or anyone could do until he had been missing for a couple of days.

David had grave concerns for his health in spite of the fact that he had taken his medication with him apparently. That was an extremely unusual event for Jonathon and was the only thing that gave David much hope. Jonathon had a history of 'forgetting' his insulin.

'Oh David, I am so sorry. I really don't know how you are coping at the moment. First you were chasing around after Liam, then it was Robbie you got involved with and Genevieve says you've been spending time with Ivy, then Jonathon and then me and now Jonathon again. You could give up work and just spend the rest of your life looking after all the people that need you for free.' Helen didn't mean to make it sound like a joke, she meant it as a heartfelt thankyou but David chuckled anyway.

It was lucky that he was someone who seemed to take it all in his stride and never seemed to become hassled, thought Helen although she had often seen him very thoughtful and concerned.

'Well I hope he turns up soon,' said Helen, as they rang off, although it did occur to her that the sooner he turned up, the sooner David would be running backward and forward to Brisbane or wherever again to try to reach him and talk some sense in to him.

Breakfast and morning necessities over and done with,

Helen decided to ring the office. It was early, but she knew it was probably the best chance she'd have of catching Liam, since he often came in to the office before heading out in the field for the day. She couldn't for the life of her remember what either of them were meant to be doing that week, not day by day anyway. She did know there was a meeting in Riswell that they both would have attended but couldn't remember what day it was supposed to be, so she did expect to see Liam at some stage. She also knew there was a field day on Friday and today being Monday, she thought Liam would probably be finalizing some details for that.

The phone rang out and Liam's mobile informed her that he was either on the phone or not in a mobile reception area, which was not unusual given the location of some of the properties they worked on. Still, it was very early for Liam to be out on a property. *Oh well, try again later,* she thought.

Jenny, the morning nurse arrived and Helen watched her pick up the chart. 'Well, it all seems OK, and I'll bet you'll be heading home soon,' was her opinion, but you'll be on crutches for a little while and need to have that knee checked by a physio when the swelling goes down a bit more. I assume you have a physio in your town.'

'We have a very good physio,' Helen assured her 'and I promise to be a good girl and go along to him. Besides, my next door neighbor is a doctor and I have no doubt he will make sure I do.'

Helen remembered the night before and asked, 'How is the young man they brought in last night?'

'Well, he's a lot better this morning but I don't think he'll be going anywhere for a while.'

'Why's that?'

'We all thought he was drunk when they brought him in but it turns out he was in a diabetic coma when they picked him up and although the helicopter guys did manage to stabilize him with an emergency needle, he still wasn't too good. He hadn't eaten much all day and wasn't testing they reckon, and add to that he didn't have any water in the car. He was pretty much a mess, when they brought him in.'

'Is he a local boy, or local to where they found him, I mean?' Helen's mind flew straight to Jonathon, even though she knew it would be very unlikely.

'No, but he won't tell anyone where he is from so just at the moment they're concentrating on getting him right and then I guess they'll have to search through his stuff. He must have a license somewhere. Apparently it was a hire car.'

Helen's skin began to prickle. 'What does he look like?'

'About twenty two, a good looking young fellow with blond hair and quite tall. Not carrying any weight and he has a couple of tattoos.'

Helen thought back to everything she had heard about Jonathon but it would be a huge coincidence for this to be him, probably too huge but she definitely felt that she needed to make the effort to find out. Just in case. It was the least she could do for David, even if it did feel really, really awkward and there was the possibility of making a total fool of herself. But the worst he could do would be to tell her to get lost, surely. She was sure she could survive that.

'You know, I'm not sure but I may know who he is,' suggested Helen. "Is there any way I can get to see him or talk to him, without making a fuss about it?'

'I'd have to ask the doctor about that and it could take a

while before he gets here, but I'll go straight away and see what I can get going. Maybe they'll find his identification before then. You'd think he'd have to have some, wouldn't you?'

Jenny hurried off and Helen lay back in bed, wondering if she should try to talk to Liam or David about this or wait until she knew more. She hated the thought of David being anxious any longer than he had to be, but she decided he would have to wait until she knew.

How she was going to know, even if she talked to him was a little bit problematic. She'd heard a little about him from Liam and knew that in fact he was blond and quite tall but she really didn't have much more information than that. It could be extremely embarrassing if he was not Jonathon or if he would not admit that he was. She thought about the fact that he also had a drug problem and Liam had made a remark about the marks on his right arm, so she knew he was left handed as well. Maybe if she passed these facts on to the doctors first, they could decide whether it was worth her talking to him. She didn't want to talk to a total stranger and upset his precarious mental balance unless she was a little more certain of her facts. So she decided that even if, big if, the doctors decided she could talk to him, she would trawl her memory for every little physical detail she was certain of and see if they could verify them first. She hoped she could remember enough bits and pieces about him and about David that she might be able to make him identify himself, that is if he was up to talking.

There was the sound of footsteps at the door and she looked up expecting Dr James, but instead a petite blond bombshell stepped through the door quickly and scanned her face and body in one quick movement. 'Boy, you look a lot better than I expected,' and Genevieve came over to give her a hug. 'I was expecting a drugged out, beaten up carcass, not lady muck lying there looking like the queen waiting to be served.'

'Genevieve, you must have got the early plane to be here now.'

'Yep, I stayed in Brisbane last night and caught up with some of the people I conferenced with a while ago then came on through this morning. Holidays again, bless the Education Department.'

'How long are you here for?'

'I thought I'd stay until you go home and then go home and look after you.'

'You are an angel and that will make Mum a happy lady. I don't think it is going to be too long. I was sitting here trying to remember what day Liam and I had a meeting up here and was hoping it would fit in to hitch a ride home with him so no one had to make a special trip.'

'We can always hire a one-way car to Carslisle and then we needn't bother anybody.'

'It is so good to see you. What have you been up to? It seems ages since we talked and how is Ivy getting on? And your Mum and Dad?'

The girls chattered most of the morning, until lunch arrived and Genevieve decided that she would visit the great metropolis of Riswell to procure some lunch and maybe do some shopping she'd been putting off for a while.

A couple of times, Helen almost raised the subject of Jonathon but just didn't want to make more of a fuss about it than necessary in case she was wrong. Surely the doctor would have an answer for her soon or maybe they had already found out what they needed to know and no one had thought to tell her. Helen shrugged philosophically and decided not to worry about it. It probably was just one of those strange little coincidences and she was worrying for nothing.

Dr James arrived almost with the lunch tray, apologizing for being late and interrupting her sumptuous banquet. Helen laughed and forebore to point out that it was corn meat sandwiches yet again and what looked like packet soup. Still, it smelled good.

'No, they still didn't have an identification and no, the young chap wasn't volunteering any information either, not even medical. It seemed he had absolutely no desire to help them or to help himself.'

Helen explained what she knew about Jonathon and the doctor agreed that it certainly did sound very, very likely that she had identified their man but it was almost impossible without him actually admitting to it himself.

'What if I make his acquaintance and can find out in conversation?' suggested Helen.

I know quite a bit about a couple of men who know him well and maybe I can identify him well enough for David or Liam to be asked to come and identify him positively- just so we aren't wasting any more of David's time than we need to.'

'Well, I hope we can do this quickly but even then we won't know what we are dealing with as far as medication is concerned.'

'Well, if it is Jonathon, I would assume that David will be able to deal with that. He is a doctor and has also been closely involved with him in the last couple of weeks.'

'Is that the young doctor who was here with you then?'

'Yes, that would be him. I assume you got to meet him by the sound of that.'

'We've had referrals from him too. Well for this young chap's sake, I hope that's who he is and that we can work on this together. It is a huge problem if he won't take charge of it himself.'

'So what's next?' asked Helen.

'I think we'll get you in there if you think you can manage it and then we are going to have to bother David if you think there's any possibility. I can't imagine what has happened to his identification, since he had to have had some to get the car surely.'

'Maybe got rid of it deliberately and was planning to get well and truly lost and unidentifiable for reasons I'd rather not think about,' suggested Helen. 'If this is Jonathon, then that is quite probable from the little I've heard.'

'This is all starting to make a strange kind of sense.'

'Where did they find him exactly?'

'He was on a back road that wasn't that far from your hometown as the crow flies, except that it was not really on the way to anywhere much, just a small property road joining two highways.'

'That doesn't make a lot of sense either, if we assume he was trying to lose himself. David lives in the same town and surely Jonathon would have known that.'

'Hmm, I don't know, but maybe we'd better let you have a go at finding out, but you'll need to be very careful. He's pretty defensive and I would judge, very, very fragile. I'll organize a wheelchair for you and Lisa can take you in when she has a moment. I'd like her to stay fairly close to the room just in case, as well, so she may just work around in the same room or next door for a while, if that is OK with you.'

'No worries, I'll just sit here and think about what I'm going to say to a young man I don't even know until Lisa is ready.' Helen was beginning to feel doubtful of her ability to get any useful information but she knew she needed to give it a try.

CHAPTER 34

Lisa came in with a wheelchair about half an hour later and by this time Helen was well and truly nervous, giving Lisa a fleeting little smile as she helped her into the chair.

'Well, aren't you the lucky one,' said Lisa, 'all the nurses have been vying for the chance to talk to Mr. Handsome in there.'

Helen hadn't realized that Jonathon was considered attractive. It wasn't exactly something that had come up in conversation with the two other men.

Yes, the young man in the bed was certainly handsome, although a little too frail looking to suit a fond mother, Helen thought and then amended that again. He also wore an almost tortured expression that would have broken the heart of the most hardened parent.

He looked up listlessly as she was wheeled in and held her glance for only a moment. Other than that, there was no greeting and while Helen was not at all vain, she was used to a little more interest from the male members of the population.

'Hi, I'm Helen,' she ventured. 'I've got the room next door.'

'Did they conscript you for entertainment duty, to make sure I didn't get rid of myself somehow?' he asked sullenly.

'No, is that likely?" she responded.

'Well they all seem to think so, all the questions they've been asking.'

He looked at her suspiciously, but Helen managed to keep her face interested and concerned, but hopefully not as horrified as she felt, with this very direct and almost aggressive approach.

'So what did you do to merit that?' asked Helen trying to keep the nervousness from her voice. Just at the moment though, the young fellow looked rather like a very young and sulky animal. Helen thought back to the young horses she had helped with at times and this seemed to imbue her with a warmth and confidence that most young animals would respond to. With animals it was not in the words you used, since they didn't understand them anyway, but in the patience and steadiness you displayed yourself, giving them confidence and sometimes the desire to please you, if you were very lucky.

'I was just trying to get to a friend's place, but I ended up on this stupid back road and everything went wrong.'

'Where does the friend live?' asked Helen, although she was getting a sneaky feeling he may have been referring to David. He must have caught something in her face and she could almost see him shut up shop again. 'Sorry, I do a lot of driving for my job and I was just thinking I might have been able to help you find out where you went wrong, since I know a lot of the back roads around here.'

'Wasn't anywhere near here,' he said and Helen decided not to follow that unproductive line of questioning.

She decided that maybe the best way to get a conversation going was to find out what he liked doing, so she started to tell him about her accident and the brumbies, and how she had come in by helicopter. 'I assume that was you who came in the helicopter last night,' she guessed.

'Yes, that was me.'

'I wonder what has happened to your car then. What do you think they'd do?'

'I guess the police will pick it up and take it to the nearest town.'

'Have you got stuff you need in it or did they bring everything with you? I ended up in the chopper and my horse was left behind where I had the accident and my car and float were at the start line. I was lucky, the emergency people floated my horse back to the start but friends had to go and get him and my car and look after everything. I could probably organize someone to get your car and bring it up here for you if you like.'

'Doesn't matter, they brought all my stuff and it was a hire car. Guess the police will return it, if they haven't already.'

Bingo thought Helen, one more fact to add to the list.

He thought for a moment, and then gave her a small smile. 'That wasn't very polite of me, so thank you for the offer.' Suddenly Helen could see why he got away with so much in the family. Even under these conditions, and unhappy as he seemed, that one small smile had a ten thousand watt appeal.

He was like a pup or a kitten, you couldn't help but respond and Helen made no effort to resist. *After all, this was the reason beautiful young animals existed*, she thought, *so that you just watch them and smile and make your day better.*

But this was a beautiful and injured young animal and she thought about her next words carefully.

'Now, I've told you what I like doing, it's your turn,' and she hoped that he would respond with some way of identifying him from the small amount she had heard from David and Liam.

'Do you like to travel, or ride horses or motorbikes? What floats your boat?'

He looked at her quite seriously. 'Anything that gets my adrenalin going, and that is getting harder and harder to find.'

'What, you're all adventured out at 19.' Helen held her breath and waited for his response.

'I'm 22 and I've been everywhere and tried a lot of things that you might not even have heard of,' he said, not being able to resist bragging a little to a pretty and interested girl.

She looked at him questioningly, 'Try me.'

'Heli-skiing, for one.'

'You'll have to do better than that. I've heard of it and watched it on TV.'

'Base jumping, bungee jumping, rodeo.'

'With a parachute or a wing suit?' inquired Helen.

'Yeah, I haven't got around to the wing suit yet.'

'How can you afford all that? It all sounds pretty expensive?'

His face closed over and Helen felt the cold weather descend.

'Not that it's any of my business- that was a bit rude. It

is just that I would love to try some of those things and I just don't make enough money to afford it,' she hurried in with.

'I thought you must have had a sponsorship deal or something like that going.'

There was a silence for a moment and the young man almost smiled again. 'You know I'm trying to turn over a new leaf here and I'm not doing real well,' he said, 'the whole thing's been a mess from start to finish.'

'Can you tell me about it?' suggested Helen. 'Maybe we can sort it out and I can help you unmess it.'

He eyed her assessingly. 'What do you know about diabetes?' he asked.

'I'm guessing type 1,' ventured Helen.

'You do know a bit then, do you?'

'I had a friend in school who was diabetic from when she was seven. We still catch up occasionally and I spent five years in the same dormitories and classes. We went on camp together and worked our horses together.'

'Well, I've been diabetic since I was twelve, and I don't know what your friend is like but I've hated it every minute of every day. You can never forget and nor can anyone else, even if you try to lead the most normal life possible. There's always something.'

He thought for a moment. 'I had made up my mind I was going to look after myself at long last. They've been on at me forever because I don't' but I've thought about it a lot lately and maybe they're right.'

'They?'

'Oh everyone. Doctors, nutritionist, family, or so called family anyway.'

Helen could hear the defensiveness returning to his

voice so she steered the subject away from family. 'So what happened that messed it up?'

'Well I decided to visit a friend, someone I knew would help me and not nag like everyone else. Besides, he really understands it all and he's known about it since it happened.'

'What happened?'

'I got rammed by a tractor when I was ten. I had some friends over and one started the tractor and trapped me against the back wall of the shed. D…..my other friend was there, he's a fair bit older and he raced in and backed the tractor off me and called the ambulance, but it was too late. It took two years for my pancreas to give up, but it did.'

'That's terrible. I can't imagine how everyone felt when they realized what was happening. And what about you?'

'I was in and out of the mental health unit and I didn't make it easy for my family. In the end, with the drought and everything, my Dad did what I'd been threatening to do. He shot himself. Just another farmer statistic, but I knew I'd probably caused some of it.'

'No, surely you can't think that.'

'Well, if I didn't, Mum told me often enough.'

Helen looked at him in horror. 'You can't be serious.'

'Well, she didn't really say it in those words but I knew what she meant. Then she died when I was fifteen from breast cancer.'

Struck completely silent, Helen watched her fingers twist around each other. What can you possibly say to a story like that? No wonder he was so incredibly fragile.

He reached forward and touched her hands, and as he did she realized two things. He was left handed and his right arm had the needle marks of a drug user.

'I do mean to try now though,' he said. 'I was on the way to this friend's place to put myself in his care and to promise I would do whatever he said. He said something a week or so ago and it just made me realize how stupid I've been. But I got lost, and I hadn't taken any extra food and I'd left my wallet on the service station counter three hundred kilometres back, when I filled the car. Just everything went wrong that possibly could. My mobile phone didn't even work, then it went flat and the low hit really suddenly.'

'Diabetic low?'

'You wouldn't know what it's like but suddenly everything becomes too hard, like moving through thick black water.'

Helen's heart went out to him and she returned the pressure of his hands, looking up at him with a relieved smile and wide, sympathetic eyes.

'That would be such a relief for everyone who loves you, if you did decide to take a bit more care,' she said. 'I hope you get it all sorted out soon. I'm hoping to get out maybe tomorrow but I'll come and see you before I go, if I can.'

There was a knock at the door and Lisa came in hurriedly. There is someone to see you Helen and he hasn't got a lot of time, or at least he seems to be in a hurry.'

'Ok, I'm coming. She turned to Jonathon, I'll see you in the morning then.'

Liam looked thunderous as she entered her own room, awkwardly trying to work the wheelchair past the doorframe a few minutes later.

'Well you found the little beggar then,' he stated as

he moved quickly closer to grab the back of the chair and propel her towards the bed.

Helen looked around at him, 'I assume you mean Jonathon. He hasn't told me his name yet but we're getting there.'

'Oh it's Jonathon all right and it sure doesn't take him long to get everyone around his little finger.'

Helen knew Liam didn't like Jonathon much but this seemed a bit extreme.

'I'm not sure what you mean by that but I'm pleased you identified him, it will save David a trip. The hospital have had no idea who he is and he wasn't telling, although he might now,' she conceded.

'I'm not sure I want to tell David,' said Liam. 'It will just unsettle him again and he'll be running up here every day. I've seen all this so many times before.'

Helen wondered at the suppressed anger still in Liam's voice but said anyway, 'Well David will need to know, you can hardly keep it from him, especially since he is already worried about where Jonathon is.'

Liam seemed unconvinced but let it drop for the moment, 'Apart from that message to David, is there anything I can get for you? I had to come up for that biodiversity project meeting and I'll be up again Wednesday for the rangelands one.'

'I think I'll be going home tomorrow and Genevieve is here, so we'll hire a car I think thanks Liam.'

Liam's relief was almost palpable as he realized that Helen would not be staying in the vicinity of Jonathon for more than one more night. 'Well, I'll see you tomorrow evening, then and say hello to the beautiful Genevieve for me.'

Liam seemed to have recovered his good humour and gently lifted her hand and patted it before leaving, 'You look after yourself too and don't worry, I will tell David. I've no doubt he'll be up here as fast as the wagon can make it.'

❦ ❦ ❦

'Breakfast was not bad,' decided Helen 'but she could have preferred it an hour or two after 6am.' It was only a few minutes after her morning shower that there was a knock on her door and Jonathon appeared, wheeling his tubing in with him. 'I thought I'd save you the bother of coming next door and telling me who you are before you go,' were his first words. He looked at her sideways, 'Or did you think we could meet again at David's and pretend surprise?'

'How did you know?'

He grinned, 'I saw you with the "oh so jealous" Liam last night, and wouldn't he like to have torn a strip off me.'

'What, because you are going back to David's? I wouldn't think he's jealous.'

In fact, Helen had the distinct feeling that Liam would not be at all jealous, that Liam definitely did not have designs on David himself, but she kept that thought to herself, unsure where it had come from. She knew for sure that Liam was often angry about Jonathon, but it was more because he hated to see David hurt so often. She shook her head. 'I think you are way off there.'

'Well, you wait and see.'

'I hope you are not planning any mischief.' Strangely

enough Helen felt quite comfortable in her role as mentor and confidant. It was not a lot different, she decided, from the pony club kids and their concerns, except that for Jonathon, this was pretty well life or death decisions. Somehow, Helen felt that he had turned a corner somewhere, and she knew this even though she had not met him before.

'You will be good to David won't you? Not worry him anymore?' She watched him impassively as he thought about this for a while.

'I am going to try, but I might need a little bit of help,' he grinned naughtily, 'Would you like to be my mother confessor.'

Helen definitely had the feeling that she was being wound up, but she responded the same way, 'Only if you promise to obey me and not to worry David anymore, at all, ever.'

'I don't think I can promise all that in one go but I'll make a good start at least, when they let me out of here.'

'So what's the plan?'

'I think they'll keep me in for a week or so. Not that there is anything wrong, but they'll do a lot of talking to me, then they'll talk to David and anyone else that'll listen and if I'm still here, they'll talk to me again and if I'm lucky they'll let me go.'

'Jonathon, please don't let it get to you. Please take it seriously.' Helen felt so helpless as if all she could do for David's peace of mind would be to pray. It seemed a pretty slim chance that Jonathon would manage to restrain himself for the week ahead. She knew that the hospital would be intently monitoring his blood sugar levels to make certain they were as stable as they could be, before they released him, even in to David's care. And they would be making certain he didn't have access to any drugs.

'I can see what you are thinking.' Jonathon put on a serious face, 'I am not a drug addict, you know. I have used it or sometimes I should say do use a bit of heroin but I don't need to. I don't often have it really. It just all got too much for me when I got back to Brisbane and it all seemed so huge and I went to a party. That's all.'

Helen wondered how '*that could be all,*' but she kept that thought to herself. Not ever having used any form of drugs herself, she really wasn't qualified to comment.

Changing the subject she asked Jonathon what he did for a living. Somehow it had never come up in discussion and she had no idea.

'Not a lot. Some modeling that I picked up when I was in Uni, before I went overseas. Some bar work.'

Jonathon had begun at University, seeing it as a way to a new life when he was seventeen, but the diabetes was still with him. This was something that you have for life, twenty four hours a day, seven days a week and Jonathon had not really realized in his heart that it would be with him forever, even in his new life.

Helen had the feeling that he was putting this in to words for the first time, that before this he had not really thought about why he had run away and kept running for so long, so she let him talk.

'I finished first year in Engineering and did the right thing and worked for the holidays and then I just couldn't go back, so I ran away. Not that there was anything to run from really, I didn't really have my own home or parents and David was always busy, so I just left.'

He hadn't told anyone where he was going or for how long. He didn't really know himself and maybe he felt that if he kept moving, if he kept losing himself, no one including himself would ever have to know or do anything about the disease.

Helen shook her head at the illogicality of it, but then decided that there was nothing logical about Jonathon's life, right from the start. She was certain of one thing though. When Jonathon came to live in Carslisle, if Jonathon came to live in Carslisle, nothing would ever be the same again. It would be rather like entering the spin cycle on a washing machine.

Looking up, she caught a speculative expression on Jonathons' face. Turning her head she realized why, since there was Genevieve with her head poking around the door frame.

'Will I come back or are you going to introduce me?'

Helen could see Jonathon do a double take as they were introduced. Genevieve had a wonderful yellow, white and black outfit on which accentuated her blondeness and made her appear even more delicate than usual and she sparkled with genuine happiness. Helen had known Genevieve for a long time and never failed to be attracted to her deep well of joy and the aura that she had of all being right in the world. The only time this ever seemed to dim was on occasions such as when they realized the truth about Ivy's circumstances, when Gen became very thoughtful although not for long. She could be very decisive when she needed to, a fact completely belied by her air of fragility. Genevieve's mother had often told Helen about the stubbornness and determination that Gen was born with, and of the fact that no one would ever believe her about it because *'that little blonde angel just wouldn't be like that.'* Helen knew better. She had seen Genevieve persisting with an unruly pony or an obstinately unintelligent thoroughbred and knew that she had never, ever given over until the animal offered her an attempt at the desired result. Genevieve could out-stubborn anyone and any animal.

As she watched Genevieve and Jonathon introduce themselves, she realized that there were some great similarities here, like looking at twins. Both of them were aggressively blonde in a Nordic well defined way and both of them had huge reserves of stubbornness and strength with charismatic personalities. *They will take Carlisle by storm between the two of them,* she decided.

CHAPTER 35

Home seemed somehow dislocated, as if Helen had left as one person and come back as another. Her car and float were back in the sheds and Jack was there to greet her ecstatically, his plume of a tail waving madly until she reached the gate. His dignity completely in tatters, Jack performed the Sheltie dance, circling after his tail like a demented dervish and uttering little yips of delight. Helen smiled and Genevieve knelt to try to give him a hug, copping a slush of tongue on the ear as she bent. She was brushed rudely aside as Jack lunged for Helen, butting his head against her legs to propel her toward the house. Even from a distance, Helen could tell Jack had had a bath. He smelled of conditioner and sunshine and his coat shone, with traces of brush marks in the unruly hair around his ears.

The yard had been mowed and the gardens clearly watered in the couple of days Helen had been away. The mail was collected and carefully placed on the kitchen bench along with fresh produce from the garden. There was a casserole in the fridge.

'Clearly somebody was looking forward to you coming home,' suggested Genevieve.

Helen looked around and tired tears welled up. 'Maybe Josie, or it could have been the boys. I am going to owe them big time if it was them, they have been so wonderful about JJ as well as looking after Jack and everything.'

'Well, no point in crying about it so just be exceptionally kind to them. Anyway, you found Jonathon for David and that must count for something.'

Helen sat on the bed and pulled off her shoes, 'What do you think I should tell David about Jonathon?'

'I think I'd leave it alone and see what happens. There is no point in getting his hopes up, before Jonathon makes it here, if he does.'

'I guess you're right, but it seems unfair. I feel like rushing out and telling him good news.'

'Well from what I've heard, he's already disappointed David so many times that you'd only make it worse,' said Genevieve flatly.

'You've been talking to Liam, haven't you?'

Genevieve didn't answer, since she was watching the driveway from the bedroom window and a car had just driven up.

'I think you should have a rest before you come back out, so I'll go and unpack and then I'll come back and do yours. Suit you?'

Helen lay back and listened to the sounds of the car next door, aware that Genevieve had gone to the door and was talking to whoever had arrived, but she was too tired to go and investigate. She would find out as soon as she felt a bit livelier was her last thought before drifting off yet again.

Genevieve excelled herself by making a dessert that evening to go with the casserole donated by Josie, which provided enough dinner for both girls and David and Liam.

Not that they saw much of either of the men as they raced in and out at different times. Liam had a meeting of the Landcare Group which Helen had more or less forgotten and David flew in early, ate his dinner and disappeared to Riswell, to stay overnight to consult with Jonathon's doctors as early as he could in the morning.

Helen didn't hear Liam come home after the meeting, still existing as she was in a state of pain-killer induced haziness, which although it was better than it had been, definitely had the side effect of letting all her worries slide away for the moment.

She woke up next morning with a completely different attitude. Today, she would get out to see JJ if it killed her, to reassure herself, although she knew in reality that between Doug and Liam, JJ was twice as safe and comfortable as he probably needed to be. *It was a good feeling*, she realized, *to be able to trust someone as she trusted Liam*. It occurred to her that the trust had built up over the months of working together and especially during this little incident. He seemed to know exactly what action would reassure her, even to the special attention of bathing Jack for her welcome home. These were definitely thoughts she would pursue at a later date. Just for the moment, she was excited to see JJ out in the vet's paddock, his hoof in a rubber boot, taking a lively interest in all that went on over the fence.

Helen buried her face in his shiny neck and inhaled the smell of clean and healthy horse, knowing that her world for the moment was back together again.

CHAPTER 36

DAVID

In Riswell a week later, David heaved a sigh of relief as Jonathon walked around to the other side of the car and got in. Short of jumping out at high speed, this time he would definitely be taking Jonathon home with him where hopefully he could give himself some space to recreate, in the true sense of the word. Already, he sensed a difference in Jonathon's attitude, a maturity and resolution that he had never seen in the ten years since his diagnosis.

Jonathon had been an engaging boy, attached to David's family through his own hero worship of David and later through his need for a legal home. It had been a rough time and although David's parents had become the only family Jonathon had, they realized they just could not reach him to help. At seventeen he left to go to University, appeared to be settling down and then he was gone. Of course, at eighteen, he'd acquired the management of his own money from his parent's insurance, the property sale and his own accident cover. He was lucky in some ways that his parent's had had the foresight for this, but sometimes David thought he would have been better off, if he had had to work for a living. Still, he was here now and maybe, just maybe, he would be ready to settle down. David had no idea what he would settle down to, no idea beyond getting him to the security of his own home. Of course there was the small issue of Liam since Liam had always had a distrust of Jonathon, but David knew that he could trust Liam to try to make it as easy as possible for David, even if he didn't like the reason for his reticence. Liam was the most dependable friend it was possible to have, in spite of a sometimes volatile temper.

Jonathon watched around with interest and even asked a few questions. He zoomed in on Genevieve, asking if she would still be there, what she did for a living, where she lived and David answered patiently, knowing that Jonathon would let go of the subject only when he was ready and not before. His intense interest in the subject of the moment often tended to be a bit unnerving for many people and David knew from experience that the subject could be dropped at any moment and replaced by another, just as absorbing. It was when you were the subject of that interest that Jonathon had the most impact. Intense interest combined with his engaging smile and innocent looks could be devastating in a social situation, whether you were male or female. Jonathon could collect followers and acolytes faster than a jack rabbit bred kits and this had led to some very hair-raising stunts and wild, wild parties when his sense of mischief surfaced. David sincerely hoped he had grown out of some of his more innovative ideas.

Only Genevieve was home when they pulled up the driveway and after a brief chat and quick hug for both David and Jonathon, she was gone as well to meet Josie for a coffee and then out to exercise Superman for David.

David had been incredibly impressed by her ability to manage the huge animal since she was so tiny herself, but Superman had responded like the gentleman he was and they made a beautiful sight that he would never tire of watching as she put him through his paces. Helen had always said that Genevieve was an amazing rider and he had to agree. She made riding the huge chestnut, look like she was sitting on a gentle swing. All the same, he couldn't wait until life settled down a bit and he could get out to ride his own horse.

'Do you still ride, Jonathon?' he asked.

Jonathon looked at him quizzically, 'I did a summer season on the trail rides in Canada and a winter driving sleighs last year so I don't think I've forgotten yet.'

'Maybe we'll be able to find you something to ride around here. Helen might know of someone going away or a Uni student's horse you can keep exercised. If you like that is.'

David waited. There were times when an offer like this would have sparked an explosion to rival Vesuvius, but Jonathon replied quite calmly, 'I would like that, maybe we can get some mustering in somewhere too.' David relaxed a little, not believing the transition to reasonable adult could be this easy.

They were all home for dinner that evening and the girls had invited the male household over for pre-dinner drinks and dinner with the proviso that one of the men man the barbeque and that they washed up. This seemed a fair enough exchange and David wondered how Jonathon would fit in to what had become quite a comfortable circle of friends, in the brief moments they had together in busy lives. Even Helen and Liam seemed to have forged a new beginning. Somewhere on the drive down, David had realized that he would have to get to know Jonathon all over again, that he was no longer the hero worshipping child or rebellious and hurt teen that David had known. He was a young man who obviously had been able to hold down a job and was keeping himself alive, in spite of some serious lapses and desperate attempts to outrun his issues.

They could hear Helen and Genevieve laughing as they walked across the path toward the house, a breathless hearty laugh from Geneveiee as she charged around the yard playing soccer with the dog and a slightly less breathless one from Helen, who looked suitably guilty as David rounded the corner to the back yard in time to see her whacking the ball with a crutch.

'I thought you were supposed to be resting that leg,' suggested David, knowing that Helen was still suffering some pain with the bruising on her calf muscles.

She looked toward him, her face flushed and hair flung across her cheeks, while Jack sat adoringly at her side, bright eyed and sitting upright like a pre-schooler who'd completed his homework.

'The exercise will loosen it up, I'm sure, and I wasn't running. I wasn't even kicking the ball,' she said and Liam coming in behind David caught the brunt of the mischievous grin she seemed to flash in the direction of David and Jonathon. She came over and gave Jonathon a hug. 'I'm glad you made it here.'

Looking over at Liam, she continued,' Liam, I haven't

thanked you properly for everything you did for me while I was away. There was so much to look after and you had some of my work to do as well'. She reached up to give him a hug too and Liam stiffened, looking like a deer caught in the headlights. *Somewhere between anger and a desire to grab her and run,* thought David. She stepped back, giving him a puzzled look and moved off to help Genevieve in the kitchen, leaving David to watch Liam, amused at Liam's fuming at his own ineptitude, a new and disturbing experience for him. He wondered why Liam never seemed to get it right around Helen. They seemed to communicate through a sheet of water or a pane of glass all the time, except when they were working together. Then, as far as David could see they performed like a well- oiled machine and while everyone had the utmost admiration for the team perspective Helen managed to bring to every project, and for her dedication and insight it was absolutely complemented by Liam's attention to detail and broad experience every time they collaborated. It was a shame they just couldn't seem to communicate so well socially. *Awkward,* he thought.

CHAPTER 37

'Something here smells incredible, especially after hospital food,' broke in Jonathon as he went off to bother Genevieve in the kitchen. The two blonde heads bending over a recipe book gathered a halo of light visible through the kitchen window and Helen caught a look of concern on David's face, which just maybe could be interpreted as jealousy.

She shook her head. David and Jonathon hadn't seen each other for a few years. There really couldn't be any sort of relationship but she was acutely aware that David was on edge all evening and watching Jonathon carefully. And Jonathon had his sights firmly fixed on Genevieve.

CHAPTER 38

They all watched the two blonde heads bobbing in unison as they rose to the trot effortlessly, in time and in tune. Even the eerily similar chestnuts seemed to be listening to the same music and their strides matched without any obvious signals from the riders.

David, Helen and Liam were being treated to a truly beautiful display of horsemanship from Genevieve and Jonathon as they circled and returned, side-stepped and gently cantered.

The horse they had managed to borrow for Jonathon from a local student who was currently on a six month exchange abroad, was a match in every way for Superman, which was not surprising since they were half -brothers. He had the same well-bred air of gentlemanly collection and affectionate nature and he was equally as clever. They had been trained by the same family as high performing all-rounders and had also been used to muster on their properties.

Jonathon had clearly not forgotten how to ride and even Liam expressed his amazement at the skill that he was displaying, given the life he had led them to believe he

240

had been living in recent years. *Helen would be astonished*, thought David. He knew that nothing she had ever seen of Jonathon would have made her suspect that the adrenalin fired youth that she had originally met, could ever have had the patience and mental concentration to perform dressage at such a level, especially on a horse he had only ridden once before. David sneaked a look over at Helen, but to his surprise she was looking in his direction and frowning slightly, concern written across her features.

Genevieve and Jonathon didn't even appear to be exchanging commands and yet they were able to perform together without a pre-arranged plan and completely in tandem, like a choreographed dance routine.

At last they pulled up side by side, bowed to an imaginary judge, in the direction of their spellbound audience and cantered easily over to the group.

Jonathon's face was the most animated and happiest Helen had ever seen him. He glanced admiringly at Genevieve and patted the neck of Ariva. 'You are incredible Gen. That was the most amazing thing I have ever done.'

Genevieve was laughing, 'Just imagine what we could do if we had more time. David, you are so lucky, this is one of the loveliest horses I have ever ridden. I wish I didn't have to go back to work so soon.'

'You could stay. Just tell them you need more holidays,' pleaded Jonathon. 'Tell them you've got a sick friend who needs you to, I don't know, um help him put his life back together.'

There was a heartbeat of silence and David could feel a chill down his back. One of these days he was going to have to deal with Jonathon's fixation on Genevieve and the added bond of an incredible riding partnership was not going to improve the chances of it being easy. There was definitely chemistry between them, at least when they were both on horseback. David wondered how much more deeply it went and whether he should be worried about the fragile peace that seemed to be developing between himself and Jonathon when the time came to clear the air.

He dreaded the consequences. It was not that Jonathon would intentionally hurt anyone else, he had never been the sort of child who felt entitled and he didn't tantrum. It was worse than that. Jonathon simply withdrew and he always punished himself most of all for what he felt were his mistakes. As a teen, this had turned to neglect of himself as if he weren't worth looking after. David was not concerned about reproach or revenge, he was simply worried that Jonathon would turn his hurt on himself and disappear again, damaged and grieving and all the promise of the last couple of weeks would evaporate. He was worried this would be the last chance.

'Well, I won't even try to compete with that,' he joked. 'I think from now on Superman and I will stick to mustering. Trailing along in the dust is about all I'm good for.'

CHAPTER 39

LIAM

'Jonathon, do you mind if I borrow Ariva for an hour or so?' asked Liam. 'Helen, do you want to come for a ride for a while, you didn't get too much action before this pair took over the arena.'

The plan had been that all five of them would have a bit of a work out sharing the three horses, and David and Helen had been first up on their own horses while Jonathon, Liam and Genevieve sorted out a full saddle that looked like it would fit Ariva, from the bits in the shed, left over from Helen's parent's property owning days. Helen was taking it very easy with JJ for the moment and had hacked quietly around the arena while David had given Superman the rounds, clearly enjoying being back in the saddle after the past few busy and time consuming weeks, with no chance of a ride.

Once Jonathon was ready with Ariva, David had handed over to Genevieve, while Helen held JJ. She had been going to offer him to Liam but they had all become absorbed in watching the other two riders and somehow, it seemed wrong to push in with a third and completely different horse, when the others were so beautiful together. So they waited.

'Liam I'd love to, does anyone else want to come?' She turned to the others but they were already unsaddling Superman and debating the merits of saddle soap and various oils in the clean-up of the neglected saddle that Ariva still wore. A search was in progress for the necessary items.

'We'll go home and get something on for dinner. You go off and get your butt back in the saddle.' Genevieve was aware that Helen was just the tiniest bit nervous of riding out again and that she was also concerned about how well JJ had healed. It was really only a week and a half since they'd managed to extract the glass and he was still wearing a boot to keep it clean, although he seemed happy enough.

'It'll have to be a quiet one, I'm sorry Liam, but I'll take you to the one of the best spots to make up for it.'

Liam watched Helen as they rode away from the yards. She sat very straight in the saddle and her hair, which she'd braided in a single braid, swung behind her against faded blue shirt she wore. One day, he was going to talk to her about the fact that she never wore a hat, except when she was in sight of her pony club kids, when she did wear a helmet. She always took a hat in the car with her when she was on the job, but it very rarely made it on to her head and this afternoon was no exception. He could see the hints of blue-black in her hair, glinting in the sun and the roll of her hips as the horse moved was all absorbing, so absorbing in fact, that when Ariva stopped he had no idea how he'd got where they were.

Helen turned, 'This is my favourite canter, up this hill

but JJ and I might take it easy, so why don't you head off and do a few circles at the top while you wait for us.'

Giving a final glance at the attractive picture in front of him, Liam gathered the horse and then let him out, feeling the exhilaration of the powerful horse beneath him as they flew up the hill, the initial bound immediately settling in to a leaping canter that felt like flying. *This was something you never forgot*, thought Liam *no matter how long it was since you had ridden.* Suddenly he could see himself settling here, with his own horses and maybe, just maybe a black haired, long legged woman by his side. That is, if he ever had her to himself long enough to talk about it. He was deep in thought, on auto-pilot, circling on the top of the hill when the object of his thoughts appeared, laughing at the sudden fright and precipitate disappearance of a wallaby that had stopped to watch Liam fly past, then moved out straight in to the path of Helen and JJ trotting gently up the slope behind them.

Liam stopped, struck by his thoughts and momentarily sure that he had voiced them out loud. He looked at Helen and was suddenly struck by how right they seemed together, how comfortable they could be and how much he needed to say to her. 'Helen, ...' he hesitated, and she looked at him fully, interested by the intensity of his tone. He tried again, sure that he should just not blurt out what he was thinking, but not sure how to go on. 'Helen, can I come over and see you later in the week?'

Helen looked surprised but nodded, 'Anytime, I don't think I'm out at all this week.'

Liam cursed himself for his awkwardness, but there was something so bizarre about this whole situation, that no one seemed to be talking about. He had his own suspicions about what was going on but there just seemed to be a pact of 'Not in front of Jonathon', as if the boy was ten years old still. As far as Liam could see, Jonathon was a lot more capable of looking after himself than any of them gave him credit for.

He smiled hesitantly at Helen noting her confusion, knowing that he and tentative normally did not belong in the same sentence in her limited experience of him at work, but she smiled tolerantly back, lifting her brows in interrogation. Clearly she was wondering what on earth he could have to say. Perhaps she thought he was going to resign his job already and was going to try and soften the blow.

CHAPTER 40

HELEN

That thought had just occurred to Helen in fact, and she glanced at him again, the image of him leaving giving her a nasty jolt somewhere in her solar plexus. *Surely, he wouldn't do that. He must know how far forward he had helped to drag their projects in the last few months and besides, she was sure he loved what he was doing.*

Just last Thursday, he'd leant back in his chair, given her a big grin and a thumbs up and remarked that he just loved making farmer's favourite pipe dreams come true. He had just received the approval on a big project that one property owner had wanted to take on for years, but it was hard to find the money for re-fencing for conservation management projects when the market and the seasons were so poor. Most farmers had plenty of projects they'd love to do, but just couldn't justify financially. Liam and Helen both loved that they could often help to make it happen. At least Helen was absolutely certain that Liam loved what he was doing at the moment. Somewhere, buried deep in the back of her consciousness, a little hope fanned itself back to life. In spite of all their ups and downs and misunderstandings, Helen was sure that Liam had a soft spot for her and she knew with certainty that she had options she wanted to explore with him.

Suddenly, she made up her mind. No more pussy footing around, feeling like she was trying to push aside a heavy curtain. When she got Liam to herself that night, she would definitely ...do what she wasn't sure but it would clear the air, on that she was determined.

No, she thought as they wound back down the hill after admiring the view, *I really don't think Liam will be leaving. Not yet anyway.*

Genevieve had one more day and they were all determined it would be a good one. There were suggestions of bushwalking, kayaking, a trip to the beach, each one discarded as too much driving since Genevieve would still have to drive to Riswell on Sunday to catch the plane to Brisbane and then make the hop home. It would be a long day for her Sunday.

Compromise was reached at last and all five of them booked in to an apartment out at the beach for Saturday night after a day cruise across to the islands, some snorkeling and a meal in the best restaurant they could find.

Helen was not looking forward to losing Genevieve. It was strange how her near disaster had become one of the best holiday breaks Helen had ever had. Somehow, the five of them had had a wonderful time for the last few days, even if David and Liam had needed to work. Helen had to admit, Jonathon was great company when he put his mind to it. Blokus, a shape game had become one of the greatest challenges ever, in his presence and no one had ever been as inventive with Pictionary. When Jonathon set himself out to entertain, there was no resisting the impish grins and the devilish laugh that he had. His cheek and turn for dramatics had turned every outing in to an adventure and every day at home in to a holiday.

Helen didn't even mind much that she had hardly spent any time alone with Genevieve during the day, although there were times when she wondered if Genevieve enjoyed Jonathon's humour as much as she did. Occasionally there seemed to a spark of impatience or even a sharpish word, very quickly covered up but there all the same.

Helen could feel David's watchfulness as Genevieve skirted around Jonathon, and she worried for David that Jonathon would suddenly regress to the sullen and defiant almost teen that she had first met, fueling David's guilt yet again. There was nothing in the story of David and Jonathon that should really contribute to guilt in Helen's opinion, nothing that David could have done or not done differently and yet he was over protective and intensely vulnerable to Jonathon. On some levels, it just didn't make sense to Helen, but she did wonder if she would feel differently if Jonathon were her younger brother or even a past lover. She banished that thought before it could take hold and vowed to try to take some of the weight from David by spending more time with Jonathon, trying to ensure that he knew he had a place in the group of friends. This was the first time Helen had really let herself think of the group as a group of friends, but that is what they had become as surely as night followed day. She didn't think it was a passing friendship either, there were too many things they enjoyed doing together and so many things they had talked about trying together for this just to be a friendly few days and then goodbye. It just didn't feel like that at all.

❦ ❦ ❦

Saturday's early start was made easier by a bright morning, the sort of morning that made you feel ten kilos lighter and able to run miles without a break. Helen and Genevieve installed Jonathon between them in the back of Liam's new metallic blue Prado and promptly informed him he was taking up too much room, while spreading themselves as much as possible to occupy as much of his space as they could.

'It's like having a bunch of kids in the back,' remarked David, 'perhaps you should pull over and we'll jettison one.'

'You choose which one then,' grinned Liam, watching the nonsense in the rear view mirror, 'and I'll pull over.'

'I think they should all justify their existence in the back seat,' said David alluding to a game they'd played at home one night requiring tall stories and exaggeration to support claims made by the game on behalf of the players, on the throw of a dice.

'I'll start then,' called Jonathon. 'I have met the girl of my dreams,' he started, 'and she is so beautiful that every time she puts her face outside, the sun runs away and hides. When we are together and because I am so ugly, the sun comes out again and watches us together in fascination. So you see, you can't throw me out of the car since I am the only one that enables my true love to go outside in the light and sunshine.'

'Oh, that is so bad Jonathon,' laughed Genevieve 'so bad that Helen and I won't even have to try to keep our seats in the car. Liam might as well just stop now and you can get out.'

It appeared though, that neither David nor Liam were particularly amused by the silly story and somehow the game lapsed without a word being said.

By the time they reached the ferry terminal, conversation appeared to be back to normal but Helen had the niggling feeling that there was something not quite right.

After a late breakfast they boarded and spent the hour of the trip up the front of the boat getting windswept and sunburned, their dolphin watch being rewarded about halfway across. 'It doesn't matter how often you see dolphins does it,' enthused Helen, 'they are just as amazing every time.' Their sleek bodies curving in an out of the wake, the little pod followed the boat for a full ten minutes before heading off to find another boat to follow. She caught Liam's eye and they exchanged a disappointed glance as the creatures disappeared. Leaning over the rail, they watched hopefully for whale spouts in the distance since it was almost time for the annual whale migration to reach this far north, but not a single spray disturbed the glassy blue green of the absolutely still waters and Hunter Island came in to view within minutes.

'I think that is the best part of the day,' Helen said as they disembarked on the jetty, 'It is always over far too soon and I think I would rather keep cruising around the island than get off and get all sandy and sunburnt, although that water looks amazing to swim in.'

'Maybe we can get a run on the boom netting boat,

so you can do both, cruise around the island and swim,' suggested Liam.

'I haven't done that yet and I'd love to try it. I wonder if anyone else wants to.' Helen turned to David and Genevieve but they shook their heads.

"No, we want to have a look around and have a look at the resort, maybe hire a jet ski. What about Jonathon?'

Jonathon was busy talking to the captain, having wheedled his way in to the wheelhouse in the way that some people just manage to. They were talking very seriously and peering at instrumentation, so Helen just waved to let him know they were going and swung down the ramp on to the jetty.

There was a wide sweep of sand around the bay to the right to a rocky headland above which the resort sat, in amongst the trees. Helen was hoping to have a look at the resort at some stage, since it had been sold and the new company owners were proposing some serious renovating and had also been doing some work to be able to register as an eco-resort. She wondered just what was entailed in becoming eco-friendly.

In front of them a path snaked off in to the bush and up on to the verandah of a small store and office for the camping and day picnic areas. Helen knew that further over on another small bay, you could hire a jet ski, snorkeling gear, a windsurfer or a canoe but her immediate destination was the store, to see about tickets for the netting boat for herself and Liam. By the time she came out of the store, David and Genevieve had disappeared leaving Liam with the message that they could meet for lunch on the verandah at one o'clock if that suited, but otherwise they would see them at the ferry to go home.

Briefly, Helen felt a bit abandoned by the pair as if it was all pre-arranged to exclude her, then realized she was being completely ridiculous. *Everyone was just doing the things they liked doing'*, she decided, *just going with the flow*. After all, she and Liam had made separate arrangements as well, and heaven knew what Jonathon was up to. Of them all, he should feel it most as he was left to himself, but the last time she had seen him he looked totally absorbed and in no hurry to join anybody. Deciding that she should stop acting like a shepherd for everybody or as the farmers would say 'stop trying to herd cats', she put on her sunglasses and rooted around in her bag to put her wallet in the bag pocket.

'While you are in your bag, perhaps you could even find a hat,' suggested Liam, 'and maybe even put it on your head.'

Helen grinned at the exact parody of Josie, who was always reminding her to wear a hat and flourishing a very pretty and clearly unworn wide-brimmed foldable hat, she placed it on her head. Within two minutes, the hat was off again as they found a table and sat down.

She placed it carefully beside the chair, where it remained for the rest of the day, ownerless.

Since the tickets were for ten for a one and a half hour trip around the island with boom netting, Helen and Liam didn't have time for much more than a quick coffee and rest stop before heading down to catch the boat. Jonathon still hadn't come down from the wheelhouse of the catamaran so all they could do was wave and hope he saw them getting on the boat.

CHAPTER 41

David and Genevieve had staked out a spot on the hire beach, booked a jet ski for half an hour's time and settled down for a serious chat, before going in for a swim, keeping an eye out for Jonathon in case he came to join them.

'I am concerned about Jonathon, he seems to be getting very fond of you. Do you think he means anything by it?'

'Well he's never said anything to me and I don't really think ...No I'm sure it's not. In fact, he said something the other day about a girl in Canada and I thought, I really felt that maybe he was a bit serious but it's hard to tell and I didn't want to ask too many questions. He can still be a bit defensive, can't he?'

'Putting it mildly. I would be seriously worried though if he was attached to you. It might really put him back a long way. He's come so far and this is the most responsible I have ever seen him as if he has just realized how important it all is and that he just can't run and hide from it.'

'Oh, I don't think he's hiding anymore, I think he is serious about getting his control right from what he's said to me, but then I don't know him like you do.'

'Yes, but I may be seeing him through a parent's eyes. You know, assuming that your child never grows up.'

'Is that the way you see him?'

'Yes, sort of, or a little brother. I feel very responsible and he's been around my family since he was about 11 and he used to hang around behind me all the time, probably more than Luke did.'

'You know, I'm not sure but Helen may have the impression that there's more than that. She let something slip one day about what Norm thought and she seemed a bit doubtful herself, maybe.'

'Gen, you don't seriously think anything like that do you?'

'Not me, but I had the feeling Helen wasn't sure, but she didn't come out and say anything.'

'So what are we going to do? Will we fess up and take a chance on Jonathon or leave it in limbo a bit longer?'

'Here is he is. Hi Jonathon, we've hired skis for a half an hour. Are you going to join us?'

'No, no. I think I'll get a kayak and loop the island or as much as I can for an hour or so.

'I have just had the best look ever at how these ferries operate and how to get a license. I reckon I could work doing this especially since I've had so much to do with tourists in Canada. I like that sort of work.'

'Are you thinking of coming back to Australia for good then?' asked David.

'I'll see but I'd like to do something a bit more settled than work on the ski fields and tourist trails, but I like this sort of work. A qualification would be good.'

David looked a Genevieve, clearly thinking that wonders would never cease.

He was also thinking that perhaps he should have made more time to talk to Jonathon since he'd been around but they had all been so busy. 'Jon, I might get a kayak after the jet ski and come out to meet you if that is OK.' He gave Genevieve a look that clearly made his excuses in advance for leaving her alone, but she didn't appear too worried.

'Don't worry about me, I'm going to laze. This is my last day before it all starts again for the rest of the year. I'll see you at lunch maybe. If not, Liam and Helen will be back. You two should go for a long paddle.'

'And you can play piggy in the middle with them,' Jonathon suggested with a cheeky grin.

Genevieve was surprised. It hadn't taken Jonathon long at all to pick up on the vibes she thought existed between Helen and Liam and she wondered if that was the reason he had backed off Helen fairly quickly and become her new best friend so suddenly.

'I'll wait for you David,' offered Jonathon, 'especially if you are happy to go for a bit longer.'

It was clear that Genevieve had decided after the first twenty minutes that she would not be buying a jet ski. Basically it was fairly boring, although if they had been allowed out of the square between the buoys and over to the other islands, it may have been more interesting. After half an hour of going round in circles in a calm sea, she had had enough and waved the men off without a backward glance. The coffee and souvenir shop was clearly calling and she had noticed that there were some rather fetching togs on sale in there as well. She snuck off to have a girl's half hour all by herself.

❦　❦　❦

Helen was having a ball. Boom netting was the best fun she decided, but she was eternally grateful that she'd worn a one piece bathing suit. The huge nets dragged behind the boat were full of people, with a dozen or so at a time being allowed to cling on to the nets and be hauled along. It was like sitting in a horizontal salt water waterfall with the added advantage of a view of the other islands as they circumnavigated Hunter. After each fifteen minutes the boat stopped and the passengers changed places with the wet and laughing group of boom netters. Helen decided they would probably get two turns each in the net and that was fine by her. After quarter of an hour, her fingers were wrinkled like prunes and just about had to be pried from the net. She wrapped up in her favourite azure blue sarong and sat on one of the plastic seats on the upper deck. Liam came to join her, shaking his head like a dog and grinning with pure pleasure. 'It sure feels good to do that sort of thing again, I missed it so much in the last eight months.'

Helen had completely forgotten in the last month or so that Liam had been taking it pretty easy until recently and she had surprised herself as well, with how quickly she had healed in the last week. After all, she was only a week or so out of hospital.

After the second session in the net, Helen decided that perhaps that was enough and there were enough people who thought the same way that the fifth run was made up of the hardiest of the two groups who had been before, and Liam was one of them. Helen leant against the rail and idly watched as two kayaks pulled up on the beach and the paddlers walked up the beach toward the shade of a tree. She was fairly certain it was David and Jonathon and she was about to wave when the larger figure pulled the smaller in to his embrace and then held him at arm's length while they exchanged intense words, before continuing their walk to sit on a log in the shade. Even after the boat had finished the loop and passed by the same beach, the two figures were still sitting talking intently, their bodies turned to almost face each other and very little space between.

'At least that answers my questions,' thought Helen, 'I don't think I have any reason to wait for David to say anything anymore.' She realized suddenly that this was a relief rather than anything else and wondered at her own naivety in accepting what was a pressure from the community for them to be a couple. She wondered if David had ever sensed that or if she had in fact been the only one bothered by the expectations. *She wasn't hurt at all,* she thought, *but she did wonder what the future held as far as David's stay in Carlisle.* Norm wouldn't make it easy although as far as anyone else was concerned, Helen didn't think there would be any change but she found it hard to imagine Jonathon settling down there, with his itchy feet and restless mind, forever looking for the next challenge.

To tell the truth, she was so relieved that she turned and smiled happily at Liam as he climbed from the nets, clearly surprising him with her sudden unguardedness.

❦ ❦ ❦

The resort definitely needed some loving care, Liam, Helen and Genevieve decided as they wandered through for a look. What had been a spectacular pool with views of the bay and the mainland had become quite bedraggled with flaky decking and the odd lifting tile. Nothing felt particularly clean and there was an air of inefficiency and depression that permeated the whole place while the grounds had definitely seen better days. The hedges were trimmed but felt blurry at the edges, the lawns sparse with darker and yellowing spots and the flower beds untended. Helen's fingers itched to help bring it back to life as she had seen it as a child but she knew that the proposed renovations, running in to millions of dollars were stalled at the moment for Environmental approval. To cater for generations of families who expected more and more quickly, the airstrip was being upgraded to commercial rather than emergency and a myriad of other perceived necessities of everyday life were going to compromise the previous environmental sustainability of the low key resort so that it became economically sustainable. Helen sighed, and Liam looked at her with a questioning smile, clearly wondering what could be prompting such heavy thoughts.

'Are we snorkeling? Or are we going to spend all afternoon looking at this musty old place?' asked Genevieve. 'I assume David and Jonathon will find us when they're ready.'

Looking down from the head of the beach stairs toward the transparent blue green water, Helen could see the reefs and rocks as clearly as if they were encased in a glass paperweight and suddenly she couldn't wait to feel the coolness of the water again.

'Coming through,' called Genevieve who barged past and leapt two at a time down the steps with Helen hard on her heels.

'What happened to Liam?' asked Helen, 'I thought he was right behind you.'

"He said he'd be down shortly, he just wanted to take a few more photos.'

There were two canoes pulled up on the beach, just out of sight of the top of the steps and instinctively Helen knew that they were the ones David and Jonathon had been using.

'We could see you up there,' they shouted just as the girls reached the bottom 'but we just couldn't attract your attention so we came in to the beach. How many sets of gear have you got?'

'Three when Liam brings his down, but that's only one set for the men. Ours won't fit you.'

Jonathon got up, 'I'll paddle back around and then bring another set. Do you think we have time?'

'We don't need to leave until the four o'clock boat so there should be plenty. It's only two now.'

'I'll come with you, Jonathon,' called Genevieve 'I haven't used a kayak for ages. Is that Ok David?'

'Sure, I'll take your mask then and forget about the flippers for the moment.'

Helen's mask was not the best she had ever used but since the reefs were only about thirty metres off the shore and the water was incredibly clear and calm, she was not too worried about having to reseal it every few minutes. She and David swam out slowly, enjoying the feel of water at a perfect temperature combined with the sun on their backs and then swam lazily in circles taking in the reef only a couple of metres below. On a perfect day like this it was totally understandable that tourists came from all over the world to enjoy this unique experience. They drifted around pointing as they each spotted a new coral form, whether it was frilled or waving, pink or yellow, and laughing as they herded small schools of fish amongst the reef. The angelfish and clown fish were everywhere, like extras from the 'Nemo' movie while the bright damsel fish darted in and out from the reef, brave little terriers defending their territories.

Popping her head up and treading water, Helen spotted Jonathon and Genevieve crossing the top of the ridge not far from the head of the stairs to the beach and remarked to David who had come up beside her, 'I can't believe that I just never think to do this. There is all this wonderful reef almost in my back yard and I hardly ever come here.'

'I'm so glad we did,' replied David 'for more reasons than one. I really have to thank you.'

Helen could not imagine what was coming next but she was pretty certain it would involve Jonathon.

As they swam back off the reef and put their feet down on the sand he said, 'You have made such a difference to Jonathon, you and Genevieve both have, but you especially with that discussion you had with him in hospital. He's made up his mind what he wants to do and he sounds so sure now. As well as that he's made up his mind to look after himself and to let me help him.'

Helen wondered what would be coming next but she kept her face still, 'That is such good news, David, but I had very little to do with it. I think he'd almost made up his mind before he even got here. I think that's why he came but there were just a few slips along the way.'

'Yes, he was on his way to me, but I don't know, this is different from every other time he's even thought about it. This time, it's not a promise to me, it's more of a promise to himself and that is far more important and somehow you've helped him to reach that. I know it's different this time.' David touched her arm, turning her to face him. 'I really can't thank you enough for your support and friendship over the last year or so, but especially for Jonathon.' He moved closer and caught her in a gentle hug, kissing the top of her head and then her cheek as she turned her face up to him. She smiled up at him, her heart strangely light and kissed him back.

'Well, that's what good friends are for isn't it and we'll always be that won't we?'

David turned and waved to Jonathon and Genevieve, offering his mask to Genevieve, who was already entering the water with her flippers in place. Jonathon had a full set in his hand.

'Did you see Liam?' asked Helen.

'We did but he was heading back down to the shop. He said he wanted a coffee but he gave me these and said he'd see us at the boat.'

He must have changed his mind, thought Helen *or decided he's had enough exercise for the moment.*

She and David sat on the beach and idly watched the two blonde heads bobbing in the water. Eventually Helen lay down and closed her eyes, enjoying the moment just as it was.

❦　❦　❦

On the return boat, Jonathon was still bubbling over with his plans to find a job on the boats and eventually do a Master's ticket. There didn't seem to be much time between initial thought and decisive action for him and Helen wondered again, how that would work out for him and David and she was puzzled by David's calm acceptance of Jonathon's plans. Surely it would make a difference to him as well.

Beside her, Liam was silent and had been ever since they left the shore, replying to questions but not responding to the conversation that swirled around him. Helen was concerned, worried in case Liam had overdone the exercise for the day. Boom netting was quite hard on your body and already she could feel her arms stiffening up and the scrapes on her hands where she had grabbed the ropes in a hurry. She didn't think that would have worried Liam though, unless he'd bumped his leg or hurt his back as he tumbled around in the net.

CHAPTER 42

LIAM

From the moment they had ridden down the hill on Friday, Liam had focused on people as he never had before, determined to understand what was going on in the minds of each member of the group. He was determined to talk to Helen, to convince her that she was wasting her time with David but he felt powerless in the face of her loyalty to their earlier friendship. *Where were the words that other people could employ so easily, that he needed to find out where he stood? He was a lawyer, he should be able to use words to his advantage and think his way through this situation but he just couldn't.*

And then she'd smiled at him as he came in off the boom net, that one unconcealed smile of pleasure, of uncomplicated joy in his company and he knew unreservedly that she could not possibly be attached to David if she could smile at him like that. She looked so wonderful, so fresh and so alive with the brilliant blue/green sari tied over her togs and her dark, damp hair flicking back from the speed of the boat. All the way back to the pier, he watched her as she spoke with other passengers and teased a small boy who'd claimed her as his own confidant. Liam felt that he had so much to look forward to when he finally got her to himself and had her full attention. Watching her now, he didn't think she even realized how she drew people to her, how so many on the boat were taking part in the conversation she was having with a small child, even if was just to smile in passing at the nonsense. He'd noticed before that she created a bright spot in any room that she was in, not in the manner of an extrovert making an entrance but with a slow, steady light that everyone gravitated to and was warmed by. It was incredible that she never seemed aware of this, and Liam knew the depth of her own admiration for David's ability to remember people and their interests or problems. He had to admit, that together, she and David were a compelling couple in any gathering, but he was absolutely certain, as of this minute, that she didn't see David as a potential lover.

He felt he had never enjoyed an afternoon as he was enjoying this one, poking around the old resort, speculating on the renewal and how it could be done. There were so many conversations he and Helen could have, so many interests they could pursue together that he felt their lives might not be long enough to capture each one and he alternately could not wait for their lives together to begin but did not want this wonderful afternoon of promise to end. On the pretense of photographing the area so that they would be able to compare it later for the changes that were made, he documented the afternoon and every mood of Helen's as she and Genevieve enjoyed their last day of the holiday together.

He agreed absently when they spoke of the crazy, happy holiday they had all enjoyed together so unexpectedly and he listened with almost detached elation as they made confident plans for future get-togethers for all five of them. 'After all they agreed, you didn't often find five people who enjoyed so many of the same things, that there were so many more they could all try together and never run out of options.'

When the girls at last decided to head down to the beach to snorkel, Liam had finally begun to concentrate on the photography, determined that this was going to be a place that would be special to them in the future and that they might wish one day to remember it as it was now. He watched as the girls disappeared down the stairs and then went back to work.

He caught sight of Helen as she came out of the water but momentarily his mind deceived him in to thinking that it was David with her. As they kissed, he knew he was right but his mind could not accept the evidence of his eyes and he hurried toward the stairs, to meet Genevieve and Jonathon on their way down. With a startled glance of comprehension and a mutter about coffee, he disappeared in the direction of the shop.

CHAPTER 43

At six o'clock on the dot, Helen and Genevieve were sitting in the hotel foyer waiting for the men to come down, talking quietly about the day and comparing notes on plans for the next few months. There was no doubt in both the girl's minds that they would see each other and possibly the other three at some point before the next Christmas.

'And maybe Jonathon's girlfriend will be over here by then,' said Genevieve 'and we can all be together.'

'What was that? Who said anything about a girlfriend? I thought he and David were....' Helen trailed off uncertainly, surprised by the shock and then laughter that followed across Genevieve's face. 'What... What have I said?'

'I don't believe you said that! What on earth are you thinking?'

As the men walked in to the room Helen turned away, hiding her embarrassment and trying to bring her too expressive face back under control.

She wondered what it was she had seen on the beach then. Was Jonathon telling the truth, or making up a smokescreen for Genevieve? *But why would he bother*? was her next thought. If it was true, then she wasn't sure now what David's feelings would be.

It was all too hard and you could add to that the almost unfriendly way that Liam was acting, yet again. How on earth had it all fallen to bits so quickly, when they had all been having such a wonderful time? Suddenly, Helen didn't feel like dinner at all but she didn't want to spoil Genevieve's last night so she did her best to join in the conversation. At least, David, Genevieve and Jonathon seemed to be having a good time.

She sneaked a glance at Liam beside her, just in time to catch his eye as he did the same. He frowned, moving forward to David's other side so that she and David were left shoulder to shoulder as they walked along the pavement. David automatically dropped back to continue his conversation with Genevieve again, leaving Helen beside Jonathon.

Helen did not know how to approach the topic that was right at the top of her 'wish to know list' so she asked Jonathon to tell her some more about his plans for the next couple of months. 'How was he going to start? Did he want to look for a job first or did he need to study?'

Enthusiastically he mapped out a plan that include study at the marine college further down the coast and weekends and holidays spent on the tourist boats.

'You're not planning on fishing?' inquired Helen.

'No, I have absolutely no desire to fish, but I wouldn't mind taking out the scuba boats. I already have a dive ticket and have been meaning to do my instructors anyway.'

'Where'd you do that? I thought you were in Canada most of the time and I can't imagine diving is big over there.'

'You'd be surprised in fact, but I did do it in California. The water is pretty cold there anyway so I might as well have done it in Canada. You know they wear wet suits to surf in summer over there, even as far down as Los Angeles.'

'What made you decide to do it?'

'Oh, you know, a few mates and besides that the doctors told me not to a long time ago so I decided to prove them wrong.' He gave her a conspiratorial grin.

'And did you?'

'Yes but I'll admit it now, I was lucky. I couldn't let them know I had diabetes because they wouldn't have been allowed to send me down. It's a bit different now though, they've changed the rules and you just have to prove you've been controlling it.' He sighed. 'Another good reason to get control and prove it, as David would tell me.'

'Why did you come back to David, because you did, didn't you?'

'So he could tell me not to be a fool all the time maybe. I don't know, I think maybe I just needed to ground myself, although I almost didn't succeed, did I?'

'Almost permanently grounded yourself you mean,' said Helen wryly.

'True, now tell me about you and Liam.'

'What?'

Jonathon slung his arm over Helen's shoulder and leant close to her ear. 'I think it's time you two came clean and let us all out of suspense,' he whispered.

Helen glanced around, hoping no-one was within hearing distance and caught Liam's eye as he focused on Jonathon's hand trailing above her breast.

'Jonathon don't,' she tried to lift his arm away, and laugh

it off but for some reason he let it hang more heavily and leant against her. 'Get off.'

Suddenly, she felt him lurch against her and they both went down in a flail of arms and legs. Pinned beneath Jonathon's weight, Helen could feel her skirt riding up her legs in the most undignified way possible as people gathered to give advice and view the spectacle.

'It's OK.' David was calm and authoritative. 'He's just had a bit of sugar low, I'm sure. It's been a long day.'

Helen could feel hands helping her to extricate herself as David searched Jonathon's pockets for a sweet. 'Could someone get me juice from the shop, please?' Genevieve flew in to the nearby café and came out with a popper which David proceeded to dribble between Jonathon's lips while Liam supported him.

Luckily, Jonathon was not altogether out to it, and was alert enough to respond quite quickly to the commands to both drink and to sit up.

David could have kicked himself. Instead of lunch, they had been kayaking and then snorkeling. At no time did he give a thought to the fact that Jonathon probably needed to eat and obviously, nor had Jonathon. He hoped this incident would not set Jonathon off again on the path to self-destruction. At any time in the past, this would be the trigger for yet another disappearance.

Jonathon looked up at the circle of people around him and grimaced, then smiled his devastatingly mischievous smile. 'Just taking the lady for a ride. We'll see you all later.'

As the crowd disappeared he turned to the group of friends with him and said 'Look just leave me here, go on off to dinner with you. I'll get something here myself.'

'Jonathon, no.'

'Look, I said I'll eat. Just don't make a fuss OK. I want you all to go.'

David touched Helen on the arm and inclined his head toward the restaurant.

'Jono, you know where we are if you want to join us. Maybe we'll see you later.'

'David, we can't do that.'

'Yes we can. Come on.'

Helen had never seen David so determined, especially when she would have expected him to stay and tend to Jonathon. Liam and Genevieve turned and headed up the street, with Helen and David following slowly.

'David, I can't believe we did that. How do you know he won't disappear again?'

'I don't but at some stage I'll just have to trust him and just at the moment I believe he has a good reason to want to be sensible about this - in fact, several good reasons.'

Helen was having a hard time coming to grips with the steel in David's voice although she was aware that it was taking a lot of effort on his part to just walk away and leave Jonathon behind.

'Are you sure he'll be OK enough to make a rational decision.'

'Yes, he finished the juice and that will give him an hour or so to settle down and find something to eat. I'm sure he'll do that at least. The rest is up to his good sense and he's been showing a lot more of that lately than he ever has before.'

'Come on Helen, let's catch up before Liam thinks I've abducted you.'

Dinner was a much quieter affair than the group would

have expected early in day with conversation limited to generalities and not to future plans. Genevieve halfheartedly tried to introduce the topic of her next holidays but it was clear that the other three were seriously preoccupied with their own thoughts, although they did make some effort when she raised the topic of the fund raiser they had started to organize for after Christmas, in Carlisle.

Instead of the fun run for cancer, they had decided to find sponsorship for a swim for cancer, being a swimming marathon in the local pool.

Other than this conversation was strained and following the dessert menu, in honour of Genevieve, they decided that since Jonathon didn't have a key at least some of them should head back to the units in case he returned.

Pleading tiredness from an active day so soon after a hospital stay, Helen waved them all off and directed her steps back along the main street and up the hill toward the brightly lit apartments on the hill. Once there, she quickly found a piece of paper and pen, writing Jonathon a note which she left outside the door of the apartment the men were sharing telling him to come up to apartment 4a for the key when he got back.

Coming back in to the apartment she shared with Genevieve, she helped herself to a glass of the Sangiovese whimsically named 'La Vendetta' with an appropriate knife and blood on the label, that they had brought along for post dinner drinks. With Jack Johnson lilting in the background, she moved out to the deck which overlooked the park and the sea and sank in to a comfortable outdoor lounge to admire the view. It seemed as if this was the first time in ages that she had had a moment to herself and there was a lot to think about in the happenings of the last week.

Firstly, she was starting to suspect that there was something between Liam and Genevieve, although obviously Jonathon and David didn't seem to think so, but at least that let her off the hook as far as David was concerned since he'd implied that he should 'return' her to Liam. And if Jonathon did have a girlfriend, where did that leave David? In fact, why did anyone have to be with anyone, they could just all be good friends.

Leaning back in the chair, she deliberately tried to erase all thoughts and simply listen to the music, but instead there was a tentative knock on the door and she got up to let Jonathon in.

❦   ❦   ❦

He looked around, 'Are you by yourself?'

'Mmm, the others felt like a walk and I was a bit tired.' Helen wasn't about to let on that they had decided that someone would need to be there in case Jonathon came back. Leaving the door pushed open, Helen returned to the sofa.

'How was dinner?'

'Good, it was very pleasant food and Genevieve said the dessert was amazing but then she always does.'

'Look, I'm sorry, I'll bet I put a bit of damper on it for you all and I feel really terrible with it being Genevieve's last night. I was just so disappointed with myself that I had forgotten to eat, when I'd promised myself I would never do that again and I felt I let you all down too.'

273

'Only by not letting us help,' returned Helen, 'but you're here now.'

'And before you ask, I did have dinner.'

'I wasn't going to ask,' Helen replied, trying to take a leaf from David's book and indicate her trust in Jonathon. 'Probably, it was a lot easier for her than it would be for David,' she thought,' since she had only known Jonathon as an adult.

'Get yourself a wine and come and join me,' she told him, leaving him in the kitchen.

'Will I bring out some nibbles?'

'I'm Ok but you go ahead if you'd like some, thanks.'

Jonathon came out with just his glass after all and sat down facing the sea on the big lounge beside Helen. She curled her feet up out of the way and put her glass down.

'Tell me about your girlfriend. Genevieve mentioned that she might be coming over soon.'

Helen was still a bit unsure about this bit of information, with Norm's broken record attacks on David playing over in her mind, so she crossed her fingers and hoped her information source was impeccable as the media would say.

'I hope so but I've been so up and down since I came back that I wouldn't blame her if she decided not.'

'When did you meet her?'

Jonathon hesitated, 'After the accident.'

'The one in Canada?' Helen hesitated, 'with Liam?'

'mmm, that would be it.' Jonathon got up and moved around restlessly, drumming his fingers on the table and looking out at the ocean. 'All my fault and I came so close to killing us both. In the end, it was Liam who got the worst of it and I got off nearly scot free. After that, I decided to try to sort myself out a bit and I went to see an endocrinologist in Canada. God, it's so expensive over there. Nicole is her receptionist and we got to talking, mainly about Australia and one thing led to another as it does.'

'Do you talk to her much?'

'Everyday,' he looked down for a moment, 'well almost every day.'

There was a silence and they both listened to the waves against the rocks below for a while.

'I'm sure she will be coming over, we've made some pretty concrete plans and I would love to have her here.' He looked at Helen seriously, 'Do you think it is fair to her, to ask her to come here. I can't even look after myself for one day properly.'

Helen laid her hand across his and squeezed it hard. "I am certain you are Jonathon and we'll all be around to support you, especially if you stay up here near the islands. If you were over here, we would be over to stay with you all the time. You'll have to rent a three bedroom house at least to accommodate guests.' Helen hoped Jonathon knew because of friendship that she said this, and not that she meant they would be checking on him. She searched his face for any hint of concern and as he turned to look at her hesitation Helen leaned across to give him a reassuring hug.

Jonathon responded with the fervor of a small boy who had been lost for a long time and found by loving parents.

CHAPTER 44

If David and Genevieve wondered why Liam had decided to walk with them instead of returning with Helen, they were discreet enough not to ask but decidedly puzzled. It was obvious that Liam was not really listening even though he walked along beside them and nodded and smiled when he was spoken to.

They all admired the surf hitting the sea wall below them with the moonlight touching the crests, a molten golden spray accompanying every boom of the waves against the rocks.

They appraised each of the buildings, wondering about the occupants and the cost of a week or two in a rental house or in the units they were staying in. *A house would be better,'* they decided, *more friendly and they would all be able to share a kitchen rather than hopping between units.*

They wondered if Jonathon would find a job and eventually as they realized that Liam was not listening at all, David and Genevieve drifted in to the kind of conversation that could only be the result of more than a casual friendship. Liam listened without comprehension for a while, until the tail end of a sentence about the possibility of David making it down to Armidale for Genevieve's school reunion penetrated his absorption.

He listened with escalating amazement while they made plans, plans which obviously did not include any of the rest of the group. It was not that he was hurt in any way, but he was certainly puzzled and said so, 'What are you two planning?'

'Oh, he is awake, imagine that,' laughed Genevieve, 'we thought you'd left us altogether.'

'You know, I'm feeling pretty stupid here. When were you two going to tell the rest of us about your little relationship?'

David looked a bit surprised. 'Well it's not exactly a secret, but I guess we might have been a little bit discreet.'

'So was that to keep it a secret from Jonathon, or Helen? And what about Helen? When were you going to tell her?"

'Helen?'

'I thought, blow, the whole town thought that you and Helen were a pair. You even had Norm convinced more or less.'

David looked surprised while Genevieve nodded thoughtfully. 'That starts to make a bit of sense you know. I did wonder about some of the statements various people made.'

Liam turned to her, 'But you still encouraged David anyway?'

'David and I have been in touch since Christmas and I hadn't been talking to anyone else here to find out otherwise and Helen sure didn't say anything.'

'Look Liam, there is nothing between Helen and I, except we're good friends of course.'

'Very good friends from what I saw.' Liam watched him for a reaction.

'Yes, we are but I'm not sure what you are talking about at the moment.'

'Well, I hope that Helen understands what that was all about back at the island then, because I sure don't.' He clenched his fists reflexively, watching David like a big cat waiting and flicking its tail in anticipation.

David looked around for inspiration while Liam and Genevieve waited.

'Are you talking about when we were snorkeling?' he ventured at last.

Liam raised his eyebrows, 'Go on.'

'We were talking about Jonathon and how far he's come and I was just thanking Helen for her support for him. That's all.'

'Are you sure that's all? It all seemed a bit more enthusiastic than that to me.'

David thought for a moment, reliving the few moments in the water, but Genevieve broke in, 'I wouldn't have thought so, Liam, especially since I think she is not sure whether David is gay or not.'

'What?' Both the men looked at her with disbelieving expressions.

'Something she said earlier about David and Jonathon but you just walked in then and I didn't get time to find out any more. But thinking about it, she may have mentioned it earlier. In the same sentence as she mentioned Norm, I suspect so I didn't take too much notice. I didn't think she would be influenced by his opinion really.'

'What Jonathon and I? What made her think that?'

David and Liam exchanged looks in which laughter and incredulity were equally mixed. They'd known each other a long time and roistered their way through university in the same town but this was the first time either of them had had this particular charge leveled at them.

'I don't think so,' said Liam slowly, 'unless a lot has changed in the last few years.'

'Well, I don't think so either,' said Genevieve as she exchanged a small smile with David,' but for some reason Helen is not sure, so how about you go away and tell her the truth, hmm.' Genevieve gave him a look which clearly indicated that he was one too many in the group now that the air was clear.

❦   ❦   ❦

'Not you too!' Liam pushed the door further open as Helen looked up, surprised at the angry tone.

Liam backed out and slammed the door, thudding his heels as he strode back toward the lift, jabbing the button with a stiff index finger.

Helen and Jonathon almost collided in their efforts to reach the door and call before Liam could disappear.

'Liam, what is the matter, where are you going? Come back, please.'

He looked around and at that moment Jonathon shot out the door and headed toward him, hand held out to grab him by the sleeve.

Liam shrugged the hand away, 'Leave it.'

Jonathon persisted, gaining a firmer grip just as the lift door opened and two faces peered out, rapidly hitting the down button when they realized they could end up in the middle of a brawl. Liam shot his hand out as the door closed, but the shock on the strange faces on a level with his finally registered and looking extremely sheepish, he muttered,' I am sorry, don't worry I'll get it next time,' and turned to face Jonathon who still had a fierce grip on his left elbow. 'As for you, why don't you just go back inside and finish what you started.'

Jonathon frowned and then his face cleared 'It was finished. Why don't you go in and start what you should have started a long time ago?'

Liam started past him to press the lift button again, but Jonathon had parked himself against the panel and short of another undignified scuffle, Liam was not going to get his fingers on the buttons again.

Helen's patience gave out as the two men stood there staring each other down, 'Jonathon, I have no idea what you meant by that but let's go inside and try to sort out whatever is going on.'

As Liam turned toward the door, Jonathon stood watching, clearly willing him to follow Helen and watchfully ensuring that he didn't make for the lift again.

'After you,' and he smiled a little to himself, rolling his eyes in the direction of the door. 'I am sure that you and Helen don't need me but if you need help getting through that door, I can give you a kick on the backside.'

'Thank you, I am sure I can manage. Are you coming in?'

'No, Helen and I finished what we were talking about. You are welcome to the rest of my wine but I'm rather hoping you'll be there long enough to pour one for yourself,' and with that enigmatic sentence, he turned in to the lift doors which had magically opened behind him and descended to wait in the foyer to head off the other pair when they arrived.

Liam entered the room slowly and Helen watched him curiously as he crossed the tiles toward her. 'Would you like some wine before you tell me what that was all about?' she enquired.

'No, you tell me first what you were doing with Jonathon when I first came in.'

Helen eyed him narrowly, suddenly suspicious of the high points of colour on Liam's cheekbones.

It crossed her mind to tell him it was none of his business, but suddenly she decided that that was not an answer that would change anything, and that the problem was not between Liam and Jonathon but also concerned herself. *Ten points for deduction*, she thought suddenly, almost smiling at her random sense of humour.

'We were talking about what he is going to do,' she ventured.

'And what is he going to do?' Liam was also being very careful with his words.

'Hopefully get a house up here so Jenna can come and live with him and ultimately find some work on the boats.'

'Jenna? Who's Jenna?' Liam studied the tiles, thinking irrelevantly that the pattern was probably Byzantine, and simultaneously hoping that Helen was referring to a possible girlfriend for Jonathon.

'Jonathon met her in the States and she is coming out to live with him.'

Liam felt as if all his Christmases had come at once. 'I think I will have that wine after all.'

And he poured himself a very large glass of the Shiraz

on the bench top which advertised itself as having plum and berry flavours with a hint of spice. Just the way he liked it. He took his time to settle his mind and plan his next question.

'I thought that you thought that Jonothan was gay,' he commented. Obviously, his mouth was not going to obey his mind, realized Liam and he was still in the land of irrelevancy where he could avoid topics which were of extreme importance to himself.

'Where did you hear that?'

'Umm, Genevieve.'

'Well I was wrong and she should have kept that information to herself.'

'And David?'

'What about David?'

'You thought he was too.' Liam held his breath, sure that the answer to this could be important to him.

'Not exactly. Well maybe sometimes. I don't know but I'm pretty sure he's not, not that it matters.'

Liam looked at her hopefully. 'What do you mean by that?'

'Well, we'd still be good friends but it is a bit awkward as far as my work is concerned for David.'

Liam felt his heart sink. 'I don't see what it has to do with anything.'

'Oh, just Norm giving me a hard time and making it uncomfortable for David. You know the nonsense he goes on with. It's not a big deal, but he does try to make trouble for David as well in other ways and I feel responsible.

'Well, he's not you know. You can tell Norm if you

like, tell him to check with Genevieve if he has trouble believing it.'

'I don't see what it's got to do with Genevieve.' She frowned. 'Do you mean David and Genevieve? 'Clearly Helen was thinking back and possibly wondering how much blinder she could have been. 'I feel so damn stupid and she never said a word, how rude is that?' She started to smile, 'But that is so perfect, I can see it now and I can't imagine what I was thinking not to suspect. She is so dead when I get hold of her.'

CHAPTER 45

In the foyer, Genevieve and David had caught up with Jonathon, who was lurking on the settee close to the entrance. 'How about we all go out for a drink,' he suggested.

David looked at him warily, with just a hint of exasperation. 'There's plenty upstairs,' he suggested 'but I gather you'd rather we didn't go there.'

'Well yes, I should have been smart enough to grab a bottle or two before I left the apartment, then we could have had our own little party in 3B.'

'How long do you think we'll need to be gone for?'

'At the current rate, it could take a while. Those two have six months' worth of sorting out to do before they even get around to anything interesting.'

David rolled his eyes at Genevieve and shrugged. 'I have a better idea, not that I want you to take this the wrong way or anything, but how about you go for a good long walk and buy us a bottle of something and we'll wait upstairs in case Liam and Helen decide they'd like company.'

Genevieve laughed, 'Poor Jonathon, you are being horrible David. What about we all go, come back and have a quiet drink, then we'll gatecrash the other party?'

Muttering about inconsiderate friends and bossy women, David trailed Genevieve and Jonathon out the door and down the street, all the time wondering what stormy words were being exchanged upstairs. It constantly amazed him that two such sensible, intelligent and normally clear sighted people could get their wires crossed so regularly.

Once the bottle was finished, the three conspirators sat looking at each other, then both David and Genevieve turned to Jonathon.

'What? Oh no, I'm not going back up there. I almost got flattened and only just escaped in one piece.'

David eyed him.' 'You know I'd give a lot to know what this was all about, I have no idea why it has taken Liam so long. Do you know anything?'

'Well, I'm not really sure but I think that Liam thought that you might have had an interest in Helen.'

'What? Where did he get that idea?'

'Maybe because the whole town thought you did. At least those who didn't think you were gay.'

David stared at him, dumfounded.

Genevieve nodded thoughtfully. 'Yes, Helen did say something about that.' She wisely kept the information that Helen had a touch of the same suspicion to herself. Then she smiled at Jonathon mischievously, 'and when Jonathon came to town, that proved it.'

The two men looked at each other, completely nonplussed.

'OK, if half the town and possibly Helen,' and here David winced, 'thought that, then what was Liam's problem? I don't understand why it made any difference to him.'

'I told you.'

'About the whole town?'

'Well you were pretty thick for a while there, or so I was told.'

It was clear Jonathon was enjoying this, thought David, sneaking a look at Genevieve- a Genevieve, who was trying to look completely disinterested while covering a great big, smug smile. Her eyes crinkled as she watched David squirm.

'Yes, but …Genevieve, did you know about this?'

'Sort of, but there wasn't anything I could do, I wasn't even here most of the time.'

'Well, what was Helen thinking then? Just tell me that at least?'

'About Liam, I suspect and how to let you down easily, just in case you weren't gay at all,' she said helpfully.

'I am beginning to think that we had better go upstairs and do some sorting out,' said David, who was not seeing the funny side of this at all, in spite of the barely repressed snorts and giggles from the other two.

'Oh, I think you'll find it is probably satisfactorily sorted already,' suggested Jonathon. 'At least it was looking promising when I left.'

''Well, let's go and hurry them along, just in case they need a bit more of your help.'

At the upstairs door, Jonathon and Genevieve hung behind David, scuffling to be the first to look over his shoulder but the last to have to say anything.

David turned the door handle and pushed open the door to find the room completely empty, not a dead body or a passionate embrace to be seen and then hastily stepped aside as the two behind him shoved unceremoniously in to the middle of the room.

Genevieve's eye fell on a slip of paper on the kitchen table with large black letters and graphic drawings indicating the probable fate of various fair haired members of the group at the hands of a laughing dark haired couple who eventually disappeared in to the distance holding hands.

Voices from the balcony alerted the trio to presence of the architects of their illustrated fates.

ACKNOWLEDGEMENTS

Any likeness to people you may know is purely accidental, except the lovely Helen who is an amalgam of several amazing ladies I worked with. Thank you to Landcare and to vibrant country towns who throw together some of the most diverse, talented and committed people you will ever find. It is these people who keep their communities alive.

And a big thank you to Wendy, an accidental meeting that led to some great advice.

And to my beautiful Rookie, the model for Jack.

Printed in the United States
By Bookmasters